Claire
and the
Missing
Heir

AMANDA NELSON

ISBN: 978-1-7360587-4-9
Library of Congress Control Number: 2023909272

Published by

LAUREL ELITE BOOKS

Laurel Elite Books
PO Box 815
Claremont, NH 03743
www.LaurelElite.com

Additional copies of this book may be purchased at:
www.LaurelElite.com

Book Design by: Laurel Elite

Printed in the United States of America

To my loving and supportive husband who said I couldn't write a book. Ha! I did it.

Without your little challenge, I may still be procrastinating.

Also, thanks to all my family and friends who encouraged me along the way.

Chapter 1

"I'm desperate. It's a matter of life and death." I tried to sound authoritative, but it came out more like a whine. My attempt at a convincing look was met by a flat, brown-eyed stare. When there was no response, I tried again. "Please, I need it now!"

"You've had enough." After one last glare, she turned away, dismissing me as if I was not worth her time.

"Please, just one more. I really, really, really, need it."

She turned and looked me up and down as if judging my worth. The slight curl to her lip indicated she found me lacking.

I almost quivered with anticipation.

Finally, she reached into the case and without breaking eye contact selected the uppermost brownie and handed it to me.

"This is your last one."

"Of course, sure, absolutely," I would agree to anything at this point but tried to salvage at least some composure. "This will be enough."

She continued to look at me, the doubt clear in her eyes, before ringing up my brownie.

I cradled the precious confection protectively in my hand as I paid for it and then scurried to the outdoor seating area. After the ordeal, I was so looking forward to enjoying my brownie in peace, away from judgmental eyes.

However, no sooner had I sat down than an adorable blue-eyed blond urchin appeared at my elbow, staring at me. I clasped my brownie protectively and stared back. Neither of us spoke or looked away. Then, another blue-eyed blond child appeared, older, but no less adorable. I choked back a slight whimper as she stared at my brownie with hungry eyes. When a third-blued-eyed blond popped up on my other side, I clutched my brownie even tighter.

"No," I said. "No, no, no." I shook my head for emphasis. More blue-eyed blond children—who appeared angelic but were obviously spawn of Satan—kept popping up until I was surrounded by them.

"Sorry I'm late," a too-chipper voice interrupted my panic.

I looked past Satan's children to see Satan herself standing nearby. She resembled a pinup model and looked effortlessly stylish in a pair of fuchsia capris and a tropical floral print top. She was short with blond hair that seemed to glow honey and gold in the sun. Her blue eyes weren't simply blue, they were stunningly blue—almost turquoise—and surrounded by long thick lashes. Looking at her I felt self-conscious in my jean cutoffs and t-shirt.

"Auntie Claire isn't sharing," a sweet voice at my elbow declared.

Satan looked down at the youngest of the vicious monsters staring enviously at my brownie. "Auntie Claire doesn't have to share. I bought a whole batch."

She, who was previously known as Satan but is obviously an angel, pulled out a chair and sat at my table. The children dragged chairs over and settled in.

"How?" I asked, ignoring the loud screeching the chairs made when pulled across the patio. "How did you get a whole batch of brownies from her?" I placed special significance on the word her, signifying my disbelief and contempt.

I momentarily feared a case of sunburn from her radiant smile. "I asked nicely."

"Plus, she brought seven adorable children with her," said Nell, the oldest of Satan's children, and an almost exact replica of Satan.

Satan's smile slipped a little, as my own spread across my face. I leaned back, my accusing stare fixed in place.

"All right," she admitted with a shrug, "that probably helped."

Nell rolled her eyes, and the long, arched lashes reminded me of some dramatic bridge architecture I'd seen. "Of course it helped," she said, crossing her long, lightly tanned legs.

"Auntie Claire," the youngest of the children, Eve, tugged on my arm to get my attention. "Can I have a bite of your brownie, please? I'm so hungry."

Her eyes, with just a hint of tears trembling on her lower lashes, seem to cut me as they gazed into my soul. Her soft curls lifted in the slight breeze as we stared at each other, locked in a silent struggle of wills. Her will was obviously stronger than mine. Although she resembled an angel, I knew denying her request would result in a tantrum of epic proportions, but to give up a piece of my brownie would be like giving up a piece of myself.

Thankfully, a plate of brownies appeared in the middle of the table as if by magic. I seized on the distraction and took a huge bite. The once pitiless proprietor of the bakery was now all smiles and laughing brown eyes as she greeted Satan and her children. This change in demeanor made her look years younger despite her white hair, which was secured in a long braid and gleamed silver in the light whenever she moved.

"Cordelia your children are just the sweetest things," she said, wiping her hands on her retro cherry-printed apron.

Satan/Cordelia beamed at the owner of the best bakery ever. "Why, thank you, Rose! You are too kind, but these brownies are truly the sweetest things, and please call me CC. All my friends do."

They smiled at each other for a moment while the children began helping themselves to the mountain of brownies.

Rose spread her smile around the table, until her eyes landed on me. "Shame on you not sharing your brownie with poor little Eve." Her smile was nowhere in sight now. "Just look at the poor sweet dear."

We both turn to look at Eve, who was shoving a whole brownie into her kewpie doll mouth as she reached to grab another off her older brother's napkin.

Half of Kyle's darker blond wildly curling hair was sticking up as if licked by a camel and black square framed glasses sat askance on his dirt-smudged face. Neither of which detracted from his good looks. He seemed oblivious to what was going on around him while he continued to draw in his ever-present sketchbook, but I knew better.

My smile widened at catching Eve in the act, while Rose's expression soured.

Eve, sensing our scrutiny, immediately redirected her hand to grab a napkin off the table and delicately wiped her mouth. She smiled sweetly at Rose who seemed to have bought Eve's innocent act and smiled warmly at her before returning to the bakery counter.

"Have you been waiting long?" Satan asked while helping herself to a brownie from the huge plate.

Even though I had a brownie clutched in my hand I still stared covetously at the pile in the center of the table. "Not long," I said, "just a few minutes."

Satan looked at me over the top of her brownie. After chewing the mouthful with obvious relish, she asked, "Then why did Rose say you'd already eaten five—" she cast a significant glance at the half-eaten treat still clutched in my hand. "—make that six brownies?"

"You would believe Rose, a near-stranger, over your best friend?"

Every head at the table nodded, all the way down to Eve, the toddler who was finishing her brother's forgotten brownie.

As Eve turned her covetous eyes toward me, I shoved the rest of the brownie into my mouth. She puckered her lips, and a slight frown appeared between her brows.

We all breathed a sigh of relief when no screams followed, and instead she turned to her sister Jane, Satan's eleven-year-old daughter who had an unnatural ability with all animals and was currently cooing to a bird on a nearby tree branch.

Now that my brownie was safe from Satan's children, I turned my full attention to Satan, also known as my best friend Cordelia, better known as CC. "So, what's on the schedule today?"

"Let's go to Park Square Mall," Nell, CC's eighteen-year-old daughter suggested hopefully, while flipping her perfect shiny waist-length honey blond hair over her shoulder. It settled into soft curls that glinted like polished gold in the sunlight. I half expected a magazine photoshoot to materialize in the seating area.

"No. The animal shelter." Jane's soft counter didn't disturb the bird perched on her finger.

"The toy store!" said Eve. I wasn't sure the two-year-old tyrant hadn't sprung forth from the gates of hell just to torment us, despite her adorable appearance.

"There is a new exhibit at the art gallery," said thirteen-year-old Kyle from underneath his curly mop of hair.

"We could hike along the river," fifteen-year-old Frank offered as he scanned the street. "Amelia likes walking along the river," he added. His classic boy-next-door handsomeness drew the attention of females from five to twenty-five years old. His strong jaw had a hint of stubble, and his shoulders were wide enough to cast shade. Already gorgeous like his father, it was evident he would only become more so.

Nine-year-old Ann rolled her eyes so hard it caused her twin French braids to flutter as well. "Frank always wants to do whatever Amelia wants to do. He even kisses her," she said, with a look of disgust, only a nine-year-old could manage, on her adorably freckled face.

Frank colored slightly but ignored the comment.

I snickered under my breath, but when Frank turned his gaze on me, I realized it might not have been under my breath after all. I smiled shamelessly at him. After a moment he smiled back.

"Nice shirt," he said, gesturing to my fabulous t-shirt.

It read, 'you don't know me' and featured an official witness protection seal. "I know, right? I'm surprised you were able to recognize me this morning," I said, holding the hem out.

"I heard the junkyard got a new shipment in," a voice under the table interjected.

I stopped admiring my shirt to peek underneath the table. Seven-year-old Dean didn't even glance up from his most recent contraption.

"What are you building?" I asked the top of his close-cropped blond head.

"I'm trying to tie my shoe." He leaned closer to scrutinize the two straws, a stick, and a package of gum.

I squinted to be sure I was seeing things correctly. Yup, that was a 9-volt battery, too. "Huh," I said, perplexed about how it was all going to work. "Well good luck!" I sat back in my chair.

CC shrugged. "You knew they would never pick the same things."

"Well, then that means I get the tie-breaking vote." I ended my declaration with a loud victory crow, which caused a few people to look in our direction.

"Again?" Eight voices interrupted me in chorus with varying degrees of resignation and indignation.

"Again." I smiled devilishly.

"Will you at least pick one we suggested?" asked Kyle, glancing up from his drawing, with a smudge of something across his cheek. It might be dirt. How he got a smudge of dirt across his face sitting at the table will forever remain a mystery. Out of the corner of my eye, I caught three girls at another table sighing and giggling. As expected, Kyle acted like he didn't know they existed, but I suspected he could do a police sketch of all of them.

"Not a chance." I rubbed my hands together. "Let's see," I tapped my index finger on my chin, "we could go to the city."

Nell brightened.

"But I hate traffic, and we would have to take two cars."

Her demeanor immediately wilted.

"We could go to the arcade."

Nobody seemed impressed with this idea. Then I snapped my fingers as if I had just come up with the best idea ever, which I had. "We can go to the pool!"

A few sour faces glared at me, while the rest ignored me completely.

"Again?" CC asked. Her voice conveyed surprise and shock, even though we all knew I was always going to pick the pool.

"Can we change the tie-breaking rule?" asked Jane, who now had a bird perched on her head in addition to the one on her hand.

"No!" I replied indignantly. "The rule was in place before you were even born. You don't get to vote for changes." She nodded, her expression downcast, and seemed to acquiesce to my superior reasoning. The bird on her head also appeared to nod. I smiled with approval at this new ally in my life.

"We can't swim for thirty minutes after eating," the traitor under the table piped up while still fiddling with his contraption.

I squinty-eye glared at the top of his head, since he didn't bother to look up, and then smiled sweetly at the others. "By the time we get to the pool, and you change into swimsuits it will have been at least thirty minutes."

CC got a suspicious look in her eyes, which made me instantly wary. I tried to head her off, but I wasn't quick enough.

"Before we get into our swimsuits?" she asked. "What about your swimsuit?"

"Maybe she's going to skinny dip," Eve blurted out.

All of us turned to look at the angelic tyrant. Even Kyle stopped sketching to look at his baby sister. The expression on CC's face was priceless. She tried to respond but seemed to have lost the ability to form words.

"Where did you hear that term?" Nell asked.

"From Dad," Eve replied. "He asked Mom if she remembered their trip to the cabin and going for a quick skinny dip in the lake after everybody else was asleep. And then Mom said certainly she remembered because that's why they have seven kids."

All eyes turned to CC who was bright red to the roots of her hair, but a Cheshire cat grin hovered at the corners of her mouth and her eyes took on a faraway look.

"Mom!" exclaimed the four oldest kids in unison.

"Skinny dipping is why you have seven kids? Is that where Eve came from?" asked Ann with a nine-year-old's innocence.

"I came from the lake?" Eve asked, rocking precariously on her tabletop perch. "Does that mean I'm a mermaid? I'm a mermaid!" She declared loudly, not waiting for a response. Heads turned toward us again. We were drawing a lot of attention from the surrounding tables today.

Finally, having mercy on CC, I grabbed Eve off the table and said, "Then we better get you to the water before you turn into a raisin,"

I headed to the parking lot with Eve under my arm like a football, and the others fell in behind like ducklings, as I knew they would. We wound our way through the tables and eventually reached CC's minivan alongside my turquoise '67 Impala. The old chevy made me grin every time I saw her. The restored classic was immaculate inside and out. I knew turquoise wasn't a stock color, but she deserved to stand out from the rest, and boy did she.

"I'm riding with Auntie Claire," Frank, Nell, Ann, Jane, and Eve declared at varying volumes.

"I wish you could, mermaid girl, but I don't have your car seat, so into the mom mobile for you." I handed Eve to CC so she could strap the little mermaid into her car seat.

Eve puckered her kewpie doll lips but again refrained from screaming.

CC turned and locked her suspicious blue eyes on mine.

"You never said why you didn't need to change into a swimsuit." My best friend's hands were planted on her hips in a no-non-sense manner.

"Well," I mumbled, "I may have already put mine on." I turned and tried to escape into my car.

"I knew it!" she crowed before I could take two steps. "You were always going to choose swimming."

"Well, duh." I didn't sound very intelligent, but pressed on, "Swimming is the best!"

My friend shook her head. I could sense her disappointment "Claire, Claire, Claire. You really should try something new. You might like it."

"CC, CC, CC." I wasn't above a little copycat. "Nothing is better than swimming, so why bother with second best?"

Her unconvinced expression prompted me to continue.

"Why would I pick a scone over a brownie?"

Bowing to my obvious intelligence, she admitted defeat and turned to climb into her minivan. The angelic faces of Eve, Dean, and Kyle had bounced back and forth between us like they were watching a tennis match. Sensing I had won this time, they settled back in their seats.

Nell, Ann, and Jane were already in the back seat of my car, and Frank was riding shotgun. Sliding into my sweet baby, I turned the key and she rumbled to life. The 283 cubic inch V8 growled like a big cat and not-so-subtle vibrations pulsed along the chassis. The birds on Jane's head and shoulder flew out the window, obviously startled.

"What did you name them?" I asked Jane as we pulled out of the parking lot.

"Pietro and Samantha." In the rearview mirror, I could see her watching as they flew away. No fits like Eve. Jane was always serene.

"Didn't you already have birds named Pietro and Samantha?" I asked. My brow furrowed in concentration as I tried to sort through hundreds of names she had given animals over the years.

"Yeah, they're the same ones from the park last week."

I joined her siblings and nodded agreeably, because if anything on this planet was true, Jane knew her animals and, apparently, they know her too.

Chapter 2

Due to fighting a two-year-old whirling dervish of pure evil into her swimsuit and swimming wings, and getting her coated with sunscreen, it seemed an eternity before I finally collapsed onto the lounge chair next to my bestie.

"How come I always end up getting Eve ready for the pool?" I asked, still slightly winded from the exertion.

"Do you?"

I narrowed my eyes at her faux-innocent response, but my sunglasses hid the look from her. Before I could say anything else, Nell folded herself onto the chaise lounge on my other side with a good deal more grace than I managed. Her light blue bikini showed off an enviable tan as well as her long legs, but was still modest enough that I wouldn't have to kneecap any boys.

"What's wrong, beautiful? Why aren't you swimming with the others?"

She shrugged, an unconscious response that caused her already-perfect hair to somehow become more perfect. Perfecter?

"I will in a bit," she said.

I looked from her to her mom. CC was somehow both relaxing and watching her six other kids like a hawk as they splashed around with varying degrees of swimming skill. No help there. I turned back to Nell and caught her looking at something over my shoulder. I whipped my head around like a deranged owl and saw nothing but the lifeguard.

I looked back at Nell and her nonchalant pose raised my suspicions.

I craned my neck back the other way so hard I almost tipped over the lounge chair. Yup, still just the lifeguard. The really cute, teenage boy lifeguard.

I was going to need a chiropractor after this. "Oh, the lifeguard, huh?" I said in a teasing voice once I settled back into the chair and faced around to Nell. I tried to nudge her with my elbow, but since she was nearly a foot away it probably resembled a chicken dance more than anything else.

Her cheeks turned a little pink and she tried to avoid my eyes, but I'm nothing if not determined.

Trying to swivel in a lounge chair isn't easy, but I managed it yet again without falling off. I wanted a better look at the lifeguard in question.

"Aunt Claire, try to be cool," Nell said with a desperate look in her eyes.

CC said one word, just one word, but it was enough to get me leaning back in my lounger almost before she finished it.

"Sampson."

Now I was the one trying to look indifferent and relaxed while Nell stared at me.

"Who's Sampson?" she asked.

"Nobody," I practically yelled. Lowering my voice to a normal level, I tried again. "Nobody important, just a kid your mom and I went to school with."

"Oh, Sampson, huh?" Nell mimicked me, the devil child.

"You know what would make this better?" I asked. "Silence. Calm, relaxing silence. No talking."

Roughly three seconds of silence elapsed, and I cracked. "Ok, ok, stop browbeating me. Sampson was a boy we went to school with. He was an Adonis and I wanted to go to prom with him. It was my only chance at beating your mom and dad to be the king and queen, but he didn't even know I was alive. The end. Let us no longer speak of it. Ever."

"Well," the traitor formerly known as my best friend interjected, "that's not entirely true—"

"Nell doesn't want to hear this," I interrupted.

"Oh, but I do. I really, really do."

Nell the traitor stared at me with an evil grin. She obviously took after her mom.

"Auntie Claire asked him out. In the cafeteria. In front of the whole school. With rhyming couplets." She barely got the words out over her snorts of amusement that became loud guffaws, all at my expense.

I folded my arms across my chest. "Yeah, well, at least he knew I was alive." It wasn't the most mature response, but I did manage to resist sticking my tongue out at her, although the urge was overwhelming.

"He sure did!" CC said.

"What happened next?" the traitor Nell asked, eager to hear more.

"He said no," CC managed to answer between evil cackles of glee.

I looked at Nell and thought for a moment that she finally understood my pain and humiliation. Her mouth quivered as if she were about to cry, but when I looked more closely, her eyes weren't full of tears, they danced with merriment. I realized she wasn't about to cry. The spawn of Satan was trying not to laugh.

Nell's laughter fills the air. Normally, a delightful sound that brought joy and peace. Today, it was more akin to an evil witch's cackle. Gasping for breath, my two companions tried to regain some self-control.

Their laughter wound down to sporadic giggles at the same moment Eve yelled from the pool, "Nell! Swim with me now!"

Nell, of course, complied because, despite her behavior of the last few minutes, she is a thoughtful, kind, and loving girl.

"I'm going to need to know the exact wording of the rhyming couplets," she said, before sauntering away with the grace of a runway model.

"Oh, gee, I don't think I remember them."

"You don't have to," CC said. "They're in the yearbook."

Nell's eyes danced with barely suppressed glee as she turned to join Eve in the pool.

"I thought you were my friend, but you are an evil, evil woman who shouldn't be allowed around children, animals, or decent people."

"Good thing I'm just with you then," CC quipped.

My lips twitched in unwitting acknowledgment of her hit. "Touché," I said, and we smiled at each other.

Her eyes suddenly widened in either shock or she was having some kind of attack.

"What?" I said in sudden panic. "Wait, is there a bug? You know how I feel about bugs! It's a big one, right? Get it off me quick!" I flapped my hands in some deranged effort to shoo away the imagined bug.

"It's not a bug for Pete's sake, Claire. Look behind you, but don't make it obvious."

I lowered my hands to the chaise lounge and, in my attempt to look casual, almost tipped the chair over again. "Do these have seat belts?" I asked, only half-joking. I still didn't see what CC was so focused on that she hadn't glanced at her kids for a full two minutes.

"Whoa," I said after a minute, finally catching sight of what had captured CC's attention so completely.

Perhaps the most impressive six-pack abs I had ever seen strutted down the pool deck. I mean, I'm sure there were legs involved in the strutting, but my eyes were glued to the abs, so I couldn't swear to it. It occurred to me that my mouth was open, so I snap it closed. The abs were getting closer and filled my vision more completely as each second ticked by.

I knew the pool had been the right choice. I congratulated myself on the impeccable foreplaning to select it as our destination today. As the abs passed in front of me, my gaze continued to track their owner who also possessed a rather impressive back. I caught sight of CC in my peripheral vision. Her slack-jawed expression prompted me to reach over and gently close her mouth. This plus the fact that the abs had passed caused her to snap out of her stupor.

"Wow! I haven't seen abs like that since—"

"This morning when your husband put his shirt on?" I supplied an accurate reply.

"Well, yeah," She agreed, her voice dropping to a murmur. Her attention seemed to turn inward and her eyes kind of glazed over.

I snapped my fingers in front of her face. "Come back to me CC. Come toward the light."

"That's when people die," she said and slapped at my hands.

"Why do we always come to the pool if you aren't going to swim?" A sweet voice asked from the foot of my lounge chair.

"Of course, I'm going swimming," I assured Dean, CC's seven-year-old son who had some contraption on his goggles that resembled windshield wipers. I didn't ask why.

"I'll race you, Auntie Claire!" Another voice yelled from the edge of the pool, where all that was visible were nine-year-old Ann's water-darkened hair, big eyes, and her fingertips clinging to the edge of the pool.

"You're on!" I yelled, jumping to my feet. Thankfully, I avoided falling on my face when my feet became tangled in the lounge chair. After two running steps, I launched into a cannonball and thoroughly doused CC and the children.

Somehow, Nell escaped the splash zone and still appeared as if she were waiting for a photoshoot. She'd been the climbing toy of the tyrannical two-year-old called Eve for the last ten minutes or so. I honestly didn't know how she did it.

Retaliation splashing commenced until we were nearly alone on our end of the pool. Almost immediately, all the other swimmers moved away from the epic war being waged in the shallow end. A loud throat clearing caused everybody but Ann to stop splashing and look toward a different lifeguard than the one Nell had checked out earlier. Not wanting to get kicked out I tried to distract Ann.

"Hey Ann, are you trying to get out of the race because you know you can't beat me?" A pretty bold taunt for someone who had only beaten said child one out of about a million races.

"Ha!" Derision and confidence infused her reply in equal measure.

We lined up and Frank counted down. "Three, two, one, go!" he shouted.

Ann and I exploded into the pool. A splashing cyclone engulfed me as I propelled myself forward. It felt like I was flying through the water. I spared a thought for poor Ann, who would be crushed when I beat her. I wondered if maybe I should leave off performing my epic victory dance, to spare her feelings a little. I reached the other side of the pool mere seconds later and turned in anticipation of watching Ann struggle in behind me, but she wasn't there.

Now concerned that the poor girl had drowned, I begin to panic. I ducked under the surface and opened my eyes as wide as they could go to try and see if she was lying on the bottom of the pool. Unable to hold my breath I popped up to the surface, gasping. From the pool deck behind me, I heard sweet laughter ring out.

I spun around and was stunned to see Ann sitting a few feet from the water's edge in her red racerback Speedo. "But . . . you were there . . . and now you're here." I sounded a little incoherent, even to myself, as I pointed between where Ann was and where I thought she should be. My head swiveled back and forth between the two places.

"I didn't know anybody could swim that slow and not sink," Kyle said.

I fixed him with a baleful stare, and he fell silent under my death glare.

"It's because she splashes around so much," said Dean. "It keeps her from sinking."

I turned my death glare on Dean, but his attention had shifted to the skimmer basket and he didn't notice.

Frank's girlfriend, Amelia, who I realized had been here for quite a while said, "I don't think she was splashing. I think she was trying to swim."

Amelia was a pretty, petite girl with dark wildly curly hair, deep brown eyes, and a caramel latte-colored skin tone. She was very nice, but often didn't get us, or our jokes. I couldn't decide if she just knew nicer people, or if she was a little slow.

Frank puts his arm around Amelia's shoulder. The top of her curls barely reached his chin. They made a striking couple.

The rest of us glanced around awkwardly before Ann broke the tension. "It doesn't matter what she was doing, because she lost. Big time! Like I could have beat her twice in the same race!"

My laser-eyed glare returned, this time focused on Ann, who only giggles in response.

"All right team let's pack it in," CC called from the lounge chairs, already gathering up gear and preparing to distribute towels to all of us.

"Aw, Mom!" I used my best whiny kid voice. "Do we have to?" I dragged out the last word for a full twenty seconds. The traitors were already climbing out of the pool and heading toward their mom and the towels. Not a complaint to be heard, the kowtowers. Abandoned by those I held closest to my heart, I silently admitted defeat and climbed out as well.

The process of getting everyone changed and reloaded into the cars was significantly easier than getting swimsuits and sunscreen on them, but we managed it in record time anyway. Since Amelia had joined us, she climbed into the backseat with Frank and Ann, and Nell claimed the front.

"See you at home," I called to CC as I pulled out of the parking spot. A thump caused me to slam on the brakes and crane my neck around.

"I think you hit this guy," Frank said, with his arm still around Amelia.

"What?" I cried in disbelief. "What guy? I didn't see a guy." I slammed the shifter into park and jumped out, rushing to the back. Sure enough, there was a guy lying on the ground behind my car.

"What are you doing down there?" I asked. "This is a terrible place to take a nap."

"I wasn't napping. I dropped my towel," he said between clenched teeth. "And then you hit me."

"Well, if you were hiding behind my car there was no way to see you." I explained this obvious fact as if speaking to a slow-witted individual. His scowl deepened, which I hadn't realized was possible.

"Oh! It's Abs." CC said, appearing at my elbow.

"What! It is?" I squinted at the stranger on the ground. As he sat up, his shirt shifted and gave me a brief glance at the abs. "So it is," I said, nodding.

"I could charge you with assaulting a police officer," he said as he stood slowly, checking for injuries. Apparently, he didn't find any.

"Huh?" I said. "You aren't the sheriff and you're kind of old for a deputy." I eyed him from his flip-flop-clad feet all the way to the tips of his still wet brown hair, pausing ever-so-briefly at his choc-olate-brown eyes. *Mm, chocolate*, I thought to myself. Wait, was that to myself? I cast a quick glance around and since none of the blond people were laughing at me, I assumed the words were only in my head.

"I'm the new sheriff. The old one retired. His last day was today."

"Old Tom retired?" CC asked.

"Old Tom has been retiring for ten years," I said. "It's about time."

"You're probably right," CC nodded, "he didn't seem to have his heart in it the last few years. But I would have expected to hear about it way before it happened."

"You're right. I just saw Missy at the store yesterday and she didn't say a word."

"If anybody would have known it would be Missy. And she can't keep a secret," CC said.

"Well since I'm obviously not needed, I'll just be on my way before you can attack me again," The new sheriff said.

"I can't believe I didn't hear about this. I mean what is the point of living in a small town where everybody knows your business if you don't get to know theirs?" I continued as if the sheriff hadn't spoken.

"That's true," CC said, nodding again.

All the nodding made me think CC resembled a bobblehead. This thought tickled me and made it hard to keep up my outrage at being kept in the dark.

"The least Old Tom could do is have the decency to allow us to gossip about him like every good small-town citizen." I continued needling away at the subject, managing to grasp my outrage again.

"Hey, he's gone. Like, long gone. Can we go too?" called a voice from the obviously poor-mannered, moppets waiting in our vehicles.

I mean, haven't they ever heard the rule that states children are meant to be seen, not heard? Or is it heard and not seen? Either way, they interrupted an important discussion among adults. Yeah, I nod my head ready to chastise the lot of them.

"Mom bought fudge," called another voice.

"What are we waiting for? Let's roll," I said. I all but ran to my car. "Last one home is a rotten egg!" I shouted at the mom mobile as I backed out of my parking space, but not before I checked my mirrors twice.

Chapter 3

"**Y**ou're a rotten egg!" Eve said when I stepped into her kitchen followed by Frank, Amelia, Nell, and Ann. The recently remodeled room looked like it was straight out of a magazine. White cabinets gleamed against black granite countertops, shot through with flecks of silver. Black and white floor tiles drew your eye to the bright red banquet nestled under the bank of windows. Dappled sunlight streamed into the inviting space between red curtains, illuminating complimentary scarlet accents around the room including an old school clock, the bread box, and a fruit bowl.

Dean was already seated, tinkering with some Rube Goldberg device that included a marble track and strings hooked to pulleys, which were in turn attached to one of the pendant lights above the large banquette table. Jane had one of her many cats draped around her shoulders like a living stole and was reading some book about animals. Kyle had staked out a corner of the table and was drawing in his sketchbook. I noticed a red smear across one arm. Was it blood? No, I decided, probably jelly. Where the jelly came from was anybody's guess since no jelly jars were visible in the rest of the kitchen.

"Your mom cheats!" I defended my honor. "She cut me off at the bridge."

"You weren't close enough to be cut off,"The little monster said, placing her tiny fists on her hips.

"You know, I think I might have liked you better before you could talk," I said, and placed my hands on my hips as well. CC rolled her eyes but didn't intervene in our standoff. The gasp of outrage from Eve should have sucked all the oxygen out of the kitchen, but lucky for all of us it didn't. "You were so cute and tiny then."

"I'm still cute and tiny," Eve argued, stomping her little foot for emphasis, her angelic face puckered in anger. "And you love me more and more every day, so ha!"

I felt my victory slipping away.

"I've heard you tell her that." Amelia looked around the room, as if seeking allies. Poor thing didn't realize it was every man for himself. Frank wrapped his arm around her shoulder and steered her gently from the room. Probably for the best, I thought to myself. She can't handle my level of word play. I turned back to confront the little monster and realized she'd gone too. Ha! I decided she had admitted defeat and ran away to hide her shame.

That problem settled, I turned to CC and asked, "Where's the fudge?" Nell passed me the box and I opened it. "What is this?" I stared in disbelief at the green and orange fudge in the box. "It's orange and green," I said. "Where's the chocolate?" I demanded of no one in particular.

"I ate it all." Came the reply from my left. My head snapped around to see Eve, my archnemesis, petting another of Jane's cats, a calico, that had melted into a puddle of sunlight on the tile.

"What?" I didn't want to believe her. "You ate Auntie Claire's Fudge?"

"No. I ate our fudge. Mommy bought it."

Before I could leap on her, Nell handed me a box of chocolates. "Ooh. Chocolate." I completely forgot Eve and dug into the box.

Possibly the most gorgeous man alive walked into the kitchen and asked, "Who wants pizza?" He balanced what must have been ten boxes as effortlessly as if they were ten pieces of paper. His blond hair was casually mussed, creating the effect celebrities took hours to recreate. In his case, I knew all he had done was unconsciously run his fingers through it. For him, the look was completely natural and enhanced by warm, friendly blue eyes. His perfect smile put the toothpaste ads to shame. I half expected a CGI twinkle to appear at any moment.

A swarm of locusts, sometimes called children, descended on him and grabbed boxes out of his hands before he could even close the back door. The locusts settled onto various chairs, and banquette benches with their pizza. Once the kids had settled down to eat, the most gorgeous man alive dropped kisses on their heads and maneuvered through the kitchen with a single pizza box still in his hands. He planted a quick kiss on my cheek as I shoved the last of the chocolate into my mouth. When he reached CC, the kiss was on her lips, lasted a lot longer, and edged toward indecent.

"Gross! I'm trying to eat here," I said around my mouthful of chocolate.

Two sets of annoyed eyes turned to me, while the kids just ignored another in a long line of nearly constant make-out sessions. I flipped open the last pizza box and grabbed a slice.

Jake followed my lead and scooped out a slice for CC and himself. "So, what did you all do today?" he asked, sliding onto a bar stool next to me. Before I could answer, a chorus of voices—including Jake's—sang out, "Swimming again."

Amelia looked around the room with a slight frown line between her brows, seemingly perplexed as to why Jake would ask the question if he already knew the answer.

"Hey! I can't help it if swimming is simply the best," I said.

"You know if any of you could agree on something Auntie Claire wouldn't get the tie-breaking vote," Jake said, his tone reasonable.

Come on, I thought, what siblings are going to agree with each other? That's just ridiculous, man!

The sound of the doorbell caused us all to freeze. Only Amelia continued eating as if nothing had happened. When it rang again Amelia finally seemed to realize something was off. She looked around and said, "Do you want me to get it?"

That finally kicked Jake into gear. "No, of course not. I'll get it," he said and headed out of the room.

"Who do you think it is?" CC asked. "Everybody in town knows it's not locked and to just come in."

I was curious too, but not enough to walk away from pizza. I listened and tried to decipher the murmur of voices from the front door. If I wasn't mistaken, the visitor was saying, "Time the pew tariff do mimic I'm Strong."

Well, obviously their visitor had escaped a mental institute. Assuming Jake could handle a deranged visitor, I shrugged it off and grabbed another slice of pizza.

CC jumped up to mop up some juice Eve spilled, which left me alone at the counter.

When Jake didn't return and the rumble of voices continued, I finally got curious enough to slide off my barstool and go investigate. Also, I was full and didn't want to hang out in the kitchen by myself.

Rounding the corner, I saw perhaps the two most beautiful men in the world. Dismissing Jake, I turned my scrutiny on the stranger. He was as tall as Jake, so over six feet, stubble on his jaw, broad shoulders, lean hips, intelligent eyes, and a mouth that looked like it had never smiled. Ever.

"Claire, this is the new sheriff, Dominic Armstrong," Jake said. "Sheriff, this is Claire Miller, a close family friend, and neighbor."

New sheriff, I think to myself, that sounds familiar. The sheriff's eyes widened at my approach. That made me glad I had brushed out my hair after swimming, so it didn't look like a rat's nest. Thinking it was always nice to be appreciated, I added a little saunter to my walk.

"You," he said, his tone harsh. "You hit me with your car!"

His demeanor snapped me out of my preening. "That's outrageous!" I said, aghast that he would even suggest such an outlandish thing. "I've never hit anybody with my car. Except for Mr. Russell, but that was an accident, and he was able to walk again within a year, so . . . everything worked out in the end. Oh, and Mr. Johnson, but that was totally his fault. I mean who crosses the street in the middle of a block like that?"

"Don't forget Mitchell," Jake added, "and Ralph."

"I hit them at the same time, so it should only count as one," I stated for the record.

"How do you still have a driver's license?" asked Sheriff Armstrong. "You seem to be a walking hazard to the public."

I folded my arms across my chest. "If I'm a walking hazard then I must be safer when I'm driving."

He stared at me, and I assumed he was in awe of my clever arguments. Several seconds elapsed before he shook his head and turned to Jake.

"Who's that?" a small voice from the area of my knee piped in.

We all looked down to see Eve poking the sheriff's knee with, of all things, a turtle. The sheriff looked shocked. CC, who had followed Eve out of the kitchen, snatched the turtle so quickly I thought it had simply disappeared, until she handed the little reptile to Jake.

"Eve, we've talked about poking people with our pets. It's rude and the pets don't like it." Eve continued to gaze at the sheriff throughout the rebuke, so I'm pretty sure she was ignoring her mom.

"This is the new sheriff. Sheriff, this is my wife CC and our youngest daughter, Eve," said Jake.

The sheriff squatted down to Eve's eye level, which put him in a vulnerable position. If he spent any time around us at all, he'd soon learn to avoid such a rookie mistake. "Nice to meet you, Eve," he said, sticking his hand out.

Eve transferred her gaze from his face to his hand and back again as if determining whether the sheriff was worth her handshake, or if he was somehow a threat. Jake, CC, and I sighed in relief when, instead of kicking him in the kneecap or pushing him over, she finally placed her tiny hand in his and gave it a vigorous up and down shake, before dropping it as if it was contaminated.

"Are you going to arrest my Auntie Claire?" she asked.

"Of course not sweetie, why would he arrest Auntie Claire?" Jake answered, before scooping Eve into his arms.

"Because she ran him over," Eve said.

"Snitches get stitches," I whispered in Eve's direction.

"He was hiding behind her car at the pool."

The sheriff's victorious expression soured.

"He doesn't look familiar," I said, tilting my head to the side. "If he were to lie on the ground, it might jog my memory." The sheriff's expression migrated from sour to shocked. I guessed he probably wouldn't be lying down.

"Mr. Johnson was found dead in his home today," the sheriff said, cutting off any further conversation about an alleged pedestrian car incident.

"Oh, my goodness!" CC clutched her chest. "Poor Mr. Johnson, what happened? Was it a heart attack? He seemed to be in good health, but I guess you never know."

"We investigate every death, and I can't discuss open cases," The sheriff told her, sounding like an automatic message. Turning to Jake again he said, "I understand that you applied for a loan last week and Mr. Johnson denied it." Somehow a notepad and pen appeared in his hand as if by magic.

"I did," Jake said, "but I wasn't surprised when he turned me down. Mr. Johnson turns everybody down. I was hoping to do more business locally, but when that didn't work out," he shrugged, "I went with plan B. I went to my other bank in the city. Why?"

"Oh my gosh!" I practically shouted. "You're totally a suspect! He thinks you killed Mr. Johnson over a loan application!" I bounced from one foot to the other and pointed a dramatic finger at Jake.

"Ms. Miller, I understand you were also turned down for a loan last week," the sheriff said, turning his suspicious gaze to me.

I stopped bouncing and clutched my chest. "You think I killed Mr. Johnson? That's ridiculous. I mean just because I can't remodel my house and replace my lead-riddled pipes and may die from lead poisoning because he refused my loan, doesn't mean I'd kill him."

"Your pipes have lead?" CC asked, her eyes reflecting concern.

"I mean, possibly. Pipes do, you know."

"But you haven't had them tested?"

Why was she grilling me? "They're pipes. How would they take a test? They can't even hold a pencil, and they don't talk." The duh was heavily implied in my tone. CC's frown told me she knew how ridiculous she sounded and was deeply embarrassed. The sheriff's eyes which had been bouncing back and forth between us finally settled on me again.

"So, you're saying you blame Mr. Johnson for denying your loan and think by his denial your life is in danger from lead poisoning?"

I nodded my head emphatically. "Yeah totally, I mean I'm a great loan applicant. I pay most of my bills. Sometimes even on time." CC and Jake maneuvered behind the sheriff and began shaking their heads back and forth in unison. "I mean, wait, I would never hurt anybody, and Mr. Johnson denies everybody's loan, so it could have been anybody, and usually people just ask Ms. Peters, the senior teller, and she gets the loans approved, so it isn't a big deal to be denied." The sheriff's pencil continued its frantic scratching in his notepad. Maybe my belated backpedaling might not have worked, after all.

"Wait, this means you think somebody killed Mr. Johnson and it wasn't natural causes?" CC asked.

The pencil finally ceased its scratching. "I'm just asking questions to determine the events that led up to his death." The sheriff's reply was the usual bland response, like a TV detective.

"I didn't even see Mr. Johnson when I applied for a loan. I turned in my documents to Ms. Schwartz and received an email the next day denying the loan," Jake said.

The pencil was scratching again.

"Yeah, uh huh, that's what I did too." I nodded emphatically to give my words more believability, but the sheriff's raised eyebrow implied it might not have been as effective as I had hoped.

"Mom, have you seen Fluffy?" Jane asked, walking down the stairs, and then peering under the entry table.

"No, Jane, and now isn't a good time. The new sheriff is here."

"Why?" Jane barely spared a glance for any of us as she dropped to peer under the couch.

"He's just asking a few questions. Can you take Eve back to the kitchen please?" Jake handed Eve to Jane.

"I think that's all the questions I have for now." The sheriff put his notebook and pencil away.

He and Jake shared a handshake and turned to the front door. Just as Jake put his hand on the knob, I spotted Fluffy. "Don't move!" I said in a loud whisper and then froze in place.

CC and Jake immediately complied, except for their eyes which pinballed around the room trying to identify a threat.

The sheriff, foolish man, ignored my command. His hand moved to hover over the gun holstered at his side. "What?" he asked, scanning the room while moving toward me.

He didn't realize the danger was coming from above. "Don't move!" I repeated, with added emphasis.

"Fluffy," I said in the sing-song voice reserved for recalcitrant pets, "who's a good girl?" I shifted my weight and moved slowly toward the sheriff, who was still unaware of the imminent danger he faced.

"Jane," I said in the same coaxing voice, "I found Fluffy."

I had almost reached the sheriff and extended my arm, palm out. Fluffy dropped from the banister and landed like a flexible missile on his shoulder. The sheriff jerked his head away from Fluffy and his cheek slammed into my open hand. The sound of the slap echoed off the walls.

Everyone else panicked, but not me. I snatched Fluffy off the sheriff's shoulder before any more damage could occur.

"Fluffy! You naughty girl," Jane said as she took the four-foot snake out of my hands. She continued baby talking to it and left the room as if a near disaster hadn't just been avoided.

The sheriff stared after Jane for a minute before turning to me. "Fluffy is a snake that lives loose in the house to drop on visitors?" he asked.

"Hey, I don't live here, it's not my kid or my snake, why are you asking me?" I put my hands on my hips and gave him a proper glare.

"I'm so sorry, Sheriff," CC said. Her fluttering hands looked like well-manicured butterflies. "Fluffy is a bit of an escape artist and frequently gets out of her cage. I hope you weren't hurt when she fell on you, or when Claire slapped you." Her genuine concern prompted his assurance that he was fine, even though the red, hand-shaped area on his check argued otherwise.

In the aftermath, Jake was able to walk the sheriff out of the house with no further discussion.

"Whew," I said when he was finally gone. "Can you believe Mr. Johnson was murdered?"

"He didn't say he was murdered just that he was dead," Jake reminded me as he shut the front door behind him.

"Come on, why else would a sheriff need to question us at," I looked at my watch, "7:30 at night?"

Frank and Amelia walked in from the kitchen arm in arm. "I'm going to walk Amelia home," Frank said.

An ear-splitting scream sounded from the kitchen, which didn't stop Frank. He and Amelia slipped out and left the rest of us to deal with this latest situation.

Ann, Dean, and Kyle ran out of the kitchen.

"Not it!" Jake and CC yelled, mere microseconds apart.

"Oh, no. She's not my kid." I realized my hands were still on my hips. "This is not my problem."

They covered their ears with their hands and glared at me. All the while, the screams continued to escalate in both volume and anger.

"You better hurry, or there will be no calming her," CC warned.

I began to sweat remembering the great Tantrum of the Tutu.

Sensing the proverbial blood in the water, CC continued to shout over the screams. "Even if you go home, you'll still be able to hear her. All night."

Caving, as we all knew I would, I plunged through the swinging door and into the kitchen.

"Eve!" I wanted to speak in a soothing tone but had to shout over her screams. "What's wrong, sweetheart?"

The screams didn't stop but did lower in volume. I hoped I was getting through to her and she wasn't just pausing to suck in more oxygen.

"I told her she couldn't shave the cat," Nell said before sauntering out of the kitchen to join her siblings in their strategic retreat.

"Eve, sweetheart, we talked about shaving the cat, remember? The other cats would make fun of her."

The screams ended abruptly. "I would make her haircut beautiful, Auntie Claire. Don't you think I could make it beautiful?" She turned her hopeful, yet vulnerable gaze on me.

Trembling tear drops clung to her thick lashes, somehow defying gravity. *It's a trap*, I thought to myself. Still, I found myself saying,

"Of course! I think you would do a great job." Her hopeful expression caused me to realize my mistake. I continued, thinking fast. "Even so, the other cats might get jealous and be mean to her. Besides, if you start shaving her, you'd have to keep shaving her, and then other cats would want to be shaved, and they would forever be hounding you to shave them. You wouldn't ever get a moment's peace. You might even miss your cartoons."

She puckered up her adorable face—which is probably the only reason she has survived this long—and considered my argument. "That makes sense," she conceded. "Ok, I won't shave the cat."

Before she could skip out of the kitchen, I seized one last opportunity. "Pinkie promise?" I extended my right pinkie to her.

She stopped and then turned to face me. Eve studied me in silence for several seconds while nibbling on her bottom lip. After what seemed an eternity, she nodded and extended her right pinkie to me. We curled our little fingers together and shook them once before dropping hands.

I breathed a sigh of relief as she skipped through the doorway, blissfully unaware that she had just about deafened the whole town.

"All clear?" CC and Jake asked in unison, peeking around the doorframe.

"Yes," I said, and dropped into a chair, exhausted.

"Whew, that was close," Jake said. He ventured into the kitchen and grabbed three beers from the fridge. He passed them around and then sat opposite me.

We each took a few swallows, while seeming to enjoy the silence and contemplate the day.

"So, Mr. Johnson is dead," I finally said. "It's about time."

"Claire!" CC acted shocked.

After all our years of friendship, nothing I do should surprise her. "Come on, CC. He was old! He was so, so old. And crabby!"

CC rolled her eyes.

"He was old when we were kids, CC," I took another swig of my beer, "he must have been a hundred."

CC's response was to take a drink.

Obviously, she had no argument to that. Ha! I congratulated myself on my superior argument skills. The silence drug on. For my part, I contemplated deep thoughts. Like, was Mr. Johnson related to Johnson and Johnson? Johnsonville brats? Magic Johnson?

"I can't believe it," she said, interrupting my thoughts.

"I know, I mean, he looks nothing like Magic Johnson," I said.

CC's forehead wrinkled, but before she could speak, Jake said, "I don't think they are related."

See? Jake gets me. Maybe I should trade up for a new best friend. Jake and I could have a great time. We could go to the bakery and Rose would give him all the brownies—which he would share with me, of course. We could get drinks and loser guys wouldn't hit on me.

"What do you think of Coral Sunrise?" I asked Jake. His forehead wrinkled in confusion.

"Don't even think of replacing me, Loser," CC interrupted. "He can't tell the difference between Coral Sunrise, Sunset Serenade, and Kiss me Quick. Besides, he'd never be able to keep from chipping his manicure at the office. He is always tinkering with things. It would never work."

I, at least internally, admitted defeat. "Kiss me Quick is a really good color," I said, looking at my nails. "We should get manicures tomorrow."

"I already scheduled an appointment for us both."

I beamed at her. "You're the best friend ever!"

"Don't you forget it." She smiled, satisfied with her place.

"I'm sorry, Jake, you can't replace CC as my best friend," I said, trying to let him down easy.

Jake finished his beer, walked over, and put the bottle in the recycling container. "I'm heading to bed. You coming soon?" He asked.

"Jake! That's so inappropriate! You are married to my best friend, and you aren't even trying to be subtle. CC is sitting right there!" I gestured toward my friend to emphasize my point.

Jake locked his gorgeous blue-eyed gaze with mine and stalked directly toward me with the grace of a jaguar. The intensity of his gaze paralyzed me. I could only watch his approach. My breathing, like my heart rate, was suddenly erratic. He leaned over and placed his hands on either side of me, trapping me. He was so close; I could feel his breath on my lips. This must be how a cobra's prey felt.

His lips parted and then my eyes closed of their own will. The next thing I knew, in possibly the sexiest voice ever, Jake said, "I was talking to CC."

I opened my eyes and watched him saunter out of the kitchen. "Whoa, girl, he is so hot!" I said, fanning myself.

CC smiled a satisfied smile and said, "I know." She tossed her empty bottle in the recycle bin and followed her husband. "See you in the morning," she called as the swinging door closed behind her.

Sliding off my chair, I wobbled a little as my knees struggled to support me—aftereffects of Jake's attention. I finally managed to lock them in place and headed next door to my own house.

Chapter 4

The next morning, I staggered into CC's kitchen, barely alive. My t-shirt was wrinkled and had holes in it. My hair was a tangle around my face and my bare feet peeked out from my yoga pants.

The children all sat at the table with various breakfast foods. Cereal, toast, fruit, etc., and not one of them looked up at their dying Auntie Claire. The heartless wretches simply went on eating as if my life didn't hang by a thread.

CC continued sipping from her mug of coffee, unconcerned by my near-death state. However, in a moment of saving grace, she slid a steaming mug across the counter to me.

I clutched it desperately in my hands and raised it to my face. Eyes closed, I breathed in the life-giving elixir. Stirred by the perfect aroma, I finally sipped the magic liquid that would save my life.

"Auntie Claire why don't you get a coffee machine?" a voice behind me asked.

I didn't have the energy to turn and see who had made this ridiculous suggestion.

"Because then Auntie Claire would have to make her own coffee," CC said.

My best friend's deceptively sweet voice tried and failed to hide her evil black heart. A few snickers from the peanut gallery caused me to turn and cast an accusing glance at her traitorous waifs. None of the kids met my eyes. Instead, they were unusually focused on their breakfast. Turning back to my life-giving mug, I inhaled deeply before taking another large swallow. Closing my eyes in bliss, I tuned out all the chatter around me and focused on the enjoyment of the day's first cup of coffee.

After finishing the whole mug, down to the last drop, I was finally ready to join the living. I placed my now-empty mug on the counter, which CC wisely refilled. A piece of toast from Frank's plate found its way into my hand and I crammed half of it into my mouth in one crumb-producing bite.

In response, Frank shook his head, obviously in pity at my poor state, and finished the piece I left him.

After eating the rest, my attention was caught by something outside the window. I stared intently, trying to determine what exactly I saw.

Ann noticed my stare and turned to see what had captured my attention.

Silly girl.

Not seeing anything out the window, Ann looked back at me, her freckled face questioning. She was just in time to see me shove the last piece of her bacon into my mouth.

She rolled her eyes but offered no comment.

A clicking noise behind me caused me to panic and abandon my plan to steal Jane's English muffin. My eyes darted around the room, searching for an escape route, but it was too late. Next thing I knew, I was flat on my back with a hundred and fifty pounds of vicious fur on top of me. I tried to save myself from further attack and covered my face, but to no avail. A long, wet tongue probed between my fingers, taste testing which part of me to bite first.

"Help!" I pleaded. "Please, for all that is holy save me from the bear." No one rushed to my aid, the heartless curs. I managed to shove the bear off to one side long enough to stand and leap onto the counter.

"Auntie Claire, if you would just pet him he wouldn't think you hated him and try so hard," Jane said.

"I do pet him." I prepared to defend myself again as the bear, pretending to be a Newfoundland, puts his front paws on the counter, which placed him at eye level with me. His huge, fluffy tail threatened to clear the counter behind him. His hopeful eyes twinkled innocently at me, while his tongue hung out like a wet pink washrag, and he panted into my face. I reached out and gingerly patted his head twice before snatching my hand back to safety. Jane's soft sigh indicated she was unimpressed with this show of affection.

"Come on, Bear," she called. The furry monstrosity pushed off the counter and trotted after her.

"Really, Claire, I wish you wouldn't make such a commotion every morning." CC calmly sipped her coffee as if nothing life-threatening had happened.

"Me?" I was indignant. "I didn't tackle myself to the floor." My defense fell on deaf ears apparently. My best friend had already dismissed me and turned to leave the kitchen.

"I'm getting dressed and then I'll be ready. Five minutes."

I wasn't the only one to roll my eyes at her back. We all knew it would be at least thirty minutes. I finished my second mug of coffee and headed next door to shower, get dressed, blow dry my hair, start a load of laundry, vacuum my living room, take my dogs for a ten-mile run, after which I would amble over to wait for CC. Okay, I didn't start a load of laundry, vacuum, or go for a run, but you get my point about how long it takes CC to get ready.

When CC finally reappeared, she was dressed in a short aqua sundress with big white polka dots. Her hair was pulled into an updo that looked like it could tumble down at the slightest movement but was probably pinned and hair sprayed to within an inch of its life. Next to her I felt like the ugly stepsister in my black twill shorts and an emerald-green t-shirt that I thought highlighted my eyes. My tee had an awesome design that featured a hammer and read *this is not a drill*. To complete the stylish ensemble, my boring brown hair was pulled up in a ponytail. Man, why did my friend have to be so pretty? I should have found the ugly neighbor to be friends with all those years ago. Well, too late now.

CC smiled warmly. "You look so nice, Claire. I've always loved that shirt on you. It makes your eyes even more beautiful if that's possible. I should have found the ugly neighbor to be friends with."

I smiled back and realized I had made the right choice all those years ago.

"Thanks," I said, "you look amazing, too! We are going to stop traffic."

"Probably because you are a menace to society," Frank said, sotto voce, from his seat at the kitchen table. We chose to ignore his blatantly false statement.

"Have fun with Eve at her friend's birthday party. Three-year-old birthday parties are so fun."

His sour expression was all I needed to put the extra pep in my step.

"That was a little petty," CC chided as we walked to my car.

"I know, but it was fun," I replied while climbing into the driver's seat.

"You know, we could walk," CC said, "it's only like ten blocks away. And it's a beautiful day."

I stared at her as if she'd suggested we drown her children. "CC! Are you crazy? Walk instead of ride in this beautiful car?" I stroked the dashboard with deep affection.

CC rolled her eyes but climbed into the passenger seat without voicing any more ridiculous suggestions.

I smiled as we cruised down the familiar tree-lined streets on our way to the salon. We passed the usual manicured lawns, filled with children playing and dogs barking. We exchanged waves with the few people we passed. Small-town life, wasn't it grand? A few minutes later I pulled into the parking lot and found a space right in front of the salon. As we headed inside, I thought, *this day just keeps getting better and better.*

"CC, Claire, how nice to see you again!" Tina said, offering a warm greeting. She was the receptionist and the owner, a willowy redhead with a generous smattering of freckles covering her whole face, neck, arms and, I'm assuming, the rest of her. "We have you all set up with Sarah and Fern," she confirmed.

CC and I headed to our normal chairs and manicurists, while the gossip that seems to permeate hair and nail salons flowed around us.

All of it seems to be about Mr. Johnson's death and the new sheriff investigating it.

The group was split half and half on whether it was an accidental death or murder. We listened to the gossip without adding any of our own and learned that Mr. Johnson was found in his home at the bottom of the staircase. Ms. Schwartz found him yesterday late afternoon when she went to check on him. She had become worried when he didn't show up to work on Thursday or Friday and he hadn't answered the dozen phone calls she made to his house.

There was rampant speculation about the romantic relationship that may or may not have existed between Ms. Schwartz and Mr. Johnson. The opinions on the possibility of a secret illicit relationship were also about half and half. Those who believed it claimed nobody would work with such a sourpuss for so long without something on the side. I wasn't sure if the sourpuss was supposed to be Mr. Johnson or Ms. Schwartz—as it described the crotchety old man who seemed to delight in being ornery and the pinch-faced dragon lady who found fault with everybody—but I had to agree with that opinion. I couldn't imagine working with either of them for a year let alone fifty. I mean, the nitwit I had to work with was bad, but at least he smiled. He was dumb as a post but friendly. I shook my head, dismissing my boss and tuning back into the gossip. The other half of the group thought a relationship between the two was too disgusting to contemplate, which I also agreed with. I had a horrifying image of them in a passionate embrace and threw up a little in my mouth.

"What color today?" My manicurist, Fern, spoke in a soft voice and looked as if she expected a physical blow at any moment. Her eyes never made it higher than my chin and her shoulders were hunched protectively.

"Kiss me Quick, please Fern," I said, and then burst out laughing.

Fern, obviously not realizing the joke, reached into a case containing various shades of nail polish and plucked out the bottle of Kiss me Quick.

Torn between trying to explain the joke to Fern and listening to further gossip, I glanced at CC. Her sparkling eyes reassured me that she got it and considered me hilarious.

The gossip turned to the new sheriff. Apparently, Dominic Armstrong came from the big city and had been their best detective. He had served in the military before that.

After our nails looked fabulous and all the gossip had petered out, CC and I headed to the car. Lost in our own thoughts, the ride home was silent. I parked in my driveway, since the garage was full of priceless and precious treasures my parents had collected—and I had expanded on. Things like old hoses, boxes of elementary art, and Christmas lights that no longer worked filled the space.

Walking up the pathway to the front door we passed the fragrant roses my mom tended lovingly for years. I was desperately trying not to kill them. They reminded me of her with a pang of loneliness that I normally avoided by surrounding myself with CC and her family.

CC linked her arm with mine silently offering her support.

No wonder she was my best friend. I opened the unlocked door, stepped into the entryway, and dropped my keys on the small table near the door. My house resembled CC's only in basic layout. My living room was on one side of the hall and the stairs were on the other. The walls were China blue, a color many people thought overpowered the rooms, but I found beautiful. Since I hadn't added on to accommodate a growing family, the living room only had room for an overstuffed couch, coffee table, and two matching chairs. The kitchen was less than half the size of CC's, but since I didn't cook, and usually ate at CC's house, it was more than adequate.

We stepped over the hound dog, Agatha, who was spread across the floor appearing dead, but was only dead tired. We settled on the couch when, out of nowhere, a large black fur ball named Blackbeard jumped into my lap and began kneading me all over. His one green eye stared at me demanding attention. Knowing that denying him would result in harm to my person I started scratching him under his chin. A resounding purr filled the room.

CC wasn't getting off easy. My other dog, a terrier mix named Benji, sat in front of her, raised both front paws in the air, and then fell over as if shot. CC, who had probably seen this trick a hundred times this month alone, clapped and cooed over Benji showering him with praise. When no treat appeared, Benji sighed in the dejected way only dogs can and laid at her feet. "I just don't know what to think of poor Mr. Johnson's death," CC said, stretching a toe out to pet Benji.

"What do you mean? He's dead." I stroked Blackbeard from head to tail as he lay across my lap and part of the cushion next to me. He is a very, very big boy.

CC rolled her eyes and said, "I know he's dead, but how? And if it was murder, who did it? I just can't imagine anyone we know is a murderer." Her eyes took on a faraway look as if mentally going through a rolodex of town members.

"What about Ms. Schwartz?" I asked.

"Well, I suppose she might be provoked to violence."

"Provoked?" I laughed. "She hit the Smith boy with her broom when he tried to sell her candy for the school fundraiser." CC frowned, but before she could say anything, I said, "And what about when the Jenkins twins were looking for their kitten and she turned the hose on them? That lady is mean."

"I suppose," CC conceded, "but what would be her motive?"

"Well, she worked for him for years, so there is that," I reminded her. She nodded but wasn't ready to admit defeat.

"She seemed to like him. Remember how many times she was spotted with him outside the bank? That's why some people believed they were having an affair."

"A truly horrifying thought." We both shuddered. Quickly trying to change the subject I said, "Well, I'm sure the hot shot new sheriff from the city will solve it in no time."

CC wrinkled her forehead. "I'm not so sure. He's new in town and doesn't know people like we do. I mean he suspected Jake due to a denied loan. Everybody knows Jake could buy this whole town. If not for his factory, most people would be out of a job."

"That's true. I still don't know what they make there, every time Jake tries to explain it his eyes start dancing, and he uses confusing words, and I can actually feel my eyes glaze over."

"I'm not entirely sure either," CC admitted. "I know it has to do with computers."

I took the ensuing silence to ponder what I knew about Jake's career. As if by silent consent, we both shrugged and resumed the topic at hand, Mr. Johnson's murder.

"Maybe we should talk to Ms. Schwartz," CC said.

"What? Like on purpose?" I asked, a little shocked she would suggest such a bold move. "Normally we run the other way when we see Ms. Schwartz. We have jumped fences, hidden behind statues, and attended a gamblers anonymous meeting that one time we ducked into a doorway to avoid her," I said by way of reminding her.

"Did you hear Ken got his twenty-year pin?" CC asked.

I nodded. "Yeah, I talked to him last week about it. Did you know his daughter is expecting a boy?"

CC smiled. "Oh! Babies are so great! Imagine having one of your own," she said, with a pointed look in my direction.

You'd think with seven of her own she would be over the baby crazy thing, but not true. She loved babies. After a few seconds of wistful silence on CC's part, and horrified silence on mine, she moved on.

"I mean it, Claire. We should at least talk to some people about it. Sheriff Armstrong doesn't seem to really understand our town and the people in it."

I nodded my head at that. I mean, the guy thought either Jake or I killed Mr. Johnson over a loan application! How ridiculous was that? Everybody in town had been denied a loan by Mr. Johnson at least once. I opened my mouth to tell CC I wasn't going to talk to Ms. Schwartz.

At that exact moment she said, "Then it's settled. I bet she is home today. Grab your purse and you can drive."

I brightened at the prospect of driving my baby and almost forgot that CC wanted me to drive to Ms. Schwartz's house. By the time I remembered, she was off the couch and almost to the door. She probably would have made it, but she had to step over a still-sleeping Agatha, whose furry body covered most of the entryway floor. If this wasn't enough of an obstacle, Benji sat on his haunches in front of the door, a pair of my shorts hanging from his mouth. She fell for his clever trap, cooing in appreciation. As she accepted the shorts and lavished him with pets and scratches in all the right places, I silently debated whether to simply ignore her command to talk to Schwartz.

"Get a move on," she hollered, "or I'll tell Dean you need him to come over and help you with something."

I gasped in horror and outrage. "You would use your child in such an evil manner?"

She smiled. "I believe the last time he helped, you ended up with an automatic omelet maker."

"Well, it never actually made an omelet," I said, "but it did give me a goose egg when I walked into it. It also took me three days to take it all down. How did he even put it together in a couple of hours? It took up most of the kitchen."

She probably didn't hear the rest of what I said since she was already out the door. I huffed a defeated breath and followed. A quick glance at CC's smile as I fastened my seatbelt. told me she had known the outcome all along and had just waited for me to do the right thing.

Chapter 5

A few minutes later we pulled up to Ms. Schwartz's. It was hard to see the house because my eyes were drawn to the profusion of flowers that spilled over each other as if fighting to be the winner. She had hollyhocks as tall as her roof, roses that bloomed widely, foxglove spires, daisies, coneflowers, and probably a hundred others I didn't know the names of. CC was chewing her lower lip and fidgeting with her seatbelt. *Ha!* Looked like she wasn't so sure she wanted to see Ms. Schwartz now.

Because I have a difficult time keeping my thoughts to myself, I said, "Ha! You aren't so sure you want to see Ms. Schwartz now, are you?"

CC seemed to gird her loins, or whatever, opened her door and got out.

I still wasn't sure this was a great idea. "I could wait in the car," I said hopefully. "In case you need a speedy getaway."

She leaned into the car and her withering gaze hit me square in the chest. I opened my door and got out, too. I stood on the manicured lawn and shifted my weight from foot to foot while looking at Ms. Schwartz's front door.

CC linked her arm with mine and started up the path.

She was slightly hampered by the fact that she was almost dragging me along, but she still had a pleasant smile on her face.

When we reached the front door, CC poked the doorbell with her index finger. I noticed her hand wasn't quite steady and I smirked. After maybe a second I said, "Well, I guess she isn't home."

I wanted to turn and go back to the car, but CC had a death grip on my arm She was stronger than she looked.

While I struggled to break free, the door opened, and Ms. Schwartz peered out at us. None of her regular sharp-eyed gaze, steely-backed posture, or puckered mouth in sight. I almost gasped, but a sharp elbow from CC distracted me.

"Ms. Schwartz, we wanted to come and check on you after the terrible tragedy," she said in a surprisingly sympathetic voice.

"Thank you," Ms. Schwartz said softly.

I didn't even know she could speak softly. Normally her voice is shrill, like fingernails on a chalkboard, and meant to inspire fear and immediate compliance, which it does.

"Won't you come in?" she asked, opening the door wider.

My hesitation was almost imperceptible, but CC continued to drag me along. We stepped into the foyer and my eyes darted around the room trying to take in everything.

As far as I knew, nobody had ever been in Ms. Schwartz house, and I wanted to be able to recall everything. I had expected jars of eyeballs, newts, and spell books to fill the shelves, but instead there were ceramic knickknacks of shepherdesses, lacy doilies, and an alarming number of paintings of her cat, Mr. Franklin. They covered nearly every wall and shelf in the house that I could see.

She ushered us into a surprisingly girly and comfortable front room. It had a matching overstuffed loveseat and chair with a floral print. CC and I sat on the loveseat while Ms. Schwartz settled into the chair.

A giant velvet ottoman filled the space normally occupied by a coffee table. Mr. Franklin sat in the center, sphinxlike; a king surveying his subjects. I wondered if it was the same Mr. Franklin. If so, he must be over thirty years old. She'd had that cat for as long as I can remember. I tried to spot a difference between the paintings and the flesh-and-bone cat. Since he was all gray with green eyes, there weren't a lot of differences to spot.

"It's so nice of you to stop by," Ms. Schwartz said. "It's been just terrible. First, Mr. Johnson didn't come to work Thursday, nor did he answer any of my calls or reply to any messages. Then, when he didn't come to work Friday, I just knew something terrible had happened."

CC made a sympathetic face and asked, "Was Wednesday the last day you saw him? Did he seem different? Worried?"

Ms. Schwartz shook her head, which caused limp tendrils of gray hair—normally teased into an attractive beehive—to drift across her shoulders. "No. No, nothing was different. After the bank closed at five, he packed up his briefcase, told me goodnight, and left. It seemed like any other day." She looked close to tears.

I was about ready to bolt when she continued. "Wait, he did receive a phone call right before he left. It was from that awful Mr. Russell. He was yelling about the fence again. You know Mr. Russell thinks Mr. Johnson put a fence on his side of the property line, but he didn't of course. Everyone knows that Mr. Johnson had the fence put up in the exact same location as the old one, and therefore it was where it was supposed to be. On the property line. Mr. Russell was just ornery." The look she gave us reminded me of my old high school history teacher. "You remember, before the fence he turned poor Mr. Johnson into the historic society for the color he had his house painted. Of course, Mr. Johnson chose one of the appropriate colors. And before that there were the constant calls to the police about noise violations. That was when poor Bernard was alive and would sometimes bark. I bet he did it. He's a terrible man!"

The doorbell interrupted the litany of Mr. Russell's poor character traits and seemed to deflate her again.

CC and I exchanged a look and wondered who else would be paying Ms. Schwartz a visit.

For her part, Ms. Schwartz also looked surprised, but got up and went to answer the door.

While she was gone, Mr. Franklin twitched his fluffy tail and glared at me through slitted eyes. I could see the front door from the loveseat and recognized the sheriff as soon as Ms. Schwartz opened the door. I elbowed CC hard enough that she almost fell off the loveseat.

"Ms. Schwartz, I'd like to ask you a few more questions," he began.

Ms. Schwartz nodded and ushered him into the front room with us.

When he spotted us, I could see his mouth tighten, but he simply inclined his head in greeting and turned back to Ms. Schwartz.

"I just had a few follow-up questions about your relationship with Mr. Johnson," the sheriff said.

Ms. Schwartz looked confused. "I already told you. He is—" she swallowed hard before continuing, "—was my boss at the bank."

"I was speaking of your relationship outside of work," he continued, looking slightly uncomfortable.

If it was possible, Ms. Schwartz looked even more confused. "Our relationship outside of work? I don't understand."

"He wants to know if you two were smoochy-face kissing," I explained, trying to help. CC elbowed me so hard I lurched sideways into the loveseat's arm. Luckily, it was overstuffed, so it didn't hurt.

Mr. Franklin twitched his tail faster and continued to stare at me.

Ms. Schwartz's eyes narrowed, and her posture regained its normal ramrod straight bearing. CC and I froze, wild-eyed and terrified, fearing a dose of her wrath.

However, Ms. Schwartz turned that wrath on the sheriff, her mouth pinched like she just sucked a lemon. "How dare you imply I have loose morals!" She practically shouted at him. "Why I never! I've lived here my entire life! Ask anyone, and they will tell you I'm an upstanding citizen with the strongest moral fiber!"

While berating the sheriff, she backed him toward the door. I would have thought a big city cop and military man could withstand the wrath of one five-foot-nothing old lady, but he looked terrified. When close enough to the front door, she grabbed a broom, wielding it like a samurai sword.

A glance at CC revealed some concern for the sheriff's safety, but I was ready to watch him get clobbered.

Spoiling my fun, CC jumped up and dragged me toward them. "I'm sure that's not what he meant, Ms. Schwartz. You know how big city people are."

Ms. Schwartz turned toward us, and I ducked behind CC thinking she might be angry and believe I had besmirched her character, too. For his part, the sheriff opened the door and rushed out.

CC and I edged around the older woman and then bolted out after him, eager to avoid Ms. Schwartz's broom. As soon as we had gained the relative safety of the front walkway, we heard the door slam behind us.

Sheriff Armstrong glared at us. Although, to be honest, he was glaring mostly at me. From the corner of my eye, I saw CC edge away from me, just to be safe.

"Well, that didn't go well," he said.

"We noticed." I nodded my head at him, "You don't seem to have a lot of finesse when questioning people."

CC eased farther away from me as the sheriff's already-furrowed brow grew even more so, if that was possible. I was surprised to see his anger directed at me. I mean, I'm not the one who accused a little old lady of having an affair.

"I'm not the one who accused a little old lady of having an affair," I reminded him. He took a deep breath and pinched the bridge of his nose. His lips moved, but no sound came out. "Are you counting to ten? I'm only asking because that never works for me. Does it work for you?"

"I'm sorry, Sheriff, but we really must be going." CC grabbed my arm and steered me toward the car. "I have to pick up my kids, and Claire drove me so, ta-ta."

The sheriff looked like he wanted to put us in jail, although it was most likely just me, and not really us. He almost didn't seem aware of CC. We made it to the car and just as I put the key in the ignition to make good our escape, the sheriff stopped us.

"What do you know about the relationship between Ms. Schwartz and Mr. Johnson?" he asked, standing near the front of the driver's side.

"About half the town thinks they are doing the deed, and the other half of the town doesn't," I said. "I can see both sides. I mean, why would you work with such a sourpuss for fifty years if there wasn't a little something-something on the side, but the thought of them getting a little something-something makes me want to throw up." The sheriff had a pained expression on his face as if he might want to throw up too, which seemed fair.

"Stay out of this investigation," he said. It was pretty much an order.

"So, it is a murder investigation?" I asked.

He responded with a death glare, but since I have the best death glare around, his didn't faze me.

"We investigate every death," he said through clenched teeth.

"Okay, well we gotta go get CC's kids, so see you around." I cranked the car and threw in a jaunty wave. Unfortunately, the sheriff must've been standing a little too close to the front of the car and I felt a little bump as we started to pull away.

"You ran over my foot!" he hollered—loud enough to wake the dead—and started hopping on his good foot.

CC jumped to his defense. "Oh my gosh, I'm so sorry! Claire! Why don't you look where you are driving.

"Wait a minute," I said after slamming on the brakes. "He's the one who put his foot under my tire. First, he tells us to butt out of the investigation, and then he gets his panties in a bunch when I try to leave. I'm the injured party here!"

The sheriff and CC both looked at me as if trying to picture me in an orange jump suit.

Through still-clenched teeth, the sheriff said, "You are a menace!" With that, he turned and hobbled away.

"He seems fine," I said as I hit the gas and drove away. "I mean he was putting some weight on it when he limped away. I think he was just being a drama queen."

CC looked at me with a disapproving frown. "I can't believe I let you drive my children around. What kind of a mother am I?"

Her last comment seemed rhetorical, but I answered anyway. "You are a great mother! Those kids are lucky to have you!" This seemed to mollify her a bit, so I continued. "I mean sometimes you lose one or two, but you always find them. And so, what if you let them ride in a car with a person who has been stopped every week of their driving life? I never get a ticket, so it shouldn't count."

Her frown returned. "That's because you always bat those beautiful green eyes of yours and act so innocent and upset that you didn't know any better. Those poor police officers don't know what hit them. You're just lucky you always get stopped by guys."

"That's not true! I got stopped by a female officer one time in Riverton. We get coffee every time I'm in town."

CC's jaw dropped open. "You get coffee with someone else?" she asked.

"Only when I go to Riverton." It sounded a little defensive, but CC seemed genuinely upset. She huffed and turned away, like she couldn't even look at me. "Come on CC, I didn't want a ticket. She means nothing to me. It was just a one-time deal," I said, before mumbling, "one time every time I go to Riverton."

Hopefully, she didn't hear the last part. "You know you're my best friend and I could never find anyone else even half as great as you."

She looked back at me and said, "That's true, but—"

Before she could finish, we arrived back at my house. I jumped from the car as soon as it came to a stop. "I'm going to make sure Frank survived taking Eve to the birthday party. You know how awful those things can be." I said and dashed toward her house.

By the time CC made her way inside Frank was regaling me with stories about how awesome it had been. Apparently, if you are a gorgeous fifteen-year-old boy who brought his little sister to the party you are waited on hand and foot, get extra cake, and the moms of the other little monsters coo over you the entire time.

Whatever, I think. Having flashbacks to the last kids' birthday party I went to caused me to shudder.

"What's for lunch?" Ann asked as she entered the kitchen with Kyle trailing behind.

Ann looked pink-cheeked and proud of herself. Probably just beat all the neighborhood boys at whatever they thought they were good at. As usual Kyle's hair was a mess, and his glasses were askew. What appeared to be flour powdered his shirt front. I looked around for flour but couldn't see any. Shrugging, I waited for the answer to lunch.

"Grilled cheese and chicken noodle soup," CC said, opening the huge commercial refrigerator and pulling out two loaves of bread and a block of cheese. She sliced cheese and buttered bread, pausing to stir the chicken noodle soup that had begun to simmer on the stove. Watching in awe as she moved around the kitchen and food magically appeared. I didn't offer to help since I'd only be in the way. It was considered lucky if the smoke detector didn't alarm from me pouring a glass of milk.

Somehow, Nell knew to appear at just the right time to begin handing plates to CC so she could flip the grilled cheese sandwiches onto them. Nell then passed them out as the children trickled into the kitchen. By the time the first batch was distributed to Ann, Kyle, Jane, Eve, and me, Nell was ladling bowls of soup to pass around as well. Nell repeated the process for Dean, Frank, CC, and herself. Somewhere in this choreography of dining, a bowl of baby carrots arrived without me even noticing.

"You two are a well-oiled machine," I said, even though I'd watched this same dance a million times.

"I know." CC sighed. "I don't know what I'll do when she goes off to college."

"You do have six other children to choose from," I reminded her.

"I know, but it won't be the same," she said, starting to tear up.

"Mom, we talked about this," Nell said. "You can't cry until you drop me off."

I nodded, thinking this sounded reasonable. "Yeah, and it's like months away."

"It's in two weeks," Nell said.

"What?" I clutched my chest and then jumped up to hug Nell. "Two weeks? That's so soon." I held Nell's head to my chest in despair. Somehow, she still managed to eat her soup without spilling it. "I can't believe my baby is all grown up and going off to college." I started to cry.

"Umm, she's my baby," CC said, raising her hand as if I don't know who claimed the child.

It was kind of hard to see CC through my tears, but I knew who actually birthed this precious child of mine.

"Auntie Claire, you can come visit me and we can scope out the college boys," Nell offered before I could work up to a good cry.

"College boys," I whispered. "Well, I guess you have to go to college if you're going to become a doctor. Who am I to stand in your way," I said, and then let go of her head so fast she almost toppled off her seat.

Nell smirked at me, a knowing look in her eyes.

"Well Honey, I'm only here to support you. If you want your Auntie Claire to help you scope out college boys I will, but only because I love you." I pointed my spoon at her for emphasis.

She rolled her eyes and then caught Eve's bowl before she could knock it off the table with her elbow. That crisis averted, she handed

Kyle a napkin, who mysteriously managed to get peanut butter on his forehead.

We didn't even have peanut butter, I thought to myself. How that kid gets so messy I'll never figure out.

Now that everyone was finished eating, the kids trickled out to wherever it was kids go. They cleared their plates as they went, leaving CC and I sitting alone at the kitchen banquette.

"I think we should go talk to Mr. Russell," CC said.

I saw this coming, but I still wasn't thrilled. "Come on, CC, he hates me."

"I can't say I blame him," CC said. "I mean, you ran him over and it took him a year to walk again. He still limps."

I huffed out a breath and said, "He needs to let go of the past. It's not healthy to cling to it."

"Well, let's go tell him that," she said, standing up.

"What about the kids?" I asked, seeking an out. "I mean visiting Ms. Schwartz, and now Mr. Russell all in one day seems excessive."

"They're fine." CC waved away my argument. "Practically self-sufficient. A well-oiled machine I believe you just said?"

She wasn't wrong, but still. Before I could come up with another reason not to go, CC breezed out the door.

"Hurry up or I'm getting out the van."

"Not the mom mobile!" I practically ran out the door, only to pull up short when I see her sitting in my baby. I narrowed my eyes, but she pretended not to notice.

"I knew you would make the right decision," she said, checking her hair in the passenger-side mirror.

Chapter 6

Getting to Mr. Russell was more difficult than we anticipated. Since it was Sunday, we went to his house. CC breezed up the walkway to the front door. His style was utilitarian—no flowers here, just lawn.

I trailed behind like a reluctant child. Not a bad analogy since Mr. Russell had been our high school principal. I made several treks to his office over those four years. Luckily, he was clueless about basically everything. I could generally talk my way out of any consequences. Mostly, I think it was because he just wanted me to shut up and leave.

CC rang the bell and waited. And waited. She grew impatient and began to knock. When that still didn't bring Mr. Russell, she started peeking in his front window and calling his name. We started to draw the neighbors' attention and I looked around, acting guilty, even though we are just standing on his porch, not egging it. Not that I ever egged his house, nope definitely didn't egg his house. Not ever.

"CC? Is that you Honey?" called a voice from next door.

We both looked over to see Ms. Clark, Mr. Russell's elderly neighbor, standing next to the fence between the yards shading her eyes from the sun behind us.

CC said, "It is, Ms. Clark. How are you? I heard your grandson made the college football team. Congratulations!"

Ms. Clark beamed at her, "He sure did Honey! You should see him play. He might be almost as good as that husband of yours. Are you looking for Mr. Russell?"

I rolled my eyes so hard it's a wonder I didn't fall over. I mean, we are standing on his porch knocking and calling his name. What did she think we were doing? CC was unquestionably nicer than me.

"We are, Ms. Clark. Do you know where he is?" she asked without sarcasm. The woman was incredible.

"Well, he's at school of course. Didn't you hear about the vandalism? Somebody egged the mural on the gym." Ms. Clark said this last part while looking at me.

I tried to smile innocently, but innocent is kind of out of my comfort zone, so it might have looked like I had gas instead. Since Ms. Clark shifted away and made quick excuses to leave, I leaned toward the gas smile.

"Well, that's too bad. Now we won't be able to talk to Mr. Russell after all," I said without any real sorrow.

"Let's go," CC said. I squinted at her, suspicious that she didn't seem upset that I'd ruined her plans. Once settled in the car she directed me to the high school.

"Aww come on, CC." I may have whined. "We tried. Let's just call it a day. What's the point in having a sheriff if we do his job for him?"

CC's steely-eyed glare surprised me. "You could just go to bed tonight knowing somebody we know might be a killer, just wandering around? Maybe even past my house, where my children sleep. Maybe even past your house." CC was practically foaming at the mouth now and I leaned away from her, pressed up against the driver's door. "What if they don't continue past? Hmm? What if they come in? What then?"

"Okay, Okay." I said, "Fine, we can go to the high school."

CC settled back in her seat as if nothing had happened.

Meanwhile, I might never sleep again.

Chapter 7

Pulling up at the high school, I couldn't help but shiver. *Was it just me or did it look like a prison?*

"Stop it," CC said, leading me to believe my inner thoughts had become my outer words, again. "It's a school. My kids' school even." She continued, "It looks nothing like a prison. Well, except for the bars on the windows and the security guard over there, but those are to keep our kids safe." She tried to sound sure of herself, but I could hear the uncertainty underneath her words and see the frown lines between her eyebrows.

Oooh, the PTA was going on a warpath, I thought to myself.

"I don't go on warpaths," CC said as she walked to the side of the gym where we could see a group of people gathered.

Shoot. *Darn inner thoughts needed to stay in.*

"Yes, they do," she called over her shoulder.

I scrunched up my nose, afraid to think anything now for fear I'd say it out loud. Once again, I trailed behind CC towards the group. A few students were making a half-hearted effort to hose off the side of the gym. Mr. Russell was supervising, and Mr. Hill was directing them all. Mr. Hill became aware of us and as soon as he finished giving further directions to the group of students, turned our way.

He was in his late thirties with a runner's build. He was fit in an understated way with a full head of dark blond, almost brown, hair cut short, but not quite a buzz cut. His hazel eyes seemed kind but didn't miss much.

"CC!" He smiled widely. "Always a pleasure. What can I do for you?" He reached out to shake her hand.

I was completely ignored, which felt a little hurtful.

"Mr. Hill!" CC gushed. "So good to see you too! I was actually hoping to talk to Mr. Russell."

Every student turned bewildered eyes toward us. Mr. Hill seemed unsure of what to say. No one wanted to talk to Mr. Russell for any reason, voluntarily anyway.

"Oh sure, yeah," Mr. Hill stammered, gesturing toward Mr. Russell who still seemed unaware we were there, despite our conversation taking place a few feet away.

"Mr. Russell?" CC called, moving closer to the ancient principal.

I mean, he was old when I went to high school. What was left of his hair was white and mussed as if he forgot to comb it today, and maybe yesterday and the day before, too.

"Can we talk to you for a minute?" Mr. Russell jerked a little as if startled and then turned his rheumy-eyed gaze on us. "It's about Mr. Johnson."

"The fence is on my side of the property line!" he bellowed in response. "Just because he is dead doesn't mean he is going to get away with it! I will fight this to my dying day!"

He seemed to be building up to an epic rant, so I jumped in to head it off. "Did you kill him?" On second thought, that wasn't very subtle.

"Kill him? No, of course not. I wanted to see his face when the county sided with me, and he had to take his whole fence down and move it." He was practically bouncing with glee and rubbing his hands together in anticipation. More soberly, he said, "But now that victory has been denied me forever. If anyone killed him, it was probably his maid, Teresa or Tilly or something. He was forever yelling at her about everything. It was impossible to get a moment's peace with his bellowing. She probably got fed up and offed the old grump."

As if finally realizing the students were all listening, he tried to backpedal. "I mean, I'm sure Mr. Johnson, an upstanding citizen of our town, simply had an unfortunate accident." His decisive head nod indicated he had nothing more to say on the matter.

Mr. Russell straightened his ever-present sweater vest; this one was green with thin yellow stripes. He had never been seen without a sweater vest on. Even in the summer. The only childhood picture anyone had seen showed him in a sweater vest. I don't think he owned any other clothing, but no one seemed to have the heart to tell him sweater vests were not a good choice for him. It really drew attention to the belly paunch that was straining the front of his garment.

If I tilted my head a little to one side, it almost looked like his stomach was a huge watermelon, ripe for the picking.

A snicker from behind told me I might have once again said what I had been thinking.

Mr. Hill quickly redirected the students' attention to the area of the mural still in need of cleaning, and CC and I skedaddled back to my car.

"Who do you suppose is his cleaning lady?" CC asked. "I can't think of anyone named Teresa or Tilly that cleans houses."

"I guess it's a dead end. Oh well." I said with a shrug, but CC's thoughtful expression told me she wasn't dropping her investigation.

After a quiet ride back to our houses, CC started preparing the biggest pot of spaghetti ever, or at least since the last time she made spaghetti. She made her own sauce from scratch, but froze it in batches, so she only had to reheat it.

I nibbled on some chocolate and watched her move about the kitchen.

When she opened the huge walk-in pantry, a ticking noise began. I sat up straighter in my seat and looked around for what might come next.

CC simply stood at the pantry door and waited expectantly.

Curious, I slid off my seat and tip-toed up behind her. Peering over CC's shoulder, I saw a level attached to a fulcrum that nudged over a box on the highest shelf. The box fell but hit a wooden spoon that extended beyond the edge of the shelf below it. The box continued falling and the spoon lurched forward, which caused the jar resting on it to roll toward us. CC put her hand out just in time to catch the jar of French bread seasoning as it rolled off the shelf.

I waited to see if there was more, but CC turned around and almost ran into me.

"Claire!" she appeared genuinely startled. "Don't sneak up on me like that." She stepped around me and returned to the kitchen.

"What just happened?" I asked, reclaiming my seat.

"It's Dean's turn to help with dinner," CC replied, as if a boo-by-trapped pantry was normal, which in this house it was.

"Did it work?" Dean asked, coming into the kitchen.

"Perfectly," CC replied. "Don't forget to wash the salad."

Dean smiled a wicked smile and grabbed the lettuce from the refrigerator. "Watch this Auntie Claire!"

I can't watch, I thought and covered my eyes. But it was like a car accident you can't look away from. From between my fingers, I did watch as Dean moved to the sink. He reached underneath and pulled out a metal box that looked to be made from tin foil. Next, he placed the box in the sink and started attaching arms to the outside. Soon it resembled what I imagined the offspring of an alien spaceship and a mannequin's would look like. He opened the bag containing the lettuce leaves and dumped them into the box. Finally, he turned on the water.

After a few seconds of nothing I was ready to gently encourage him to try again. And then the arms started to move. I couldn't tell if they were washing the leaves or trying to kill them but either way water and lettuce were flying around the box. After a few minutes, Dean turned off the water. The arms and the lettuce both went still.

"Wow! That was awesome!"

Dean beamed. "Thanks, I worked on it all week."

"All week? That took longer than washing the lettuce by hand. Why bother?" I asked.

"Auntie Claire," he shook his head like I had severely disappointed him, which I probably had, "inventions are always worth the time."

"I know that," I said. "I just forgot, I guess. It was amazing and worth however long it took you to create it."

A proud smile lit up his face.

Frank and Amelia sauntered in and started setting the table while Dean fished the lettuce leaves out of the box. Soon everyone was seated around the table passing plates for spaghetti, bread baskets, salad bowls, and various salad toppings.

Somehow, I got the spot next to Eve and every time my attention wandered from my plate a meatball would go missing and the spawn of Satan would be trying to chew an enormous mouth full of something. Coincidence? I think not!

Wanting to catch the thief in the act, I pretended to be distracted but suddenly turned back and yelled, "Ah-ha! I caught you red handed! Get it? The meatball is covered in red spaghetti sauce so it's red."

Eve looked at me with judgmental eyes that belied her years and said, "I used my fork, so my hands aren't red at all."

"That's not the point," I said, "you're eating all my meatballs."

"Not all of them. You still have one."

"I had six," I said, glaring down at her.

"You weren't eating them."

I leaned down until we were almost nose to nose. "But I was going to."

"Those who hesitate are losers." Eve's misquote caused giggles and muffled laughter from the peanut gallery.

"For heaven's sake Claire, there are more meatballs. Would you like some?" CC asked.

"Of course, I would," I said, holding my plate out to her, "but that's not the point. She stole my food. What if this were the apocalypse and we had to survive? She is basically signing my death warrant through starvation."

"If it were the apocalypse, wouldn't you want to give Eve every chance to survive by giving her extra food rations? She is smaller and still needs a balanced diet to grow."

How had this turned into me being the bad guy I wondered?

"You wouldn't want to live in an apocalyptic world anyway," Jake said. "There would be no manicures or gas for your car, and no coffee."

I clutched my heart. "I take it all back, I want to die."

"But we aren't in an apocalyptic world," Amelia said, looking around the table with a furrowed brow.

Frank put his arm around her shoulder and whispered something to her while we all looked at her in disbelief, and then quickly averted our gaze to avoid being rude.

The awkward silence stretched for a few minutes while everybody thought about how to move on, except for Kyle. I'm pretty sure he was making a sketch in his mind. Also, he appeared to have a grass stain on his nose. That kid, he cracks me up. I smiled at him with genuine affection, even though he wasn't looking at me.

He turned his head and gave me a shy smile in return, reinforcing my belief that he always knew what was going on around him, he just mostly ignored us.

As the kids finished eating, they cleaned off their plates, put them in the dishwasher, and left the room. Soon, it was just CC, Jake, and me.

"What did you ladies do today?" he asked, stretching his long legs.

"Well, we went to our manicure appointment," I said, holding out my hand for his inspection, "Kiss me Quick."

"Claire, we talked about this. I'm a devoted husband to your best friend. Stop hitting on me," Jake said, barely glancing at my hand.

"That's the color," I huffed.

"Besides," he continued as if I hadn't spoken, "I don't kiss quick. I like to take my time and do it right," he said, staring intently into my eyes.

Was it hot in here? I had a sudden need to fan my face.

His quick wink and devilish smile did nothing to cool my temperature. I grabbed a glass and gulped some water. I couldn't help but pant a little from the increased temperature and pressed the cold glass to my face.

CC ignored us and began to clear the remaining food.

I still hadn't quite recovered when she returned and handed me a beer. After a healthy swallow, I felt well enough to answer Jake's original question. "After that, we talked to some possible murderers."

Jake choked on his beer. "What," he sputtered, "murderers?"

"Oh Jake, it's not like that." CC tried to soothe him while death glaring at me. "We went to offer condolences to Ms. Schwartz."

"Like, on purpose?" Jake asked, sounding confused. "I thought you normally ran the other way whenever you saw her. Haven't you actually jumped a fence, hidden behind statues, and attended a gamblers anonymous meeting to avoid Ms. Schwarz?"

Jake gets me, I thought. "That's what I said. By the way did you hear Ken got his twenty-year pin and has a grandson on the way?"

"That's great news!" Jake said. "Next time you talk to him tell him I said hi."

"Will do," I said.

"Honestly you two!" CC huffed. "Ms. Schwartz is not some evil old lady. She just found her boss dead, perhaps brutally murdered, and you can't even find it in your hearts to pay a call on her." She looked at us with eyes full of disappointment, hands on her hips.

Me and Jake hung our heads in shame. But then mine started nodding. "Yeah, but what about when she went after the sheriff with a broom?"

Jake nodded at that. "She's seriously scary," he added.

We clinked beer bottles in solidarity.

CC threw up her hands and continued putting food away.

"That's not all we did today," I continued. "After Ms. Schwartz implicated Mr. Russell, CC wanted to talk to him, too. I'm sure she would have insisted we talk to Mr. Johnson's housekeeper after Mr. Russell fingered her as the culprit, but we can't figure out who she is. Mr. Russell said it was Tilly or Teresa, but we don't know anyone in town by those names that cleans houses."

CC dropped down at the banquette next to Jake, who immediately wrapped his arm around her and pulled her close.

They are just too cute I thought to myself. When neither of them said anything, I felt more confident that my inner thoughts were no longer my outer words. Score!

"I think I heard the Garza girl Tessa was doing some house cleaning to help her family out and pay for school," Jake said.

"That's right!" I snapped my fingers. "I remember her putting up flyers a few years ago. I bet it's her. Mr. Russell was never good with names."

Noticing the gleam in CC's eyes, I knew what we would be doing tomorrow.

Chapter 8

Tomorrow came way too soon. I breached CC's kitchen like a zombie looking for a miracle cure. Coffee would have to do. Its steaming warmth filled me with happiness, and I savored every drop like the precious elixir of life it was. Since it was Monday, I had to go to work, so I didn't have a lot of savoring time to spare. CC handed me a plate.

"Hey, did Dean's omelet machine work?" I asked.

"No, but don't remind him."

I quickly stuffed the omelet into my mouth and took my now-refilled mug home so I could shower and dress.

Hurrying through the back door, I nearly tripped over the Agatha-shaped puddle of bloodhound lying just inside. Benji ran into the room and did a backflip. I sipped more coffee and returned his "treat now?" stare. Finally giving in, I grabbed a biscuit from the picnic-basket-shaped cookie jar and tossed it in his general direction on my way toward the stairs. I didn't watch to see if he caught it, but I was sure he did.

Fortunately, I made it to the shower without Blackbeard tripping me as he wove between my legs. However, I wasn't lucky enough to avoid him joining me. They say cats hate water, but apparently nobody told Blackbeard. He loved the shower spray, and even took a bath with me once—before I began locking the bathroom door. I showered in record time, and he seemed as disappointed as a cat could be when I turned off the water.

Taking pity on him, I turned it back on enough for a slow drip. It's enough to occupy him while I get dressed. I pulled on a pencil skirt and silk blouse. Deciding on an easy hair style, I twisted up my still-damp hair into a chignon, swiped on some minimal makeup, and slipped on a pair of flats. About twenty minutes after returning to the house, I turned off the dripping water, leaving a damp Blackbeard licking himself dry in the tub, and rushed downstairs. I stepped over Agatha—again—and am greeted by Benji, proudly holding a remote in his mouth.

"Thanks, Benji," I said patting his head and accepting his gift. I grabbed my purse off the entryway table and shoved the remote in as I breezed out the door.

CC was standing next to my baby with a commuter mug and lunch bag. *Boy, am I spoiled*, I think to myself.

"Yes, you are." CC smiled.

"Dagnab it." This was getting annoying. "I've been working hard on keeping my thoughts to myself."

CC's smile widened. "You did," she said, "I just know you so well."

I kissed her cheek. "Bye Honey. I'll be home for dinner."

"Have a good day, Dear," she countered with a wink before sauntering toward her kitchen door. Pulling into an open parking space at work, I turned the car off and took a deep, cleansing breath. It's not that I don't like what I do, it's not my passion, but I don't hate it. My boss on the other hand. I kind of hate him. He is the big boss's son and had his life handed to him. He knows nothing about insurance, managing an office, people, life, the list goes on and on. Basically, he knows nothing.

As soon as I walked in, I groaned. My desk, which had been clear and organized when

I left on Friday, is stacked with folders, loose papers, and a banana. Before trying to figure out the mess on my desk I headed to the break room and dropped off my lunch.

Mentally girding my loins, I marched toward my desk to try and make sense of what could have happened. Immediately, I threw the banana in the garbage and dropped my purse in my desk chair. I picked up all the folders that were scattered haphazardly on my desk and stacked them on one corner. The remaining papers were gathered and stacked on another corner. With the desktop mostly cleared, I stowed my purse in the desk drawer, took another breath, and sat back in my chair. And then Brandon, uh Mr. Brown, walked in.

"Good morning, Ms. Miller. I worked on Saturday to get you caught up a little." He smiled eagerly, not unlike Benji when he presented me with a present.

"I saw the files on my desk but haven't had a chance to look through them." I tried to be diplomatic. He might be clueless, but he was my boss. Brandon was so nondescript it was hard to describe him even when looking right at him. He had slightly wavy brown hair that was brushed back off his forehead. I was always hard pressed to remember his eyes were brown. He was about 5'9" or 5'10" not fat, not thin.

He had just graduated in June and walked into a job as my boss. I imagined his GPA was barely high enough to graduate. He had no real skills. Nell had known him for a while, and since she couldn't say an unkind word about anyone, simply didn't speak of him, which was very telling.

"What exactly did you work on this weekend?" I asked, working to keep a calm demeanor, at least on the outside. "I thought we agreed you wouldn't do that anymore."

He wilted slightly under this criticism. "I just wanted to help you get caught up," he replied, a little too eagerly.

I took a deep breath and said, "I know, but remember my filing system can be tricky for others to understand." It was a lie. It was basic filing, not rocket science, but every time he touched the files, he messed them up, which took me hours, sometimes days to fix.

"Well, it's done now, so why don't you tell me what you were working on?" I tried to soothe his hurt feelings and hoped it wouldn't result in another phone call from his father, reminding me who was in charge. It wasn't me.

"I was looking into Mr. Johnson's policy."

I raised my eyebrows at this unexpectedly correct action. "Well, that makes sense." After a moment to process the surprise, I said, "But why so many files and papers?"

He shrugged. "They seemed out of place."

The amount of effort it took to not roll my eyes gave me an instant headache. "I'll be sure to put them back where they belong." I hoped that would end the conversation and that he would go back to his office and practice his putting, or whatever he did in there.

An awkward silence followed as we stared at each other. The phone rang and I jumped to answer it hoping it would clue him in that I needed to work and, more importantly, he needed to go.

"Brown and Son insurance company, how may I help you?" I could feel Brandon watching me while I plucked a pen out of the holder on my desk.

"Auntie Claire, can I take Benji for a walk?" a sweet voice asked.

Well aware that Brandon was still hovering I said, "We certainly can help you with a policy. We have all kinds. Whole life, term life, medical, home insurance, car insurance...." As I droned on, Brandon wandered into his office with slightly glazed eyes.

"Is he watching you?" the voice asked.

"Not anymore, Sweetheart. Sure, you can take Benji for a walk. As long as it's okay with your mom," I added as an afterthought.

"Thanks, bye."

The line disconnected before I could say anything else. I hung up the phone and sighed.

It took most of the morning to sort and refile the mess on my desk, but I left Mr. Johnson's file out to look at later. I also checked messages and either returned the calls myself or took down messages for our insurance salesman, Steve Tuttle. Steve was our only salesman, but nothing special. He did his job, but nothing above the minimum expected. Which with Brandon at the helm was not much of anything. Steve wasn't there, surprise surprise, so I put the message slips on his desk and returned to mine.

Whew, what a morning, I thought, dropping into my chair. I fired up my computer and updated the calendar appointments for the office, most of which were for Steve, and then took my lunch break. Alone in the break room, I warmed up my lunch. CC had packed me some leftover spaghetti with eight meatballs—got to love that woman—some garlic bread, and a bowl of salad. I dug in and enjoyed the peace and quiet almost as much as the food. Okay, I enjoyed the food more, but the peace and quiet was nice too.

After lunch, I returned to my desk. No new emergency had occurred while I was at lunch, so I decided to peruse Mr. Johnson's file. I was shocked to see the life insurance policy. It was for five million dollars. Most of our policies were modest, meant to cover funeral expenses and that was about it. I knew Mr. Johnson had been loaded, but even with that this seemed unusually high. He didn't even have family, did he? Reading further, I saw that the beneficiary was Jamie Wilson. I frowned at the folder. Jamie Wilson? Who the heck was Jamie Wilson, and why did Mr. Johnson leave five million dollars to him? Her? I got up and walked to the copy machine, intending to make a copy and doing my best to be nonchalant.

"What are you working on?" A voice asked from right behind me.

I made a little jump, probably because I felt guilty. I spun around and came nose to nose, almost literally, with Steve.

Steve was in his late forties, about my height, with prematurely thinning hair and dull gray eyes. To compensate for his hair loss, he had a thick mustache, that lacked Tom Selleck's sex appeal, and almost completely covered his mouth.

"Geez, Steve! Have you ever heard of personal space?" I asked, before pushing him gently so he'd back up a few steps. "I'm making a copy of a file. Don't you have phone calls to return and an appointment with Ms. Downing to prepare for?" I asked, hoping to encourage him to leave me alone. I grabbed my copies and the originals and headed back to my desk, fervently hoping Steve wouldn't follow. The man had a tendency to get a little handsy sometimes. Unfortunately, Steve followed me, but I was able to sit down before he could make a grab for me.

Ms. Downing chose that moment to enter.

I smiled warmly at her.

She seemed slightly surprised by the intensity of my welcome but returned my smile anyway.

"Good morning, Ms. Downing. Mr. Tuttle was just telling me how excited he was to be meeting with you today." It was a shameless lie but had the desired result.

Ms. Downing turned her attention to Steve and began talking a mile a minute, asking questions, but not waiting for the answers.

Steve shot me a look that promised retribution. He had no other choice but to steer Ms. Downing toward his office.

I piddled around with basic office management tasks until five o'clock, when I could finally escape. I set the answering machine and logged off my computer before grabbing my purse from the bottom drawer. Steve and Brandon had already left, so I locked the office door behind me.

Chapter 9

"**H**oney I'm home!" I hollered as I entered my house. Agatha didn't even twitch, but the sound of nails on hardwood told me Benji was on the way. Sure enough, he rounded the corner dragging one of my scarves behind him. He proudly presented it to me as I dropped my purse on the entryway table.

As if by magic, the TV came on. Surprised, I looked to see which urchin was hiding in my house and playing with my remote. Seeing no one, I tried to figure out how my TV had turned on by itself.

Still puzzled, I bent down and accepted the scarf from Benji, scratching him behind the ears. Then I remembered the remote he had presented to me that morning before I left for work. After a thorough whole-body petting, Benji allowed me to fish the remote out of my purse, turn off the TV, and head upstairs to change out of my work clothes. I stripped off the silk blouse and pencil skirt with relief and replaced them with well-worn denim cutoffs and a t-shirt.

After I had changed, I headed next door to CC's with Benji at my heels.

"Honey I'm home!" I yelled as I walked into the kitchen.

Dean smirked at my t-shirt but said nothing. Disappointed, I turned to the others in the room. Kyle didn't even look up from his sketch pad. Eve couldn't read, so she wouldn't get it anyway. CC was standing at the stove with her back to me, cooking something that smelled heavenly, and Nell was reading a book.

"Really? Nothing? Your best friend, and super, most, bestest Auntie shows up after being gone forever and I don't even get a 'hello, how are you doing?'" I said, trying to guilt them into some sort of response.

Eve didn't even look up when she said, "We saw you this morning, it wasn't that long ago. And we see you every day. Maybe learn a new trick. I like Benji's tricks," she said, dropping to the floor and scratching Benji's shamelessly offered belly.

I turned in time to see Jake stroll in behind me. Maybe he missed me.

"Honey, I'm home," He called out.

Every person in the room greeted him. Eve abandoned Benji and latched onto his leg like a leech. Nell put her book down long enough to ask about his day. Kyle handed him a picture from under his sketchbook.

I peeked over Jake's shoulder and saw that it was a portrait of Jake so detailed it almost looked like a black-and-white photo. Man, that kid was an amazing artist!

Dean launched himself at Jake—who caught him in mid-air—and started talking a mile a minute about his latest invention, and CC turned to offer him a kiss. It didn't have a chance to turn R-rated since Dean was practically smashed between them.

"Well," I said, "I see how it is. You don't father any children and you might as well be invisible."

"Did anybody hear anything?" Jake asked.

The evil man. Before I could offer a scathing response, he winked at me.

"Great shirt."

Mollified that at least someone noticed the epic shirt I had on, I pulled the hem out so the whole shirt was easy to read and looked down at the animal pictures with labels on the front. The snake was a danger noodle, an alligator or crocodile—I never could tell which was which—was captioned murder log. The rest were hilarious, too, a skunk called a fart squirrel, a hedgehog named spiky floof, while the bear was, oddly, danger floof. The last was my favorite: a kangaroo labeled as a velocirabbit.

"I know right?" I said proudly as I dropped the hem and give him a high five.

He struggled to return it with Dean squirming in one arm while the other tried to keep Eve from bumping her head on the counter when she started to climb up his leg.

I was so distracted by the family show that I almost didn't hear the tell-tale clicking noise that never failed to strike fear into my heart.

Whirling toward the kitchen door as it burst open, I could only see the danger floof bearing down on me. Too late to run or hide, I braced myself for the attack. With commendable bravery, I faced my imminent demise. The sound of whimpering reached my ears, and I was comforted by their sympathy. In the split second before being eaten I realized it was me whimpering. Apparently, no one else cared.

In a flash, Benji sprang from behind me and barked sharply at the danger floof. The attacking beast tried to stop and sit down, but his momentum carried him along until he skidded to a stop a foot in front of me, and mere inches from Benji.

"Huh," I said, rising from my half crouch. "Good dog!"

Both dogs' tails wagged like mad propellers, and I reached out to pet them. Benji with deep affection, danger floof with ill-disguised trepidation.

"Auntie Claire, really. There is nothing to be afraid of. Bear won't hurt you." Jane said, walking into the kitchen like I hadn't almost died. A squirrel peeked out of her front shirt pocket, a raven perched on her head, and a raccoon ambled along at her heels.

"Easy for you to say," I said. "He doesn't flying tackle you to the ground every time he sees you."

She shook her head, as if observing a sad but avoidable situation. The raven wobbled without losing its perch.

Frank appeared out of nowhere to set the table and then we all sat and dug into CC's meatloaf, with mashed potatoes, peas, and cornbread.

Man, I loved living next door. I loaded my plate, taking some of everything. Conversations overlapped and interrupted each other as ten people and a few stray animals all shared the room. I enjoyed every minute of it.

CC and I were both only children and our houses always seemed so quiet. Especially CC's. Her parents weren't exactly what you would call touchy feely. Soon enough everybody seemed full, and the kids drifted away to various activities. As was normal after most dinners, Jake, CC, and I were alone in the kitchen. CC and Jake started putting leftovers in containers and into the refrigerator while I watched. No longer able to contain my news I said, "Guess, what I found out today?"

CC seemed unimpressed with what I might have found out. She barely even glanced at me as she asked, "What?"

Not one to be daunted by a lukewarm response I dropped the bombshell. "Mr. Johnson had a five-million-dollar life insurance policy with a beneficiary named Jamie Wilson!"

CC spun around so fast she knocked one of the containers off the counter.

Showing off his reflexes, Jake caught it before it could hit the floor.

I applauded with what I thought was appropriate decorum. I would've hated to miss leftover meatloaf for lunch tomorrow.

CC yelled, "Five million dollars. Oh, my goodness!"

"Lower your voice for goodness' sake. The whole town can hear you," I said. "It's not exactly public information here. Brandon had pulled a whole bunch of stuff over the weekend and left a mess on my desk, including Mr. Johnson's policy. You can't tell anyone." I said in a tone that conveyed national-secret-level importance.

CC nodded emphatically. "Yeah, sure, nobody, cross my heart. But who is Jamie Wilson?" she wondered aloud.

"It doesn't sound familiar," Jake said.

"Not to me either," I said. We were all glum-faced, trying to figure out who Jamie Wilson might be.

After a few minutes of this, Jake went to the refrigerator and pulled out a pitcher of lemonade. He brought it to the table with three glasses and poured us a round.

"Somebody should tell the sheriff about this," CC said after taking a sip.

I'd already half-drained my glass. "I'm sure he'll investigate," I paused and looked at my friends, "you know, on his own. Like maybe as a job?"

"Maybe somebody could help him." She wasn't going to let this go.

"Come on, CC, he hates me." I hated it when I whined. "He thinks I ran over his foot."

"You did!"

"That is not the point," I said.

She regarded me with the mom glare, clearly believing that it is, in fact, the point.

The stare off was interrupted by the baying of a thousand hell-hounds. It was horrible. The echoes reverberated around the kitchen, and inside my skull. I couldn't help but cover my ears and shrink down as if that would protect me from the relentless howls coming from my house. With hands over my ears, I rushed out of the kitchen and headed back next door.

Sneaking in the backdoor I grabbed the picnic-basket-shaped cookie jar of dog treats off the counter and dashed toward the front door and the siren like howl of Agatha.

"It's ok, Agatha," I said, my voice between a croon and a shout to be heard over her continued howls. She paused mid-howl and snatched the cookie I held out. Crunching contentedly, as if she hadn't just deafened this whole part of town, she turned back to the front door. Afraid she was only taking a break before kicking off another howl session, I tossed a handful of cookies into the kitchen. It worked! Benji and Agatha dashed after them and seemed to make a game out of which could get the most cookies in their mouth at the same time.

I snuck out onto the front porch and closed the door as gently as I could.

When I turned around, the sheriff was standing there. Nearly jumping out of my skin, I wondered why the sheriff was on my porch at eight o'clock at night.

"What in all of creation was making that noise?" He asked.

"Agatha," I said. He looked at me. I looked at him. "Was that all you wanted?"

"No, of course that's not all I wanted. Agatha wasn't making any noise until I rang your doorbell," he said in an exasperated tone.

"Well, that makes sense," I explained. "She hates the doorbell. It sets her off every time. That's why no one rings my doorbell anymore."

"Then why don't you disconnect the doorbell?" He asked through clenched teeth.

Honestly, he seemed a little stressed. It must be because he had just moved. Boy, I hate moving. Even just going to college was so much work. Lost in my reminiscing, I realized he was waiting for an answer.

"People wouldn't know the doorbell was disconnected and would just think I wasn't home." Feeling like a needed to explain further, I continued. "Like this time, I was over at CC and Jake's." I gestured next door with the arm not holding the jar full of dog biscuits. "But sometimes I might be home and wouldn't know someone was at the door if they didn't knock after trying the bell."

The sheriff pinched the bridge of his nose and moved his lips, but no sound came out.

I hoped silently counting to ten worked better for him than it did for me. I waited, rocking back on my heels. It seemed to be taking a long time. I wondered if he was a little slow in the head and had to start over or something. I squinted at his lips to see if I could tell what number he was on. *Dippy drive*? Huh, that's not a number at all.

"Do you need help counting to ten?" I asked.

His chocolate-brown eyes narrowed. *Mmm, chocolate*, I thought.

Before I could say anything embarrassing out loud, he said, "Ms. Miller, I understand Mr. Johnson had a rather large life insurance policy, payable to a Jamie Wilson."

Obviously, he was able to count to ten after all. "I knew you could do it." I beamed at him.

He looked confused, but otherwise ignored my outburst and waited, an expectant look on his face.

"What? Oh yeah. He did." I nodded. He was still looking at me. Not sure what to say, I waited.

"Well, where is Jamie Wilson?" He asked. His tone sounded quite temperamental.

"Geez, not much of a people person," I thought to myself. No! I said it out loud again.

"Only when dealing with menaces to society," He said.

He had sort of growled at me. I mean, I've read books where it said someone growled a response, but I never understood what it would sound like. Now I knew.

"That's not fair! I only ran over your foot when you stuck it under my wheel and hit you with my car when you were hiding behind it. Those are both on you, mister." I poked his chest to emphasize my point. I couldn't help but notice that it was a nicely muscled chest. And then that made me remember the abs.

He grabbed my finger and pried it off his chest.

Probably for the best, I thought. It might have moved from poking to stroking if left unattended for long.

"Ms. Miller—"

He was trying to sound patient, but I knew he was still mad.

"—it's been a long day and I just want to go home. Please tell me where I can find Jamie Wilson."

"I don't know," I replied, knowing it wasn't the answer he wanted to hear. "I'm just the office manager. Why don't you ask Steve Tuttle who wrote the policy, or Brandon Brown who is the boss?"

"I did," he said, "that's why I'm here so late. I started with Mr. Brown, who told me he had reviewed the file in preparation, but then couldn't tell me anything about it and suggested I ask Mr. Tuttle, who wrote it. When I finally managed to track him down, he didn't even remember the policy until I reminded him of the payout amount. Then he remembered, but suggested I talk to you as you would have been the one to notarize the policy and file all the necessary paper- work. I have been all over town tracking people down and I know the exact same information I knew before I started!" He ended the results of his investigation so far at a near-bellow.

"It's not my fault I work with incompetent and lazy people, you don't have to yell at me about it."

He took a deep breath and let it out slowly. "I'm sorry," he said, "it's been a long day and I haven't eaten. Can I have one of those cookies?" he asked, already reaching into the cookie jar.

I opened my mouth to stop him, but it was too late, he had already popped one in his mouth.

His face contorted as he rolled the taste around on his tongue. I could tell he was trying not to hurt my feelings by spitting it out. A bubble of laughter escaped. His shocked gaze in response made me laugh harder.

"It's a dog cookie!" I managed to say between peals of laughter.

He looked shocked, angry, and then chagrined before swallowing with an audible gulp.

"Mmm, liver?" he asked with a wry twist to his lips.

I nodded, still convulsed with giggles, and clutching the porch rail for support. "Oh, your face," I finally managed to say once I could catch my breath.

Since I had met the sheriff, his lips had always seemed like they never smiled, but through my tears of mirth, I could have sworn I saw a hint of a smile appear.

"I suppose that will teach me to take a cookie without permission."

I smiled shamelessly at him, and in the biggest surprise of the day, he finally smiled in return. We grinned at each other for a few moments before a loud thud reverberated through the front door.

He reached a hand toward his gun, but I had already turned to open the door. Benji was sitting on the other side, proudly holding my red lace bra. I tried to snatch it from him before the sheriff could see, but Benji darted past me to present his gift to the newcomer. He settled back on his haunches and put his front feet in the air, striking the traditional dog-begging pose. Sheriff Armstrong looked shell-shocked as he stared at Benji proudly presenting him with his prize.

"Benji," I hissed, "give it to me, now!"

The sheriff reached out to accept the bra and gave him a nice ear scratch while he was at it. Happy with himself, Benji turned and barked sharply at me.

I threw a treat into the house—which he immediately chases—and I slammed the door behind him. I took a moment to gather myself before turning to face the sheriff. When I did, I couldn't raise my eyes beyond the top button on his shirt. He seemed happy to wait quietly for me to gather my courage. Foolish man. That could take days. Wishing I was in the house with Benji, I eventually forced my eyes up to face level. The previous hint of a smile has transformed into a huge grin that reveals dimples in his whiskery cheeks. That smile, which extended into dark eyes, drew a reluctant grin from me as well. It also raised my temperature a few degrees. I might find him exasperating, but there was no denying his hunky good looks.

"I believe this belongs to you," he said, handing my bra over with almost as much pride as Benji had when presenting it to him.

I snatched it from his hand and shoved it into the cookie jar. Out of sight, out of mind, right? "Was there anything else Sheriff?" I asked, pretending a nonchalance I don't feel. His eyes are locked on the cookie jar, and he seems to have lost his train of thought. I glanced down to see that only half of my bra had made it into the jar, and one lacy cup was blowing in the breeze.

I shoved it in and tried my best to beat a strategic retreat. "Well, got to go, have a good night, Sheriff," I said, all but running into the house and quickly closing the door behind me. As soon as I heard the latch click, I leaned my back against the door and sunk to the floor. I couldn't see it, but considering the flush I felt, my face was probably beet red in humiliation.

"Well, that must be one heck of a story," CC said from the kitchen.

My eyes flew open. "You have no idea," I said. I stayed where I was and took deep breaths, leaning my head back against the door and trying to regroup.

CC disappeared from view, but I heard her clanking around in the kitchen. Soon enough she reappeared with a huge margarita glass in each hand. She passed me one and then joined me on the floor. We sipped our drinks and I told her the whole embarrassing story. By the time I finished, it didn't seem nearly as bad as it had in the moment, but that was probably the margarita talking.

"I guess Tessa will have to wait until tomorrow," CC said, staggering ever so slightly out my backdoor. I just hoped she made it. The backyard can be tricky when you're tipsy. I giggled as I hauled myself up—a tad off balance myself—and took the stairs to my bed.

Chapter 10

The next morning started like every other workday, with me staggering into CC's kitchen for coffee before I could attempt to get ready for work. I managed to avoid danger floof, grabbed a fantastic breakfast, and topped off coffee. Back home, I could not avoid a morning shower with Blackbeard—again. That is one weird cat. I wasn't sure how Jane had talked me into keeping him. I mean, he has one eye, weighs almost a hundred pounds—okay probably no more than thirty—and likes to shower with me. Why would I say yes to all of that?

I made it to the office without incident, which for me is not always the case. I had been the last one out yesterday and the first one in this morning, so I didn't have to clean up anybody else's mess.

The day progressed like most: allowing Brandon to think he was in charge, avoiding Steve's wandering hands, and doing all the work.

Finally, after an eternity of soul-crushing drudgery it was five o'clock and I all but run out of the office. Unfortunately, the sheriff happened to pass by at the precise moment I rushed out, and the edge of the door caught him squarely in the face.

We both froze, but I recovered first. "Oh, my goodness! I'm so sorry!" I said, trying to assess the damage. His face was beginning to swell already. "I think we should put some ice on it."

The need to wring my hands was strong, but in that moment, I was stronger and squelched what would've been a helpless gesture. Instead, I grabbed his arm without waiting for an answer and dragged him into the office. I pushed him into a chair in the breakroom and filled a towel with ice. I placed the makeshift ice pack across his left eye which was red and continued to swell.

I peered with some concern into his remaining eye. Oddly, it wasn't staring back at me. I followed his gaze and realized my bent-over position had caused my shirt to gap and he had a front row view of my bra. The same red lace bra Benji had presented to him last night.

"Is that…," he swallowed convulsively.

I straightened so fast I dropped the towel, ice and all, into his lap. He yelped and tried to grab the ice while standing up. Acting on instinct, I reached to scoop it up. Our simultaneous actions caused me to punch him in a very delicate area.

My eyes widened to what felt like the size of the moon and I jerked my hand back immediately.

The sheriff gasped in pain, grabbed the front of his pants, and hissed through his teeth as he dropped back into the chair.

"Oh my gosh, Oh my gosh, Oh my gosh!" I chanted, wringing my hands. I was unable to stop myself this time. "I'm so sorry," I said and covered my face, as if that would undo the damage. The silence stretched out for what seemed like an hour, interrupted only by the sheriff's labored breathing. Not wanting to look but needing to see if he was preparing to shoot me, I peeked through my fingers like a scared five-year-old.

"It's fine," He said between gritted teeth. "I'll be all right in a minute. It was an accident." He seemed unsure of whether to put the ice on his eye or his lap and finally settled on his eye.

"I really didn't mean to," I said, apologizing again.

He sighed. "I know, but I think I'll just head on home anyway. Whatever I was going to ask can wait."

I stood back to prevent any further damage.

The sheriff walked out with a slight limp, and the rewrapped towel of ice pressed to his eye.

I waited until I was sure he gone and headed home with a lot less pep in my step. I trudged into my house to find Agatha, again, melted across the floor and Benji rushing to bring me a present. This time it was the bathroom soap dispenser. Still distracted by the afternoon's events, I pet him, but my heart's not in it.

After changing clothes, I wandered into CC's kitchen.

"What's up buttercup?" she asked with concern in her voice.

I spilled the whole embarrassing story. At the end, I looked up and saw tear-filled eyes and a red face. Obviously, she was moved to tears by my experience. I nodded in sympathy as she began to sob.

Wait. That's not sobbing, she was laughing! Now I knew she was Satan, laughing at my pain.

"Sorry," she said, between peals of laughter, not sounding sorry in the least. "I can just picture the whole thing. Oh man, I wish I had it on video."

She continued to laugh but since I wasn't joining in, she sobered immediately. Ok, not exactly. It was more like five minutes, but in the grand scheme of things five minutes wasn't that long.

"Tessa can wait another day, let's go to Bake my Day and get a batch of brownies. That will cheer you up." She patted my hand in that comforting way mothers have.

"I don't think it will," I said, "but there's only one way to find out." I slid off the barstool and headed toward the driveway. On Tuesdays, Jake and the kids have a father-daughter-son bowling thing, so we didn't have to worry about sharing any brownies.

We arrived at the beautiful brick building with its cheerful striped awnings and huge plate glass windows. I can see Rose, the tyrant who denies sweet, kind, upstanding, citizens (me) brownies, at the counter wearing her ever present retro cherry apron. I hesitated outside, but CC breezed through the doorway without the slightest hesitation.

Rose looked up when the bell above the door rang. "CC!" She smiled in greeting., "What brings you in tonight? Is it my brownies, or my lava cake?"

"Lava cake?" I whispered. I'd heard somewhere that he who hesitates is lost, so I rushed in behind CC. "You have lava cake? Please, for all that is holy, I need five!" Realizing how my booming request might be received, I said. "I mean, hi, Rose. It's always nice to see you again. May I please have five lava cakes?"

CC whispered to Rose, "She had a really bad day. She's desperate."

Rose scrutinized me and I tried not to fidget under her steely gaze, but I failed. Her eyes traveled from the top of my head to the toes of my sneakers, stopping only briefly to take in my fantastic shirt. This one read *don't hate me because I'm a little cooler* and has a picture of a small cooler on it.

"All right," she relented, "but not five. Start with one and we'll see how it goes."

She walked down the glass-fronted display cases to the lava cakes and plucked out two. My eyes tracked her every move as she carried them toward the register. When she paused before ringing them up, I may have whimpered softly.

"Let me warm them up for you," she said and then she whisked them off to somewhere in the back of the store.

I tried not to whimper again as my precious lava cake disappeared from view.

Moments later Rose was back, without the lava cakes, and rang up the sale.

CC handed her the money and ushered me to a corner table.

An eternity later—or maybe it was two minutes—Rose brought us warm lava cakes and set them down with a flourish.

"Ooh," I cooed at the plate in front of me. I grabbed my fork and prepared to dig in. Just before my fork descends toward what I know will taste like heaven, I flashed Rose a huge smile and said, "Thanks, your baked goods are the best thing I have ever put in my mouth."

Despite the slightly awkward wording of my heartfelt praise, Rose smiled warmly at me, for the first time ever, and then moved back to the register.

I eagerly dug into my cake and put a huge forkful into my mouth. I closed my eyes in lava-cake bliss and may have moaned, too. I savored the taste, chewing slowly and with relish. Stray crumbs were plucked from my lips by my greedy tongue with what may have bordered on lust. After a satisfying swallow, I opened my eyes to see those of the sheriff—well at least the one that still worked—staring back at me. His other eye was almost swollen shut from where I hit him with the door.

Even though he was across the room at the counter, I could see the slightly dazed look on his face. His mouth was slightly ajar, his eyes—eye—burned with a strange intensity. Judging by the movement of his chest, his breathing was a little rapid, too. I swallowed again and returned his stare, unable to look away from the intensity in his gaze. I felt my face heat up and licked my lips. His line of sight lowered to my mouth and seem to follow the motion of my tongue, which I promptly ordered back into my mouth. It felt like Rose had just put me in the oven.

Our intense staring contest was broken when Rose smacked his shoulder with her wooden spoon. I winced in sympathy as he turned toward her. They were too far away to hear anything, but that was probably for the best.

"Girl, I think he was checking you out!" CC said, looking toward the counter. "I got a little turned on just watching him watching you." She said while fanning herself.

I tried to shrug it off and took another bite. Despite the fact that I know how good it will be, I barely taste it. I was too confused by what had just happened. We didn't even like each other, at least I didn't think we did.

Rose handed the sheriff a box and he left the store, limping slightly. But not before one last, long look at me. He looked as confused as I felt.

Rose, however, frowned at me.

Even more confused by this turn of events, I barely managed to finish my lava cake. But I powered through. Hey, I'm confused, not stupid.

CC allowed me to finish in silence, but as soon as I put the last bite in my mouth, she pounced.

"What is going on with you and the sheriff? I thought you didn't like each other, but he looked like he would rather nibble on you than whatever Rose sent him home with."

"I don't know," I answered honestly. "I mean he was really mad when I hit him with my car, and when I slapped him reaching for Fluffy, and when I ran over his foot, and earlier today when I hit him with the door, and then punched him in the balls." I finished the laundry list of physical harm I'd caused the sheriff staring at the two small remaining crumbs on my plate.

Despite being absorbed by recent interactions with the sheriff, I felt as if someone was staring at me. I looked around trying to find the source of the feeling.

Rose stood behind the counter and was definitely staring at me, almost like she was trying to read my thoughts.

"Why is Rose staring at me like that," I asked CC out of the corner of my mouth, while at the same time trying to clear my mind of anything Rose might find offensive.

CC frowned as she noticed the look Rose was casting our way. "I don't know," she finally said, "she seemed happy when we got here, but after she talked to the sheriff, she seems ... different. Do you think the sheriff said something to her?"

"She seemed happy enough to send him home with a box of treats," I ventured a thought, "but he frequently displays poor people skills, so maybe." I shrugged.

Rose seemed to be arguing with herself, but finally pushed off the counter and walked toward our table.

I found myself shrinking down a little in my seat as if the few inches I skootched down would prevent her from seeing me.

"How was the lava cake?" She asked. It was a casual question but lacked the previous warmness.

"It was wonderful Rose. Just like everything you bake. You have a real talent." CC's comments weren't just empty praise.

Acknowledging the compliment with a nod, Rose turned to me and with what seemed like forced nonchalance, said, "Claire, I hear you have met the new sheriff." Her tone was surprisingly accusatory, and I couldn't shake the thought that she was eyeing me suspiciously. I felt the need to confess but wasn't sure what I was supposed to confess to.

"That's right," I said, "I've run into him a time or two."

CC choked on my choice of words but held her tongue.

"And what do you think of him?" Rose continued in a tone that sounded more like an interrogation than polite chitchat.

"Umm, he's tall?" I tried responding with something generic, unsure of what to say.

Rose narrowed her eyes.

"He has great abs," I blurted out, and then felt my cheeks color, "He works late so he's probably a hard worker." I threw that last point in to distract her from the abs comment.

Rose and CC wore identical smirks at my embarrassment.

"He's a nice man," Rose said with a strange twinkle in her eyes. "Handsome, hard worker, makes good money, cares about his family."

She continued listing his good points although I wasn't sure why. I found myself nodding at her. "That's great," I said. "Well, we have to go. CC needs to get home to her kids. So, bye," I said, grabbed CC by the hand, and hauled her to the door.

"That was weird right?" I asked CC once we were outside. However, we weren't out of sight, because I noticed Rose watching us from the window the whole way to my car and even as we left the parking lot.

CC tapped her mouth, deep in thought. "I think she wants to set you up with him," she finally said.

"What?" I yelled in surprise and swerved out of my lane. "That's ridiculous! I don't think she even likes me," I said, steering my baby back into the right lane.

"Maybe she doesn't like him either," CC mused.

I thought about that possibility, but finally shook my head. "No, I don't think so. Rose gave him that big box of heaven, and he didn't even pay for it. She must like him. Wait, how did he get a box of heaven without paying for it? Even when I do pay, she tries to cut me off from her brownies. How does he get free stuff?" Now I was mad. I wanted free baked goods.

We fumed in silence the rest of the way home.

Once in the driveway CC exploded. "Well, how do you think Rose knows the sheriff?"

"Wait, what? Why aren't you complaining about not getting free baked goods?" I asked, perplexed.

CC's sigh expressed her exasperation at me. "Let it go," she said, "and focus. Rose has been in town for four months and the sheriff has been in town for less than a week. Do you think they knew each other from before they moved here?"

"Where would they know each other from? He's a sheriff and she's a baker. He's what, thirty-five? And she's like eighty? Where would they have met?" I asked, not really caring. I mean, unless there were free baked goods involved, I didn't care.

"Well, I think this is a problem for another day," I said with a yawn. We said good night and I went inside.

Chapter 11

S till in a stupor over the lava cake from last night, I staggered into CC's kitchen for coffee and breakfast. It was quiet since the kids were sleeping in after their kid's night out with Jake. Once I had consumed enough of the magic brew to function and not stab people, I went home and quickly showered, dressed, and grabbed my lunch from Benji. Why Benji had my lunch was beyond me, but for once he had brought me something I actually wanted, so I decided not to think too deeply about it.

Work was the same grueling drudgery it always was. I managed to avoid Steve's wandering hands and Brandon stayed in his office, so he didn't mess up anything, both of which were a nice change. I was the last one in the office, again, so I turned on the answering machine and turned off the lights on the way out.

Remembering the incident with Sheriff Armstrong, I carefully opened the door and made sure no one was lurking around outside before locking up. Once in my car, I took a deep breath and dropped my head onto the steering wheel trying to gather the will to go on.

A knock on my partly opened window caused me to scream while digging in my purse for pepper spray.

Over my pounding heart I heard the sheriff say, "Relax, it's me. Dominic. Sheriff Armstrong."

Lucky for him my purse was so messy I hadn't found my pepper spray and therefore couldn't spray him in the face. I think we both breathed a sigh of relief about that.

"Why are you trying to give me a heart attack?"

He rubbed the back of his neck. "I didn't mean to. I just wanted to ask some more questions about Mr. Johnson's life insurance policy. Remember, I came by yesterday, but—"

I winced. "Your eye looks," I struggled to find the right word, "almost back to normal?"

He stared at me for a minute, mostly out of the eye that wasn't still swollen and red, which made me squirm a little. But then the mouth that I thought never smiled, like not ever, curled slightly at one edge. *Smiling might become a habit at this rate* I thought to myself.

"Thanks. I think. Getting ice on it quickly helped."

Now he squirmed slightly, and I felt my face flush as I remembered the inadvertent flashing I had given him while putting ice on his eye. The uncomfortable silence stretched, well, uncomfortably long, before he broke it.

"I wanted to know how a beneficiary can be on a policy, but nobody knows who they are? Don't you need them to sign something? Fill out forms? Anything?"

"It's not that uncommon for people to be named as a beneficiary without even knowing it. As long as the person filling out the forms has all their information…." I shrugged. "Again, you should probably talk to Steve. He's the one that sells the policies and fills out forms with the families." I couldn't help but make a face as I said his name.

"You don't like him much, do you?" he asked.

"You should be a detective with those skills," I replied sharply. "Sorry, that was uncalled for." I continued before he could say anything. "It's been a long day. Week. Month. Look, I just want to go home and get out of these clothes." The spark in his eyes, well, eye, told me I might have worded that a little too suggestively. "I mean, and into something more comfortable." That didn't sound much better. "Like a t-shirt and cutoffs," I finished, still thinking it sounded lame.

His eye still had that spark in it, but he continued with his questioning. "Does the insurance company contact the beneficiary?" He returned to the topic that brought him here after closing time, again.

Hmmm. Why was he stopping by after hours? I realized I hadn't answered yet. "Usually, we don't need to as we mostly deal with locals, but in this case yes, we are using the information on the policy to try to contact them. So far, we haven't been successful."

"What happens if you can't contact them?" He asked.

I shrug. "Normally we don't have a problem. With locals' policies we all know each other. I'm not sure what the company has planned."

He nodded as he processed my answers. He must be a slow processor because he kept standing there nodding. I wasn't sure if I was still needed.

"Well, I'm going to head home," I said and rolled up the window to cut off anymore conversation. When I started the car he stepped back quickly, as if afraid I'd run over his foot. I narrowed my gaze at him before pulling out of the parking spot and didn't runover his foot, so ha!

I was lost in thought as I drove home. It was weird that nobody knew who Jamie Wilson was. In a town this size everybody knows everybody and their dog.

"It's weird that nobody knows who this Jamie Wilson is," I said, walking into CC's kitchen having already changed into cutoffs and another fantastic shirt. "Don't you think that's weird?"

"Of course, I do. What are the odds that Mr. Johnson had a social life outside of town? He barely had one in town," she said turning to me after giving one last stir to something on the stove. "Honestly, Claire. Don't you think that is in bad taste?" She asked gesturing to my shirt. This one has two crows and reads *attempted murder*.

The rest of the family started to trickle in allowing me to avoid answering her question, which may have been rhetoric anyway. The volume increased with the number of people in the room, and I smiled, happy to be surrounded by them. That is, until Eve slid in next to me again.

"What's for dinner?" I asked, eyeing Eve.

"Tacos," CC answered as she brought bowls of meat and cheese to the table. Satisfied that Eve can't steal my food, I smiled at her as she squirmed around next to me. Everyone settled into their places and started passing bowls of food.

"So," I began, pausing to pile meat, cheese, lettuce, tomatoes, salsa, and sour cream on my tortilla shell. Trying to wrap enough of the tortilla around the mound of food so I can pick it up without spilling the insides everywhere proved difficult, but I'm nothing if not committed. I finally managed it and continued, "How are we going to find Jamie Wilson?" Nobody jumped in with an answer. They were all obviously stumped.

Finally, a voice piped in, "Who is Jamie Wilson and why do we want to find him?"

"Jamie is a girl's name," Ann said, while finishing her taco. "There is a girl in my class named Jamie."

"A boy on my football team is named Jamie," Frank said.

"That's a good point," Jake said. "We don't even know if Jamie is male or female. That will make it harder. Do you know anything besides a name?"

"Well, there should be a relationship listed and social security number, but it was left blank. Which is odd as that should have flagged the file. There was an address, but it was a college dorm and out of date."

"Mr. Johnson left a five-million-dollar policy to a college student?" Nell asked.

I glared at CC. "How does Nell know about the insurance policy?" I asked.

Luckily for CC Nell keeps talking. "How does he even know a college student? What college?"

"That's a good point," CC mused, obviously trying to deflect my attention. "Mr. Johnson never had kids, and he was an only child. Who would he know in college? It's not a local or we would know them."

We all nodded, knowing that was true. Everybody knew everybody in our town.

"Let's drive to the college and ask around!" CC said. "It's only a couple hours away."

"Uh, some of us have to go to a soul-stealing job tomorrow." I reminded her.

Her face sours as she processed my employment status. "And we haven't talked to Tessa yet, either." She paused, tapping her lips.

"Ok," she said, standing and putting away food, "let me put these away for leftovers, and I'll be ready to go."

Jake tried to grab a bowl before CC could clear it. Sadly, he missed and now his second taco won't have lettuce. I smirked and popped the last bite of my lettuce-covered taco into my mouth.

Realizing that dinner was over, the kids began to clear their plates. Jane asked if she could get a ride to the pet store.

"I want to go! I want to go!" Eve yelled, bouncing up and down.

Jake sighed and tried to finish his lettuce-less taco with a bouncing dervish on one side but nodded.

I slid out of the banquet and linked arms with CC. We sauntered out of the kitchen leaving Jake with his lettuce-less taco and the kids.

Tessa lived across town, so it took about twenty minutes to get there. It would have taken less, but we had to stop and chat with a couple of people on the way. Rush hour in our town is when everyone is outside. Folks in our town are physically incapable of passing another person without stopping to chat.

One day it took me thirty minutes to make the five-minute walk to the shared mailboxes. I did learn some juicy gossip, but I didn't spread any rumors. All I can say is that a hasty wedding and a couple of high school students were involved.

Tessa still lived with her parents, which is not uncommon for kids who don't leave town for college. Their house was small and simple, but well maintained. A few balls and bikes were spread across the yard, but it was mowed and trimmed with tidy flowerbeds. Walking up the front walk we could hear what sounded like the whole basketball team inside. We knocked and a dog began to bark immediately. I heard it getting closer and cowered behind CC.

She shot me a look that implied I was a big chicken, but before she could say anything the door opened to reveal an older woman.

She was shorter than me by a few inches, but her presence made her seem taller. Dark hair was pulled back into a braid that wrapped around her head like a crown. Shots of silver-white wove through and made it look even more stunning. She had a plain white apron wrapped around her and a surprised mien.

"Hi Angelica, we don't mean to intrude, but we were hoping to speak with Tessa," CC said.

Angelica smiled warmly, "Don't be silly. You're not intruding. Come in, come in. Do you want some coffee? Tea? I just made cookies. Come into the kitchen and I'll get you a plate."

She said all that while ushering us inside. Angelica was like that. She wanted to feed everybody and views everybody as family. As we passed through the small living room stuffed with furniture and the high school basketball team—which explained why it sounded like the basketball team was there—Angelica managed to pick her oldest son out of the throng of boys reclining on every available space, including the floor,

"Rick, go and get Tessa, please. Ms. Moore and Ms. Miller are here and would like to speak to her."

She also snagged three empty glasses and a platter with only crumbs left on it on the way by, without even breaking stride. I was impressed. Settling us into chairs at the kitchen table in the bright and cheerful kitchen, she bustled around pouring coffee for us and loading a plate with chocolate chip cookies. She placed all that on the table before refilling the platter with what must have been a thousand cookies and whisking it out to the basketball team.

"Sorry about the boys," she said as she returned and settled across from us.

I hadn't even had time to pick up my cup and began to think Angelica had superpowers. It wasn't natural for somebody to move as fast as she did.

"How have you both been? You both look amazing."

"We are just great Angelica, and I love your hairstyle," CC answered. "I could never get my hair to cooperate like that."

I eyed CC's mass of beautiful blond hair as it shimmered around her head in some sort of updo that looked like something an animated princess would have. At the same time, I was pretty sure my hair looked like I was pulled through a hedge backward. I patted my hair and tried to determine how bad it looked but realized there wasn't really anything I could do about it now anyway.

"Oh, CC," Angelica said while she waved a dismissive hand, even though she is obviously pleased by the compliment. Realizing no one was going to compliment my hair, I grabbed a cookie and took a huge bite.

"Oh, man, this is delicious," I said around my mouthful of cookie.

Angelica beamed at me. "Thank you. The recipe has been in my family for generations."

"You wanted to see me, Mom," Tessa asked as she entered the kitchen. She paused when she saw us. "Hi, Ms. Moore, Ms. Miller." She smiled as she greeted us but looked nervous.

I briefly wondered why but was distracted by the cookie and took another bite.

"Yes dear," Angelica said, now standing next to Tessa.

How she got there in the time it took me to blink reinforced my belief that her superpower was speed.

"I'll let you three talk while I take these sandwiches to the boys." She grabbed another giant platter, this one piled high with sandwiches, and disappeared into the living room.

I swiveled my head around trying to determine when she could have made a platter full of sandwiches. Or where the platter came from. Honestly as fast as she moved, I expected her back before Tessa could join us at the table.

Tessa slid into a chair at the kitchen table, but she still looked unsure.

"Tessa, we understand that you cleaned Mr. Johnson's house," CC said.

Tessa looked really scared now.

"Yes." She drew out the word as if unsure if she should admit to it. "I've cleaned his house for the last couple of years," she said. "Why do you ask?"

Deciding we should tread lightly so as not to scare her or upset Angelica, I asked, "Did you kill him?" Wait. That wasn't treading lightly. Shoot.

"What? Of course not!" Tessa leaned back and crossed her arms protectively in front of her chest.

CC shot me a look and tried to smooth it over. "She is just kidding, Tessa." Another glare came my way. "We just wanted to ask if you saw or heard anything out of the ordinary before Mr. Johnson died."

Tessa relaxed a little, enough to grab a cookie off the plate in front of us. Thinking that was a great idea, I also grabbed a cookie.

"No," Tessa said, "I tried to avoid being there at the same time as Mr. Johnson. He always yelled at me or criticized my cleaning. The last time I saw him was three weeks ago. He usually left a check for me, but I hadn't been paid in a couple of weeks. I made sure I was there to remind him about it, and he started yelling that I wasn't cleaning to his satisfaction, I was trying to steal from him, and other hateful things. And then he fired me. I came home crying and Mom drove right over there to confront him. She returned with a check for the two weeks I had cleaned, that he hadn't paid me for, but neither one of us wanted me to work there anymore. That's the last time I saw him." When she finished her story, she looked down and picked at her cookie.

Mine, of course, had already been eaten. "I'm sorry that happened to you Tessa. You don't deserve to be treated like that." I said and reached out to cover her hand as a comforting gesture.

She seemed surprised at first but then gave me a small smile. "Thanks. That's what my mom said too, but she's my mom. She has to be nice to me."

"Can you think of anybody who would want Mr. Johnson dead?" CC asked.

Tessa looked at her like she had grown an extra head. "Everybody who has ever met him." She said with conviction and, I thought, an implied *duh*.

I nodded. I'm mean I'd met him, and I wasn't exactly crying about his death. He wasn't a very nice man. Angelica bustled back into the kitchen with the two empty platters. The basketball team was like a plague of locusts I thought as I snagged the last cookie.

"Does anybody need more coffee?" Angelica asked, already holding the pot.

I reached for my mug, but CC intercepted my hand, stood, and dragged me to my feet, too.

"Oh, no thanks Angelica, we have to be going, but thank you so much. It's always so nice to visit with you."

CC and Angelica beamed at each other while I silently mourned the loss of a cup of coffee.

"Well, stop by anytime," Angelica said and then walked us toward the front door.

On the way back through the living room, one of the boys called out, "Nice shirt Ms. Miller."

I smiled at the group, unable to pick out who said it. "Thanks," I said, looking down at the two crows on my shirt. "I just got it a couple weeks ago and I—" CC pushed me out the door before I was able to share the life story of my shirt. Rude!

"What do you think?" CC asked as we drove home.

"That it's rude," I said.

"I know. It's shameful the way Mr. Johnson treated poor Tessa," CC said, shaking her head.

"What are you talking about? I'm talking about dragging me out before I got another cup of coffee and not letting me finish the story about my shirt."

She ignored my outburst and continued as if I hadn't spoken.

"Tessa is a sweet girl. She would never shirk her job or steal."

Her passionate defense of Tessa is touching. "We don't have anyone left to talk to," I said, not entirely unhappy with the situation. "Ms. Schwartz pointed the finger at Mr. Russell, who pointed the finger at Tessa, who basically pointed the finger at everyone in town. We can't go around asking every person in town if they killed him." About the time I reached that conclusion, I pulled into the driveway and turned off the car.

CC glared at me. "We shouldn't ask anyone if they killed him, that's not very subtle, and is considered rude."

Well, I thought, *it's a lot faster than her ideas.*

We returned to CC's empty kitchen, grabbed big glasses of iced tea, and then retreated to the backyard. We plunked down in yard chairs set up in front of a plastic kiddie pool and dipped our feet into the tepid water, gently nudging the ducks out of the way. I had checked out the water first, just to be sure it was clean enough to put my feet in. Ducks have a habit of making their pool water disgusting. You stick your feet into one duck-infested kiddie pool without checking and you never forget to check again. An involuntary shudder ran down my spine in reaction to the memory.

"We should go to the college," CC said, staring across a yard scattered with various kids' things. There was a bike tipped on its side close to the side gate, a complicated system of pulleys, blocks, wind spinners, wood arms, and various other items that stretched from the wooden playground to somewhere behind the garage. I'm not sure what they are for or why they take up most of the yard. I thought about asking CC but figured it would be best to wait until Dean finished and tested it out. There was also a collection of dolls seemingly having some sort of epic tea party/war in the sand box, and about a thousand birdfeeders, bird houses, squirrel feeders, bat houses, and other animal-inspired items I couldn't name scattered around. And in between all the debris associated with raising children, and perhaps starting a petting zoo and inventors' laboratory, are beautiful flower beds spilling late summer blooms in a rainbow of colors.

Feeling content, I sighed and relaxed for perhaps the first time all week. A scratching thud noise comes from the direction of my backyard and repeats itself a few times before Benji can open the door and join us. He sits next to me with a doggie smile on his furry face. Turning to him, I said, "Well, go close the door. Do you want to let the flies in?"

He waited half a beat as if to decide whether he wanted to let the flies in. Finally, he jumped up and ran back to the door. Jumping at the partly open door, he is able to push it closed. I heard the latch click and Benji gave one sharp, happy bark and then returned to sit by me again. The three of us are content to sit quietly and enjoy the moment of peace offered us. It lasts all of about seven minutes before Frank and Amelia come in through the side gate and step over the bike discarded there. They are followed shortly by Ann and Jane, followed by a young deer.

"Don't let it eat my flowers again," CC called to Jane, without even turning to fully look at the deer. Kyle dropped to the ground on the other side of Benji, who immediately rolled onto his back for a belly rub. Eve climbed into my lap almost spilling what was left of my iced tea, but I managed to catch both the tipping glass and the squirmy child. Dean slid behind the garage with an intent look on his face and a toolbox in his hand. Only Nell didn't come through the gate.

I started to wonder where she was when Jake appeared with a big bag of dog food slung over each shoulder. They are nice broad shoulders, too. I enjoyed the view as he headed into the house with his load with barely a glance our way.

When he reappeared a few minutes later, he also has a glass of iced tea. On his way to a chair on the other side of CC, he leaned down and started an epic make-out session. I was actually afraid the water in the kiddie pool would start to boil from the heat of their kissy-face session.

"Where's Nell?" I asked loudly, making a point to stare at the two of them.

Jake pulled back slightly from CC's face and turned to look at me, clearly disgruntled.

I smiled unabashedly at him, waiting.

Finally, he dropped into the chair on the other side of CC and answered my question. "She met up with some friends and they went to get ice cream and talk about college."

He said this with complete disregard for my feelings. As if my precious baby leaving for college didn't tear the heart from my chest.

I felt moisture gather in my eyes, prompted by the anticipated loss of my beloved baby girl. I took a deep breath.

CC reached over and held my hand in solidarity.

I knew she couldn't understand the depth of my pain. I mean, she's not a mother. Wait. That's not right, she's my best friend, we probably have a psychic connection.

"What am I thinking?" I asked CC as I focused really hard on projecting my thoughts to her.

"Chocolate, you will miss Nell, and chocolate again."

"Wow! You can read my mind." I said, impressed.

"Nell isn't gone forever, Auntie Claire. She's just going to college. It's not even that far away, just an hour's drive."

Eve thinks she is being reasonable, but who listens to a two-year-old. Everyone knows they aren't very smart.

"Besides you'll always have me." She added, wrapping her arms around me in a hug.

"You make an excellent point, Eve," I conceded and hugged her back, "You are so smart."

We sat in the back yard as the kids came and went doing kid stuff and simply enjoyed being together for another thirty minutes before my fidgeting finally drew a comment from CC.

"What are you doing?" she asked, turning her head to look at me.

"Nothing," I said, and settled back in my chair from where I had been craning my neck to look over the fence toward my house. She narrowed her gaze as if trying to read my thoughts. I started humming to block any connection.

"You're looking for someone," she said.

I felt myself begin to panic. "No, I'm not! You're looking for someone."

Her gaze sharpened. "But who?" she wondered aloud. "We're all here and you didn't say anything about expecting someone. So, you're keeping it a secret. You're keeping a secret from me, your best friend!" She clutched her heart as if she has been mortally wounded. "We tell each other everything," she said, her voice a near wail. "I even told you I was pregnant before I told Jake." She finished with a shriek filled with pain and disbelief.

"What?" Jake asked in a shocked voice, "you told Claire we were expecting before you told me? I can't believe that!" After a pause, he continued in a more normal voice. "Wait. I take that back. Of course, you told her first. Carry on."

CC and I both ignored his outburst anyway.

"I'm not expecting anyone." I realized CC wasn't going to let this go and mumbled, "The sheriff has come to see me every night since we met. I just don't want him to ring the doorbell again and upset Agatha. That's all."

"I think there's more to it than that." CC said. "I think you might like him." Her Cheshire cat smile, usually reserved for thoughts of Jake, spread across her face.

"I do not!" I said, perhaps a little too much desperation in my voice. "He thinks I'm a menace." I sunk back into my chair and pondered why that thought bothered me. A lot of people thought I was a menace, and it has never bothered me.

I stewed over this turn of events until I headed home to bed. I have a hard time falling asleep and not just because Blackbeard slept on top of me. Not to mention, Agatha hogs most of the bed and snores. She slept all day, quiet as a mouse, but when she got into bed with me it was like sleeping with a chainsaw. Benji slept curled around my head. All that made it hard to toss and turn, but somehow, I managed. It must be because I'm such an overachiever.

Chapter 12

When my alarm clock started blaring, I felt like I hadn't slept a wink and looked even worse than normal, I was sure. I didn't bother looking in a mirror, I figured it would just depress me further.

Staggering over to CC's took a herculean effort and I almost didn't make it. After getting a little tangled in the gate latch, I had to tear my way free and ended up leaving a bit of t-shirt fabric on the latch. Still, I somehow mustered enough energy to trudge the last few feet, where CC met me at her kitchen door with a full coffee mug.

While I'm downing my coffee, which probably sounded like a dehydrated horse at a water trough, CC said, "You look terrible. Even more so than usual."

CLAIRE AND THE MISSING HEIR

See, I could always count on my best friend to lift me up and make me feel better.

She wrapped me in a hug and asked, "What's wrong sweetie?"

"I don't know," I said and flopped onto a stool at her counter. I didn't have the energy to stand. "I couldn't sleep last night. I just kept tossing and turning."

CC stared at me as if trying to read my mind again. I didn't have the strength to block her and sipped my coffee while she sifted through my thoughts to find what she was looking for.

"You were thinking about the sheriff," she said in the same way Hercule Poirot might announce that he'd solved a murder.

"Why?" asked a sweet voice behind me.

I didn't have the energy to turn around and see who it was.

"Auntie Claire has a little crush on the new sheriff is all," CC told whichever of her spawn had asked.

"He has a crush on her too," Kyle noted from his seat at the banquette.

I turned to look at him, wondering if he was serious. The thing was, I believed him. If Kyle said it's true, it's true. That kid noticed everything, but still, this was completely unexpected.

"When he doesn't think you're looking he gets this look in his eyes, like mom and dad when they look at each other," he said. He continued sketching and didn't bother to look up.

Huh, I thought. When did Kyle see the sheriff look at me? I mean, besides when I hit him with my car or maybe when I slapped him when reaching for Fluffy. He wasn't there when I ran over the sheriff's foot, or hit him with the door, or even when we were at Bake my Day. Regardless, this cheered me somewhat, and after CC refilled my now-empty coffee mug I headed home to get ready for work.

I was running late and took my shower in record time but left the water running for Blackbeard while I pulled on a black skirt that swirled around my knees. Whenever I moved, the black panels parted to reveal brief bursts of jewel-toned color from the under-skirt panels. A black sleeveless top with a black lace overlay completed the outfit. I pulled my hair into a chignon to keep it contained and, after a quick swipe of mascara and lipstick, I turned off the water, which severely disappointed Blackbeard. Some strappy sandals were easy to slip on while I shuffled over Agatha and headed out the door. CC wasn't there but a lunch bag rested on the passenger seat so, good enough.

I cringed to see Brandon, uh, Mr. Brown's car already in the lot when I arrived. I breezed in and dropped my lunch in the break room before tackling my desk. To my surprise, nothing marred the organized surface I had left the night before. Frowning despite this welcome sight, I approached my desk slowly, half expecting a trap. From my chair, I still didn't see what Brandon might have messed up. I shrugged and then turned on my computer. Instead of the typical welcome screen, a warning flashed continuously.

"What!" I said with a gasped. "What happened to my computer?" No one was around to answer my question, so I began jabbing random keys to try and fix whatever had gone wrong. After a minute or so, the flashing remained.

"Oh, yeah, it started doing that about ten minutes ago, so I turned it off," Brandon said from behind me.

"What did you do?" I said with a half-shriek, still pushing random keys.

Brandon had the good sense to at least look chagrined. "I thought I'd update your computer for you. I don't think it did what it was supposed to do. You can fix it, right?"

His hopeful puppy dog face was the only reason I restrained myself from bashing his face with the keyboard. "No, I can't fix it!" I shouted in response. "I'm not IT."

"Oh, bummer," he said, and then just sort of drifted away to his office, where he should have stayed in the first place.

Desperate, I grabbed my phone and dialed from memory. "Jake, it's an emergency. I need you to fix my work computer." I said in a rush, talking over his hello. Dropping my voice until it was barely a whisper, I said. "He touched it. Brandon touched it and thought he updated it, but I think he cursed it instead. Help!"

"I'll be there as soon as I can," Jake said, his tone reassuring.

I was trying to stop hyperventilating. "Please hurry," I said in what sounded suspiciously like a whimper, "everything is on this computer."

Jake murmured some reassuring words and then hung up. I didn't know what to do while I waited for him. I fidgeted with my hands, rearranged the things on my desk, paced in front of the door, and generally had a panic attack.

Hours later, okay, maybe it was only thirty minutes, he finally arrived. I practically ran into the parking lot and grabbed his arm. Dragging him into the office, I ushered him to my desk and basically shoved him into my chair.

"Help her!" I said, "I can't lose her!"

"Okay, Okay," Jake said, "give me a minute."

He typed quickly while keeping an eye on the screen. I watched, wringing my hands. After about a hundred years, he gave one final keystroke and my screen stopped flashing.

I exhaled in relief, but then it went black, and I gasped for air, clutching the edge of the desk to stop from falling. Dots danced across my vision and I felt lightheaded. Before I could succumb to despair, my computer screen flashed again and then displayed my familiar home screen. I took several calming breaths, although I was still nervous and didn't want to get my hopes up. By the time I could stand unassisted, Jake was also standing. Even more important, my computer was, too. The home screen was reassuringly stable, not a flicker in sight.

"Thank you, thank you, thank you," I chanted and threw myself into his arms, hugging him as if he was the only thing keeping me alive. Jake's arms wrapped around and held me secure while I continued to calm my earlier panic.

"I hope I'm not interrupting anything." A harsh-sounding voice spoke from near the entrance.

I looked up from where my face had been pressed against Jake's chest to see the sheriff glowering at us.

"Not at all," Jake said. He untangled himself from me and gathered his bag. "I was just on my way out."

He leaned down and kissed my cheek, "See you for dinner," he said, before slipping out the door.

The sheriff's scowling face turned to me and I frowned at him in return. *What has got his panties in a bunch*, I thought. Seeing his face tighten, I realized it might not have been to myself after all. Geez, just when I thought I had it under control.

"I came by to find out if you had managed to contact Jamie Wilson," he said, his voice tight.

As hard as his jaw was clenched, I was a little worried he would break a tooth. I wasn't sure what had him so upset. "I'll let Mr. Brown know you're here," I said, using my office voice. Turning on my heel, my skirt flared around my legs. I smoothed it and sat in my chair to call Mr. Brown's office. He had this thing about using the intercom. Apparently, it was in a movie he saw, and he thought it made him seem more important or something.

Since I could see Mr. Brown at his desk as I rang him it seemed ridiculous, but whatever. He picked up the phone and I said,

"Sheriff Armstrong is here to see you."

I replaced the receiver and we both waited in tense silence for Brandon. I did my best to ignore the sheriff's scowling face.

"I thought Ms. Moore was your best friend," he said, breaking the silence.

I looked up, a little shocked. "She is," I said.

"Then why were you hugging her husband and making dinner plans with him?" He asked.

My mouth dropped open. I stared at him for a few seconds before dissolving into peals of laughter. "Oh my gosh," I said between fits of giggles, "you think I'm seeing Jake?" I used air quotes around the word seeing to emphasize how ridiculous that sounded. I wiped away the tears that had gathered in my eyes at the absurdity of this accusation.

Finally composed enough to continue, I explained, "My computer crashed. Jake is a whiz at everything tech. He came to fix my computer, which he did, saving all my files. I'm having dinner tonight with Jake, and CC, and their seven children. I am not seeing Jake."

I looked him dead in the eyes, so he knows I'm not lying. When he seemed to waffle about whether to believe me or not, I added, "Besides, if I was seeing Jake do you really think I would invite him to my glass-fronted office and hug him where anyone could see? CC will know he was here before he even gets back to his office. This is a small town. Everybody knows everything."

He ran a hand through his hair and finally seemed to believe me. "Then why doesn't anybody know who Jamie Wilson is?" he asked, his tone frustrated.

"Sheriff, so nice to see you again. Why don't you come into my office?" Brandon said when he finally emerged from his office to greet his guest.

The sheriff shot me one more long look that I couldn't decipher, and then followed Brandon into his office.

No sooner had they settled into their seats than I watched Brandon pick up his phone. The light on mine flashed. With a sigh, I answered.

"Ms. Miller, please bring some coffee into my office. I'm meeting with the sheriff."

I managed not to roll my eyes through sheer force of will—and the desire to continue receiving a paycheck—I answered with, "The sheriff is here? I had no idea. Of course, I'll be right there with coffee."

Brandon didn't recognize my sarcasm and hung up the phone. I watched him steeple his fingers and direct his gaze toward the sheriff.

I headed to the break room to get coffee for the twit and the sheriff. Pouring two mugs, I grabbed them with one hand and the sugar and creamer tray with the other. Lucky for Brandon his office has a push-open door, because despite seeing my full hands, he doesn't bother to get up. I leaned over and placed the cups and tray on the desk. As I straightened and turned to go, it was clear the sheriff's gaze hadn't been on Brandon pontificating behind his desk, but on my behind. I smirked and his cheeks colored slightly. He knows I caught him staring, again, and studiously avoids my gaze.

Heading to the break room for my own cup of coffee, I noticed Steve pulling into the parking lot. For the umpteenth time that day, I sighed, about Steve being late and about him being here at all.

I sipped my coffee, lost in contemplation over the sheriff checking out my butt and his weird reaction to me hugging Jake. Steve eased up behind me and pinched my butt. Whirling so fast half my coffee paints a brown stripe across his shirt, I was ready to tear into him about inappropriate touching and sexual harassment.

However, before I could say anything, the sheriff appeared out of nowhere and grabbed Steve's shoulder. "Would you like to press charges, Ms. Miller?" the sheriff asked.

Based on Steve's grimace, it wasn't a gentle grip. Understanding dawned when Steve realized what the sheriff had just said, and his eyes bugged out. "What? I just gave her a friendly pinch. It's a compliment, really." Trying to find some camaraderie with the sheriff, Steve turned as far as the hold on his shoulder would allow. "It makes them feel pretty."

I'm shocked speechless that Steve actually believed what he is saying.

The sheriff stared at him like a frog had just spoken, and then looked at me. "Is he serious?" he asks, "Does he really think that?"

"I think he does," I said, nodding slowly.

"I'll take him outside for a little chat. Let me know if you would like to press charges," he said. And with that, he turned and half-dragged Steve out behind him.

Still shocked, both that Steve believed I liked him grabbing me, and that the sheriff was taking such a personal interest in Steve grabbing me, I didn't realize Brandon had come up behind me until he spoke.

"What is the sheriff doing with Steve?"

I was so startled I screamed and almost spilled the rest of my coffee. Turning to face him I clutched my chest with my free hand and yelled, "Don't do that! You scared me half to death. Why is everyone sneaking up on me today?"

"Sorry," Brandon said, looking like an abused puppy who just got scolded, "I didn't mean to sneak up on you." He shuffled his feet with his head bowed.

"I know," I relented. "I'm sorry I yelled. You just scared me."

Hearing my apology, he raised his head slightly so he could look at me to determine my sincerity.

"The sheriff just wanted to talk to Steve for a moment. I'm sure he'll be back soon."

Brandon nodded and waited. After several long seconds he began shifting his weight back and forth.

Realizing we might be here a while if I didn't do something, I asked, "Did you need anything?"

"No, I guess not," He said, still looking lost. When I don't respond he turns and heads back to his office.

I went back to my desk but couldn't see the sheriff or Steve through the front window. Sitting in front of my now-working computer, I tried to focus. My attention strayed to the window every half second trying to figure out what the sheriff and Steve were doing. The sheriff looked really mad when he dragged Steve out. I couldn't concentrate while waiting to see what would happen next. After about twenty minutes, Steve came back in, shadowed by the sheriff.

My subdued coworker came and stood a respectful distance from my desk and addressed his shoes. "I'm sorry that I touched you without your permission. I now realize it might—" Sheriff Armstrong cleared his throat, which caused Steve to flinch and hunch his shoulders. After looking behind him, he continued. "I now realize that it was unwanted, inappropriate, and illegal. I will no longer subject you to my inappropriate advances." With that, he turned and shuffled off to his office like a dog waiting for his next beating.

"Wow!" I said, staring at the sheriff, "I've been trying to convince him of that for over a year. I'm impressed." His face softened, but was still a little scary. I was just glad he wasn't mad at me.

"It should never have happened. There is no excuse for mistreating women," he said, his voice forceful.

"Brandon's dad adheres to a boys will be boys ideology and didn't see anything wrong with it. Brandon follows his lead." I shrugged.

The sheriff's jaw tightened again. "It should have been handled right away," he said.

Raising my hands in surrender I said, "Hey, you're preaching to the choir."

Realizing how harsh his tone was, he unfolded his arms from the intimidating across the chest pose he had been holding, perhaps to keep from throttling Steve. He rubbed the back of his neck. "Sorry. I guess it's a pet peeve of mine."

We stared at each other as if trying to figure out what to say next. I wasn't sure how much time passed, but the ring of my phone startled me and broke the spell.

"Have a nice day," the sheriff said and left quickly, as if relieved by the excuse to flee.

Through the front window I watched him walk away as I answered the phone. It was CC.

"Why were you making out with my husband at your office?" she asked, a trace of laughter in her voice.

"Well, he is gorgeous," I answered. "I couldn't help myself. It's been going on for years. The truth is, he loves me and we're running away to Jamaica together."

No longer able to hold in the laughter that bubbled up from the absurdity of the story I had told, I dissolved into giggles. Hearing CC's giggles on the other end of the line kept me in helpless laughter for several minutes. Finally, we were both able to control ourselves and I told her what really happened. We had a nice chat and I filled her in on Brandon trying to update my computer and the whole Steve and the sheriff thing.

"I told you he was checking you out at Bake my Day the other night. I think he likes you," CC said when I finished my story.

I didn't know what to say to this. I was starting to think she might be right, but wasn't sure how I felt about it.

"I have to go. I have a ton of work to do."

"Liar," CC said. Dag Nab It! She knew me too well. "But we'll talk about it later." She hung up.

I stared dumbly at the phone for a second before hanging up and tried to get back to work.

Brandon left at noon for lunch and didn't return. I didn't see Steve for the rest of the day, but when I went to lock up, I realized he was gone too. Mentally shrugging it off, I headed home.

Agatha was spread across the entry floor like melted chocolate, which gave me an idea. I detoured into the kitchen for my secret stash of candy bars. I guess it's not much of a secret since I live alone and nobody else goes through my cabinets, but it sounded cool. I grabbed a bar of the good stuff and opened it. Taking a huge bite, I moaned in pleasure at the rich taste as it melted over my tongue. Quickly finishing the candy bar, I tossed the wrapper in the garbage and headed upstairs to change.

Blackbeard was sprawled across my bed and his one eye opened to examine me as I walked in. Obviously finding me lacking he closed the eye, at least pretending to be asleep. Benji, however, jumped up and down all around me. Not getting the reaction he wanted, he stretched out his front paws and bowed. Hey, I liked that. Everyone should bow before me.

"Good boy!" I said, and leaned down to give him an approving pat.

I pulled my shirt off and dropped it on the bench at the foot of the bed. That was followed by my skirt and then I padded over to the dresser for my jean cutoffs. I didn't know what it was about being dressed up all day that made me want to dress down after work. I sifted through all the amazing shirts in my drawer for just the right one and finally settled on the one that read *dear math, solve your own problems*. Checking myself out in the mirror, I pulled the pins from my hair and allowed it to cascade down my shoulders and back. Realizing it would drive me crazy if left down, I pulled it up into a high messy ponytail. Now I could drop to the floor and give Benji the belly rubs he'd been begging for.

After several minutes I hop to my feet and ask,

"Do you want to go see the kids?"

Benji hopped to his feet and started jumping around, running back and forth to the door.

"Ok, let's go," I said, heading for the stairs. By the time I reached the bottom Benji had already opened the backdoor and was sprinting toward CC's kitchen door. I reached the low gate between our yards and saw Eve open the door for Benji, and he trotted right in like he owned the place. Eve shut the door behind him, and I thought to myself, *Did she just shut the door in my face? And steal my dog?*

The nerve of some children! I strode across CC's yard and flung the door open with as much drama as I could muster. Nobody noticed. I walked over and confronted the offending urchin.

"You closed the door in my face!"

"No, I didn't," Eve replied without even glancing my way, "You were so far away it couldn't possibly have been in your face."

"But you saw me coming. Why didn't you wait and let me in?"

"You can open the door all by yourself, Benji can't. Our door has a knob, not a lever like yours. He doesn't have hands and can't turn the knob."

She was trying to use logic against me. Before I could launch into a full rebuttal, Nell handed me a chocolate bar. "Oooh, chocolate."

Around a huge bite, I said,

"What will I do when you're gone?" Nell rolled her eyes and I wondered where she had picked up that habit. I, of course, would never be so rude as to roll my eyes at someone. Wasn't CC teaching her better?

"I'm pretty sure any of the others can hand you chocolate," she said, as if she wasn't an integral part of my life.

"But can any of them do it as well as you?"

She scoffed at me and then began to set the table without further comment. Obviously, she agreed with me.

It was hard not to jump in and start hashing out the sheriff situation with CC immediately, but I didn't want to have that conversation in front of the kids. It might shake their belief that I knew everything. It could scar them for life and cause trust issues that would follow them through the rest of their lives. We wouldn't want that. Lost in this train of thought, I realized we were all sitting at the banquette. I wasn't sure how I had gotten there. Yet here I was, eating CC's delicious pork chops, mashed potatoes, and green bean casserole while the usual dinner conversation swirled around me.

Jake was recounting the threat to my computer that he was able to neutralize. The rest of us appeared to only understand a few words, but Jake and Dean were having an intense conversation. I wasn't entirely sure they didn't lapse into a foreign language at times.

Apparently at her breaking point, Eve said, "This is boring I want to talk about something else."

Silence met her outburst before CC said, "Eve, that is rude. Your father was telling us about his day."

"No, he wasn't. He was telling Dean. No one else knows what he's talking about."

We all knew this was true, but CC trudged on. "Your father listens to you when you tell him about your princess movies, and he doesn't know about them." Proud of her analogy, CC waited for Eve to apologize.

I knew that would never happen. Eve never apologized, for anything.

"Yes, he does," Eve said. "He can sing all the songs too."

We all turned to Jake who was blushing.

"Well, be that as it may, you need to listen politely to others." Not wanting to lose this small victory, CC continued. "Since you're done, why don't you go play with Benji?"

Eve brightened and immediately slid from her place at the table and left the kitchen with Benji at her heels.

"You sing all the songs?" I asked the still slightly pink Jake.

He is saved from having to respond by the rest of the children clearing their plates and tromping out of the kitchen. CC followed suit and began clearing dishes. Jake stood to help and they moved as if dancing around the kitchen, passing bowls, plates, and containers for leftovers. I was glad my friend had this. Her childhood was lonely and sad. Well, the parts that I wasn't in, I mean, I make everything better, right? I was happy with how our lives turned out. My best friend had an amazing husband, the houseful of children she always dreamed of and, of course, me. I had the best friend a girl could want, surrogate children who were loads of fun—with none of the childbirth pain and only a bit of the responsibility—and I was as welcome into their family as any of the rest of them. Even though

I was happy alone and don't want children of my own, I heaved a wistful sigh as I watched them.

CC passed the last of the containers to Jake to put in the refrigerator and he wrapped his other arm around her, dropping the container on the refrigerator shelf. He danced CC around the kitchen, holding her close.

I sighed again. Jake sang softly and spun her as if they were in a grand ballroom. A few lines into the song I realized it was from one of Eve's princess movies. Jake's eyes twinkled with merriment as I laughed, and then he dipped CC low before kissing her with fairytale passion. I wanted that too. Not from Jake, of course. He was married to my best friend and that would be inappropriate, but with someone equally great.

Meeting the right person was hard when you'd known every guy in town since kindergarten. Finally raising CC from the dip, Jake spun her toward me as he headed out of the kitchen and gave us our space. See, he knew what we needed. If he had left chocolate, that would've been perfect.

Jake poked his head back in the kitchen and said, "I'm going to take the kids to get ice cream, I'll bring you back some death by chocolate."

"He's perfect," I said.

"I know," she said with a smile that was half contentment and half slightly dirty leer. "Now tell me again about the sheriff and Steve," she said, returning to the banquette and handing me a beer.

I rehashed the whole incident while we sipped our beers. "The strangest thing was his face. He looked so angry. It wasn't like he was just upholding the law; it seemed personal. For a minute I actually thought he was going to kill, or at least hit Steve." I said, still perplexed.

"I think he likes you," CC said. "He keeps showing up to see you. He didn't make a big deal when you hit him with your car, slapped him, ran over his foot, and hit him with the door--"

"I get it," I interrupted her.

"I think he—"

CC's eyes widened and her focus shifted. Instantly alert, and afraid, I almost didn't hear her finish.

"—is outside right now." She slid from her seat and opened the door.

Sure enough, the sheriff was standing at CC's kitchen door

"Sheriff, please come in. Can I get you something to drink? Lemonade? Beer? Tea?"

"Thank you, ma'am, I sure could use a glass of lemonade," he said, stepping inside and then shifting from foot to foot as if nervous about something.

CC smiled and gestured toward me. "Have a seat and I'll get you a glass."

The sheriff looked toward where CC had gestured, which was next to me. After a brief hesitation, he took a seat. Since the banquette was designed to seat about fifteen people, he didn't crowd me, but I could still feel his body heat.

Returning with a glass of lemonade for the sheriff, CC settled across from us. "What brings you by tonight sheriff?" CC asked, taking a sip of her beer.

"I wanted to talk to Ms. Miller about pressing charges against Mr. Tuttle." The sheriff said. "I knocked at her house, but when there was no answer, I thought I'd check over here."

It made sense, but at the same time it didn't. Why not wait until tomorrow? He could have called me. Or sent a letter. He had deputies, well, one deputy, and he was more of a deputy in training, but still. I squinted my eyes trying to decipher his hidden agenda, but nothing occurred to me.

CC beamed at him, which caused him to get the slightly shell-shocked look all recipients of CC's full charisma tended to display.

Blinking, he shook himself slightly as if to dispel the magic of CC's smile. "Well, I'll leave you two to talk," CC said, sliding out of her seat and somehow casting me a conspiratorial wink without the sheriff seeing. "I need to check on the kids anyway."

Before I knew what was happening, CC had gone and I was left sitting next to the sheriff, alone.

"Ummm," I started intelligently, but then didn't know what to say next. The silence stretched, making me squirm a bit in my seat. The sheriff didn't seem any more comfortable than me. He fidgeted with his glass as if unsure what to do with his hands. They were nice hands, too. Big and long fingered, with nails trimmed short, and calluses that showed obvious signs of work.

Clearing his throat, he said, "I did talk to Mr. Tuttle about his inappropriate behavior, and I feel sure he won't repeat it, but you have the right to press charges against him." He seemed relieved to have gotten that out and took a huge gulp of lemonade.

"I don't think that's necessary," I said, still trying to process all that had happened this week—and it was just Thursday.

We sat in silence, both unsure of what to say next. We both talked at once, and then stopped when we realized the other was talking. We both laughed.

"I really appreciate you handling Steve," I said. "He's mostly harmless, but really annoying."

"Nobody should be allowed to treat a woman like that. You should feel safe and know your personal space is respected," he said, his tone vehement.

I was surprised by the force of his words, which must have shown on my face because his demeanor softened.

He said, "Sorry, I can get a little . . ." he struggled for the right word, "zealous."

I waited in silence, hoping he would expand on his statement, but he sat quietly, sipping his lemonade.

"Well, I guess I should be going," he said, and drained the rest of his lemonade.

I slid out of the banquette and trailed him to the door.

He opened the door and stepped through, before turning back and saying, "Nice shirt, but I liked the *you don't know me* one best so far."

With those parting words he disappeared through our backyards and into the night. I felt even more discombobulated than before he stopped by. Ha! *Bobulated, that's a funny word*, I thought.

"Well?" CC asked when she came into the kitchen.

She had probably been listening at the door. "Well, what? You heard the whole thing. What do you think?"

CC smiled. "I think he likes you," she said with a knowing smile.

I felt myself wilting, "I just don't know CC. I just don't know." Before I could get too down in the dumps, Jake strolled in and handed each of us a quart of death by chocolate ice cream.

"Oooh." I hugged the ice cream to my chest as I practically skipped to the bar and claimed a seat. CC joined me as Jake passed us spoons.

He leaned against the counter across from us. "Did you figure it all out?" he asked.

I was too busy digging into my ice cream to answer

CC, eating with a little more restraint answered, "I think so." She cast a sidelong look at me.

I ignored her and kept shoveling chocolate into my mouth, hoping it would clear up my bewilderment and confusion. It didn't, but I'm no quitter, so I ate the whole thing.

CC, being ridiculous, shared hers with Jake.

"I better head home," I said. "It's been a long, weird day."

Jake came over and wrapped me in a hug. He whispered, "It'll get better, I promise." He released me with a quick kiss on the forehead.

Comforted, even though I didn't know how much Jake even knew about the situation, I called Benji and headed home to my dark—and suddenly lonely—house.

After climbing into bed around bed-hog Agatha, and with Benji curled against my stomach and Blackbeard sleeping on my head, I lay awake for some time while I mulled over the enigmatic Sheriff Dominic Armstrong. Unable to figure him out, I finally fell asleep, but was plagued by dreams I couldn't remember when I woke up, and that left me feeling off kilter.

Chapter 13

The next morning when I arrived at CC's for my coffee, I was subdued and felt itchy in my skin.

CC passed me my coffee without noticing, but when she handed me a plate with some sort of cheese, sausage, egg, hash brown breakfast casserole, she tilted her head and asked, "What's wrong sweetie? You look out of sorts."

I put my now-empty cup down and grabbed the plate. I was out of sorts, not dead, and said, "I didn't sleep well. Do you ever wake up and feel like you were dreaming, but you can't remember the dreams? I think whatever I was dreaming made me uncomfortable and now I just . . . I don't know." I ate my breakfast with little enthusiasm or enjoyment, even though I knew it was delicious, and then headed home to dress for work.

While I was getting ready for work, I kept trying to remember my dreams. When I looked in the mirror, I noticed my brow was furrowed as if I was deep in thought. I gave up. I stepped over Agatha and headed out the door. Walking up to my baby, I was startled to find CC standing there with a cup of coffee and my lunch. I must really be distracted to almost bumped into her before I realized she was there. CC passed me the coffee and lunch, and then gave me a hug.

Having somehow arrived at work, I have no memory of the trip, I sat down at my desk and turned on my computer before remembering I had left my lunch in the car. Standing with a sigh, I retrieved my lunch and dropped it in the break room before returning to my desk. I had been working for about an hour before Brandon called to say he wouldn't be in today. I rolled my eyes with enough force to actually tilt my head. *Gee*, I wonder, *how will we manage without him?* Even in my head it sounded sarcastic. Hanging up the phone I realized Steve's line was lit up indicating he was in his office. I frowned, wondering why I hadn't seen him come in.

The day was quiet with Brandon gone and Steve not paying me his normal five-times-a-morning visits. I got so much done. Who was I kidding? I was still too distracted by dreams I couldn't remember to do anything more than sit and stare into space. The rumbling from my stomach surprised me and made me realize it was after lunchtime. With nothing better to do, I headed to the break room to eat lunch.

The afternoon was more of the same. I sat at my desk and stared into space until something caught my eye. Turning my head, I saw Steve frozen, peeking around his office door.

"Oh! You're still here. Sorry. I was just leaving." Despite his words, he stood undecided, half-hidden behind his door.

I blinked slowly at this new, almost shy Steve. Realizing he was waiting for some kind of signal from me, I nodded, automatically glancing at my clock, and startled to realize it was almost five-fifteen.

"Sure, yeah," I said, "me too."

This kicked him into gear, and he scurried out as if afraid of me.

I froze in the act of gathering my things to leave. Steve was afraid of me? Steve was afraid of me! I leaned back and pondered this revelation. Smiling for the first time today, I quickly gathered my stuff and headed to CC's. She would be worried that I was late. I didn't want a repeat of the great search party of '09.

"I was worried! You're late!" CC said as soon as I walked in wearing my super cool, and apt t-shirt. This one had two stick figures. One figure held the straight line that was supposed to be the other's back and it read, *I've got your back*.

She was already seated at the table with her family. Jane had a small rodent, possibly a rat, on her shoulder. It was distracting Eve, who kept squirming around to try and see it as it hid in Jane's hair. Frank, Nell, and Dean were having some sort of serious discussion on the merits of wooden versus plastic clothespins. Ann was telling an uninterested Kyle about the pickup baseball game she won that afternoon.

"I tried calling your office and got the machine. If you hadn't gotten here soon, we would have started a search party." CC said, which confirmed my earlier suspicions.

I slid into the banquette and start eating from a plate someone had already served with a pile of parmesan chicken, rice, and broccoli with cheese sauce. *I'm so spoiled*, I thought, and smiled at everyone.

"Sorry. It was a weird day. Brandon called in again, which wasn't surprising since it's Friday, but Steve literally hid from me in his office today. I didn't see him all day, until after five. I don't even know if he went to the bathroom. He used his door as a shield when trying to leave, and then ran out as if I would attack him!"

"I guess the talk with Sheriff Armstrong made an impact," Jake said.

I nodded enthusiastically and shoved another bite into my mouth. When I congratulated Ann on her win, she turned to me and allowed Kyle a respite from her play by play. He cast a brief smile at me and melted my heart. He didn't say much with words, but his smiles and art told a whole story. I smiled, wondering where the shaving cream-like substance in his hair came from, before turning my attention back to Ann as she droned on.

As Ann's story rambled on, I finished my dinner. Ann only required a few head nods here and there to keep going. As she wound down, everyone started clearing the table and then trickled out of the kitchen, one by one.

Eve demanded Ann and Jane play with her, and we heard the three of them tromp upstairs to the huge playroom that housed a toy store. Well, not quite, but when you had seven kids even if you didn't spoil them, they had a lot of toys.

Nell and Frank were meeting friends and headed out together. Dean pulled Jake into the backyard to work on his Rube Goldberg project behind the garage, while CC put the food away. Kyle pulled out his sketchbook and started drawing.

"What'cha drawing?" I asked, peering over his shoulder. I was shocked to see an image of the sheriff. It wasn't finished, but Kyle had the basics of the face down, and his eyes. The sheriff stared out of the sketch with such intensity I felt like he was looking right at me. Except I'd never seen that look on the sheriff's face. It made me feel warm and I realized my breaths had become shallow and were coming a little faster. I was glad the sheriff had never looked at me like that or I might have embarrassed both of us by throwing myself at him.

"You're drawing the sheriff?" I asked. My voice sounded a little squeaky, so I cleared my throat and tried again. "I didn't know you had met him."

"I haven't," Kyle confirmed, still sketching, "I just saw him the other night and his expression was so intense I had to draw it."

I ran my fingers through his soft curly mop of hair. Kyle wasn't much of a talker. He added a few more details and then tore it out of the book, handing it to me before he left the room. I barely noticed the streak of red down one whole side of his shorts because I was staring at the sketch.

Kyle had focused on the eyes, capturing them with such detail it was hard to look away. The rest was vaguely complete. Oh, he had included all the parts: nose, ears, and mouth. And they were drawn well, but the lack of details left the rest of his face as a background to the eyes.

"Whew," CC said from over my shoulder, "I told you he was into you."

I couldn't tear my eyes from the sketch and the intensity I saw there. "I'm starting to believe you."

Chapter 14

C and I went line dancing every Friday night at a bar outside
of town. We started going as a lark in high school and never
stopped. I put my boots on when I changed after work, so
I was ready to boot scoot, which was good, because the sketch of
the sheriff had really thrown me for a loop. CC didn't take long to
get her boots on, but it was enough for me to compose myself. Not
really, but I was ready to fake it.

We arrived at the bar and greeted the other regulars as the band
warmed up. They had all heard of the death of Mr. Johnson and
were curious about the mystery surrounding whether it was murder
or accidental. We weren't able to tell them much, but I still felt like
a celebrity. Expecting paparazzi to spring up and snap my picture,

I start fixing my hair. It fell in a dark tangle around my shoulders thanks to riding in the car with the windows open.

Hearing the band start, I stifled my disappointment in the lack of paparazzi, and we fell into the dance lines forming on the floor. I lost myself in the repetitive motions of the dances I knew by heart. When the band finally took a break, so did everyone else. We ordered drinks from the bar, then CC and I found a table as far away from the speakers as we could to hear each other talk. In between sets, the DJ played loud recorded music that made conversation impossible if you were close to any of the million speakers. It took a few minutes of simply catching our breath and quenching our thirst before we could speak.

The other regulars flitted to the bar as well as our table, the various conversations swirling around us and changing subjects as quickly as the people coming and going. The chaotic atmosphere made it hard to keep track of any one topic. Enjoying the break from my own thoughts, I caught snatches of conversations from a dozen different people. One in particular caused my head to swivel and my attention to zero in on who had said the terrifying words. My panicked gaze fell on the copper-haired Judas headed my way with a loose-limbed cowboy wanna be at her side. I locked eyes with her and realized it was too late to run and too late to hide.

Her satisfied smile told me she knew it too. "Claire," she practically purred, before latching onto my arm as if to prevent an escape. "I want you to meet Matt. He works with my boyfriend at the mechanic's shop. Matt, this is my dear friend, Claire. I'll let you two talk while I get us another round."

"No thanks, I'm good," I said to the air where Judas used to stand. Realizing I was stuck with Matt, I turned to CC, who had also disappeared into thin air. Unable to escape I returned my gaze to Matt. His gaze traveled up and down my person, making me shudder. He smiled what I supposed was meant to be a winning smile. His self-assured manner made my skin itch.

Frantically, I tried to think of a getaway strategy and blurted the first thing that came my mind. "I have to go to the bathroom!" I stepped away quickly and made my getaway.

Or so I thought. As I turned to close the bathroom door behind me, I saw that Matt had followed me. Ewww, who did that? Well since I was here anyway, I figured I'd take advantage of the facilities. While washing my hands, I wondered how long Matt would wait for me to reappear. Hearing the band start to tune up, I cracked the door a millimeter and snuck a quick peek. No luck! Matt was still standing there. I hopped on the counter and settled in for a long wait, swinging my feet in rhythm to the music now blaring from the band. After counting all the cracks in the tile, twice, CC finally came into the bathroom.

"Where have you been, young lady?" I hopped off the counter and steadied myself.

"Geez, Claire, why are you hiding in the bathroom?" CC shot back while checking her reflection in the mirror.

"Because Judas, sometimes known as Dana, left me with Matt, the wanna be cowboy skeevy guy who is currently staking out the women's bathroom." I was almost shrieking by the time I finished, and my voice echoed off the tile, to near deafening levels.

"Nobody is out there," CC said, unconcerned as she finished fixing her hair. "Dana left in a huff with some cowboy fifteen minutes ago. I'd watch your back next week. She did not look happy."

I felt my jaw drop open. "I've been in this bathroom for over fifteen minutes for no reason?" Again, the shrieking and the echoing.

CC linked arms with me and steered us through the door, ignoring my outburst.

I tried to hold onto my outrage, but back on the dance floor I lost myself in the music and the dance steps. During one energetic, hip-swaying dance I felt like someone was watching me. Fearing Matt and Dana might have returned, I glanced around and saw the sheriff frozen in place, a glass half raised to his mouth. His gaze burned intently. The fire was back and I was reminded of Kyle's sketch. I stared back, trapped by that gaze.

We might have stood there for all eternity, but the dance continued on around me, and then other dancers began to bump into me, which broke the eye contact. Luckily, I managed to right myself before causing a domino-style debacle. I worked to find the rhythm and synchronize the familiar dance steps, but with a lot less dedication than before I had spotted the sheriff. Realizing my eyes kept scanning the crowded room searching for him, I forced myself to stop. My willpower was strong, so I was able to completely focus on the dance—for about two seconds, before I began to scan again. Lucky for me and everyone around me, the dance came to an end.

CC hissed in my ear, "What is wrong with you? I almost tripped over you twice."

"The sheriff is here and he's looking at me like Kyle's sketch," I said. My head continued its dizzy swivel trying to locate him. For some reason I couldn't fathom, I felt the need to find him. I wasn't sure what would happen when I did, but the compulsion was too strong to ignore.

"Oh!" CC relaxed. "I wouldn't have pegged him for a line dancer." She joined my search and swept her eyes around the room.

Just as the next song began, I spotted him. He was in a far corner, deep in shadow. He sipped his drink and, as far as I could determine, was studiously avoiding my gaze. I wasn't sure how I felt about it but automatically fell into line with the rest of the dancers.

My gaze wanders to that corner every time the dance faces me in that direction, but those darn shadows kept me from seeing his eyes. My enjoyment of the night was marred by confusion over the sheriff's motives. Why did he turn up wherever I was? Why did he look at me with such intensity? And what did it mean? Why did people keep trying to set me up with guys? Why did my crazy cat, Blackbeard, like water? Why couldn't I wear t-shirts to work? My mind might have wandered, but as my line swung around and we faced the sheriff's corner, I remembered what I was supposed to be thinking about.

Deciding I probably wouldn't be able to figure it out while dancing, I mentally shrugged and threw myself into dancing with gusto. Fortunately, it was an exuberant dance that left little time for thought. I managed to avoid thinking about the sheriff for the rest of the night. Not really, but I at least kept from making a fool of myself on the dance floor again. I was almost surprised to see him at the bar after the last set.

I pretended not to see him and left with CC and the other regulars before I could make a fool of myself. Outside, I enjoyed the refreshing night air and was saying goodbye to the rest of the regulars when he walked by. Had he waited for me to leave before he left? Was he following me? Or was it just a coincidence? Was there such a thing as coincidences?

Although he didn't break stride or even look at me, it was almost like a physical touch as he passed. The others didn't seem to notice, but CC glanced at me, maybe prompted by my sharp intake of breath. She glanced around nonchalantly and stiffened when she saw the sheriff getting into his car.

For my part, I continued to studiously not look at the sheriff or his car. Okay, I was totally watching the sheriff and saw him get into his car. A quick hug from one of the regulars—I wasn't sure who because I was watching the sheriff and not them—broke my eye contact with his rapidly retreating car.

Pulling way, I realized it was Gwen, one of my favorites. She had never tried to set me up with anyone. CC said it was because she wanted me for herself, but I was just glad I didn't have to fend off another guy who thought I'd been wandering the Earth just waiting for him. Besides, Gwen was smart, kind, and gorgeous. She was a petite brunette with storm gray eyes and a curvy figure. She was a neonatal nurse in a neighboring town who loved to cook. I could do worse.

After saying our goodbyes, CC and I headed to my car.

"Are you okay to drive?" CC asked.

"I only had one drink before the second set. I think I can handle it." I said before turning the key.

"That's not what I meant," CC said, as if somehow disappointed in me. "I meant seeing the sheriff seemed to shake you up."

"I've seen the sheriff every day since he came to town. It's no big deal." I was lying shamelessly to CC and myself.

CC looked unconvinced but let it go. "So, what was up with Dana and the guy she brought you?" CC asked after a few minutes.

"I don't know. Why does everyone think I need a man? Can't I be happy alone? And did you see him? Is that really what people think I want? A puffed up, cocky, Lothario?"

CC smirked. "Well, you've turned down so many guys they're starting to scrape the bottom of the barrel."

The image of our friends physically bent over a barrel scraping guys off the bottom tickled my funny bone and I giggled. It proved contagious and soon we were both chortling uncontrollably. The laughter eased my ire and confusion. I was in a much better mood when I pulled into the driveway.

That mood soured when CC said, "Remember, tomorrow we are going to visit the college and try to find this Jamie Wilson."

Before I could recover my wits—and let's be honest, that could take hours—she was already breezing through her kitchen door. I saw Jake wrap her in a hug that morphed into a lewd display. I turned away before it became X-rated. I made a mental note not to look out my windows tonight so as not to scar myself for life. CC and I were close, but I had to draw a line somewhere.

In contrast, I trudged into my house where I was exuberantly greeted by my main man, Benji. He jumped all around me barking happily. I caught him in mid-air and cradled him like a baby as I headed upstairs. Agatha was already snoring in my bed and all I got from Blackbeard was a monetary crack of his eye from where he lay draped across my pillows. Between the two of them I didn't see any room for me. I decided a quick shower was in order, set Benji on the bed, and headed to the bathroom.

Before I could even get in, Blackbeard was twitching his tail impatiently and meowing at me. It sounded suspiciously like *hurry up*. I squinted at him trying to decide if my cat could speak, but when he narrowed his eye at me in return, I decided turning on the water was more important right now. I stepped under the spray and allowed it to wash my stress, and probably a fair amount of sweat, down the drain. Rather than fall asleep in the shower, I turned off the water leaving Blackbeard licking himself dry in the tub, and toweled myself dry. Deciding that blow drying my hair would take too much effort I padded into the bedroom. I found Agatha had rolled onto her back and I fell into bed, missing her by inches. Benji immediately curled behind my knees, which was the last thing I remembered before sleep claimed me.

Chapter 15

Something smelled like heaven. I could feel my nose twitch, which pulled me from sleep. Realizing someone was in my house, in my bedroom in fact, I came awake with a start, reflexes ready to kill—or at least maim—the intruder.

"Gah!" was my battle cry as I launched myself at the threat. I missed them by at least a foot and fell flat on my face, tangled in bedsheets.

"Oh, for pity's sake," CC said, staring down at me. "I brought you coffee."

I was torn between anger at her for scaring me, embarrassment at my uncoordinated response, and joy that she had brought me coffee. Coffee and joy won. I staggered upright and reached for the coffee.

CC handed it over without further comment. It wasn't long before, I returned the mug, empty.

"Get dressed," she said, "and you can have a second cup before we hit the road. Nell is coming with us," she called from the stairs, presumably on the way home to get ready. Knowing I had plenty of time before that happened, I don't exactly rush. Still, I'd been promised more coffee, so I didn't dawdle either. Pulling on cutoffs and a t-shirt I headed next door.

Jake was at the stove flipping pancakes. He was pretty good. Only one missed the pan and hit the floor.

I smirked while taking the plate stacked with three pancakes that sat on the counter next to him.

He smiled at me while he cleaned the floor.

"You seem chipper this morning," I said, pouring syrup on the stack. "Maybe like you had a really good night." I gave him an exaggerated eyebrow wiggle.

His smile widened into a very self-satisfied expression. "I did," he said, almost purring.

I watched his expression become almost lascivious as if was recalling specifics. "It is safe to eat here, right?" I asked, indicating where I'd set my plate. "I mean nothing happened right here, did it?"

Jake started whistling a tune and turned back to his pancakes without answering.

"Jake! I'm serious! I'm trying to eat here. Please tell me you made it to the bedroom, or at least disinfected the eating area." Jake continued to ignore me and I felt irrational panic welling up.

"Relax, Claire," CC said, sauntering into the room in a chic pair of bright red capris and a black and white striped shirt with a boat neck collar. Her hair was pulled back in a high ponytail causing the curls to bounce and sway with every movement.

"Our children eat here. Do you really think it's not safe to eat here?"

Still suspicious, but hungry, I resettled into my chair to finish breakfast.

"You're going to change before we go, right?" CC asked.

"What is wrong with what I'm wearing?" I looked down at my shirt. There was a taco and a pile of nachos, both with serious, frowning faces. One was saying, 'I don't want to taco bout it' and the other replied 'It's nacho business.' I thought it was great. I looked to Jake for support, but he was necking with CC.

Nell breezed in wearing a pair of short robin's egg blue twill shorts that showed off her legs and a white eyelet shirt. Her hair was also in a high ponytail that stopped its happy swing when Nell stopped.

She eyed my outfit with little enthusiasm. "You're going to change before we go, right?" she asked.

Amid a sense of déjà vu, I mopped up the last of my syrup with the last bite of pancake and then slunk off next door to change.

Who knew tracking down an insurance beneficiary had a dress code? I exchanged my cut offs and t-shirt for a pair of turquoise twill shorts, a little longer than Nell's. I had great legs, but they couldn't compete with an eighteen-year-old's. I added a scoop neck black sleeveless top. Deciding to join the ponytail team, I also pulled my messy brown hair up in a high ponytail and added a statement necklace that matched my shorts. Satisfied, I grabbed my purse and headed back to CC's. On the way, I noticed CC and Nell waiting by my car, so I changed directions.

About an hour later, we reached the college town of McKinley. We decided to grab lunch before heading to campus and stopped at a café we always enjoyed. After ordering sandwiches with homemade chips, we settled back with large glasses of iced tea.

"How are we going to find Jamie Wilson?" I asked. "I mean, we don't exactly have any helpful information. And don't they have rules about giving out information?"

CC looked displeased, "I'm sure we will find a way." She said, her tone implying she would accept nothing but success.

Nell and I both looked away from her mother's almost zealous gaze. I think we were both relieved when our sandwiches arrived, preventing further conversation. They were piled high with meat, cheese, and vegetables.

These sandwiches were worth the drive even if we don't find Jamie Wilson, I think. Nell's frozen, panicked expression was offset by CC's determined, almost fanatical gaze.

Looking back and forth between them, it dawned on me that I'd spoken out loud. I panicked and tried to smooth things over. "Which of course won't be a problem. We are going to find Jamie Wilson. For sure. Absolutely. Without a doubt." Nell and I were nodding our heads like deranged bobble heads. CC seemed to accept our exaggerated and fearful reassurance and we managed to finish lunch without further incident.

We bused our own table, and then headed back to my car for the short drive to the campus. Nell was smiling and trying to take in everything as we drove along tree-lined campus streets.

"Look. There's my dorm over there." She pointed with enthusiasm. CC and I stared at the beautiful brick building partially covered by ivy. The building that will house my sweet baby. Hours away from her home. Okay it's an hour, but it felt longer. Tears welled up in my eyes. CC sniffed. I reached out and took her hand in mine, which she clutched with surprising strength.

"Come on guys," Nell said from the backseat. I swear I can hear her eyes rolling. "People go away to college. It's normal. Auntie Claire, you went away to college."

As if anything she said would make it better. We pulled into a parking spot and piled out. Nell seemed shocked when I clutched her to my chest fighting back sobs.

"Be cool, Auntie Claire," Nell hissed from the area of my belly button where her mouth was pointed due to my awkward hug. "I'm going to go to school here. I'd like to not start class being known as the weird girl with the psycho family."

I released her momentarily and said, "They would call my sweet baby weird? You shouldn't go here. Come on CC, let's get my sweet baby home before the monsters can hurt her." I turned and walked toward the car with Nell once again clutched to me. It made for an awkward shuffle more than anything else.

"Heads up," a voice called, which prompted me to release Nell and look around for an incoming projectile. I spotted a soccer ball headed our way and snatched it out of the air before it could hit us.

"Nice catch!" the same voice called. I looked past the ball and saw some hunky college boys approaching. A couple were shirtless, all were gorgeous. I smiled warmly, and maybe a little lecherously, at them.

"You must be new here," the obvious leader said, coming to a stop a few feet away.

Nell smiled. "I'm starting this fall," she confirmed.

The boys tried to check her out discreetly, but they weren't very discreet.

"What about you?" a boy on the side asked, lifting his chin, and casting a suggestive smile at me.

I returned his smile and couldn't resist a quick gloating glance toward CC.

"That's my Aunt Claire," Nell said. "She graduated years ago."

The emphasis on years was a little insulting. Before I could do anything I might regret, CC grabbed my arm. "Not that many years ago," CC said. Bless that woman.

"That's too bad," said the same guy.

I smiled again. "But I'll come and visit Nell often," I said, checking him out right back.

"In that case, I hope to see you both around," said the ringleader. He held out his hands in the pass me the ball gesture.

I tossed it to him and watched them walk away. "Ok, you can go to college," I told Nell without looking away from the group of guys.

Tugging on the arm she still clutched, CC steered me toward the building and away from the retreating boys.

I swiveled my head to keep them in view and tripped over the curb. I decided to watch where I was walking. It would be harder to pick up college boys with a skinned-up face. With a wistful sigh, I allowed myself to be steered along.

We entered the building and CC marched with purpose toward the information desk, situated off to one side of the entrance. A young woman, probably a student, was sitting behind the desk. Her short pixie cut was dyed a shade of red not found in nature. CC smiled at the young woman—forever to be known as Red—and immediately launched into conversation.

"Hi, we're here to see Jamie Wilson. Can you direct us to their room please?"

Wow! I was impressed. I would have given us the information.

"I'm sorry ma'am, we don't give out that information," Red said.

Oh, Red's tough.

"I understand, but this is very important. This is Claire Miller," I straightened my posture and tried to look important and official, "and she works for the Brown and Son Insurance Company." I winced at the terrible name, but CC soldiered on. "She is tracking down a beneficiary of a life insurance policy. The name is Jamie Wilson, and the address on the forms is for this college, but the dorm information is out of date."

Red stared at me, and I fidgeted under her scrutiny. Not the professional appearance I was striving for. CC's death grip on my arm, just below the counter and out of Red's sight, stops my fidgeting.

Red seemed undecided for a moment but then turned to her computer and started typing. I panicked, thinking she was calling security, or the police, or maybe even the National Guard. After a few keystrokes, she looked up and said the horrifying words that would seal our fates, "She shows as graduated."

Wait, that didn't sound like she was calling the police. That sounded like she was giving us the information. Score one for CC. It didn't help us, but hey, good try. I turned to go but was pulled up short when CC grabbed my shirt and stopped me in my tracks.

"Do you have a forwarding address? Or phone number?" CC asked, still holding my shirt.

Red looked back at the screen and typed some more. "Sorry. She hasn't updated her contact form." Red said, not sounding sorry at all.

"Is there anyone here who might know how to contact her? Maybe a roommate?" CC asked.

Red sighed a deep sigh worthy of Eve in a moment of pique. I was impressed papers didn't flutter and blow away. After still more typing, Red finally said, "Her roommate last year has checked into campus already." Red placed a map on the counter and then started explaining where we were and where we needed to go, while drawing the path on the map.

CC smiled her million-dollar smile and thanked Red who, as if finally realizing it was the most important thing she'd do today, handed over the map.

With her prize firmly in hand, CC turned and drug me along in her wake. I tripped over my own feet while Nell fell effortlessly into step beside her mother. CC didn't slow her stride, while I bumbled along in her wake and tried not to fall flat on my face.

We pushed through the double doors and stepped outside. CC and Nell slid on sunglasses while I squinted like a suspect under the glare of an interrogation lamp. Where did they even get sunglasses from? And why didn't they share with the rest of the class? Mainly me. Blinded, I had no choice but to follow where CC dragged me. When we turned a corner and the sun no longer mercilessly attacked my corneas, I blinked repeatedly to try and clear my vision and the tears that threatened to run down my face.

"I can't believe you got the information just by asking?" I said, wiping my eyes.

"You know what they say, it never hurts to ask." She turned another corner. I bounced along in her wake, like a dinghy behind a luxury yacht.

Now that dots were no longer dancing in front of my eyes, I noticed Nell was getting checked out by almost every boy we passed. She placed more distance between us the further we walked. Coincidence? I think not. I tried to catch her eye, but she studiously ignored me, while simultaneously returning the guys' stares. Before I could embarrass her, I mean, I would never embarrass Nell but before I could do anything, CC stopped. We faced a huge brick building and heard various strains of music blasting from the open windows.

"Doesn't it seem odd that so many students are here?" I asked. "I mean Nell doesn't start for another couple weeks."

"One week," Nell interrupted. "I start in one week. You guys are dropping me off next Saturday. A week from today."

I felt like she was trying to tell me something, but I wasn't sure what.

"Since all students reside on campus, a lot of them come early to get settled. Especially if they are from further away." CC said, unconcerned.

She started up the short flight of steps toward the front door. Since she still had my arm, I had no choice but to follow. CC breezed through the empty foyer and made for the stairs.

"Isn't there an elevator?" I asked.

"The stairs are good for you," CC said, "and no."

Rounding the third flight of stairs, Nell was pulling ahead. She took the stairs effortlessly while CC had slowed slightly but was still climbing. Bringing up the rear, I clutched the handrail and panted for breath. I could feel the start of a good sweat coming.

A voice called down from somewhere above, "Come on. You're almost there."

"Is that you, God? Is it my time?" I asked, out of breath.

"Auntie Claire, you're being dramatic," the voice replied.

"Huh. God, you sound a lot like Nell," I said in between wheezes.

"For Pete's sake, Claire. You're being a drama queen," CC said.

At last, I staggered onto the landing. I bent over at the waist and put my hands on my knees, working to catch my breath.

CC, without an ounce of pity in her black, black soul, didn't wait but started down the hall. She left me! What if I died?

"Auntie Claire, if you die from walking up a couple flights of stairs, it will be really embarrassing," Nell said before following in her mother's footsteps. Her voice echoed from somewhere down the corridor, "They would probably write a really embarrassing news story about it. People would laugh."

The heartlessness of today's generation, I groused to myself. But it had the desired effect. I staggered upright and followed, just in time to see Nell turn a corner. CC was already out of sight. Hurrying to catch up, I realized I was breathing mostly normal. Perhaps I had been a bit of a drama queen after all.

I caught up to them just as CC raised her hand to knock. Joining them, we all stared at the door, waiting. And waiting. And waiting. Losing patience, I raised my hand and knocked. Only I didn't stop.

Eventually, the door was wrenched open by a bleary eyed twelve-year-old with her hair in a tangled mess. She was wearing a plain blue tank top and black running shorts and staring at us like we'd killed her cat.

"What!"

"We're looking for Jamie Wilson and were hoping you could give us her contact information," CC said, adding a friendly smile to help smooth things over.

"No." The crabby twelve-year-old stepped back and tried to close the door.

Not one to be put off, especially after climbing a mountain's worth of stairs, I stepped closer and blocked it with my shoulder.

"It's important we speak to her," I said through clenched teeth.

"Not my problem." She countered with a pugnacious expression and moved closer.

"It's really important we speak to her." I shifted closer and hoped the additional emphasis would sway the girl.

"She graduated last year. I am not her answering service."

By this time, we were nearly nose to nose. Well, her nose to my sternum. She was too short to reach my nose.

"Do you know how to contact her?" I asked, teeth still clenched.

"If you give us the address, we will be on our way," CC said trying to interrupt our impromptu staring contest.

Sensing she could get rid of us, the ornery twelve-year-old broke eye contact with me and looked at CC. "I probably have her phone number in my contacts. Hold on." She pulled a phone from her pocket and started tapping keys with a surprisingly well-manicured finger.

"Hey, is that Kiss me Quick?" I asked.

She looked surprised, but then smiled. "It is," she confirmed, holding her hand out for me to inspect.

"Ooh, I love that color," I said, holding out my own manicured hand for her inspection.

"Nice," she said. "It's getting hard to find the color, but I really like it. It's subtle, but also eye catching. You know?"

I nodded along with her every word. "Totally," I agreed. "I like Coral Sunrise and Sunset Serenade, too, but there's just something special about Kiss me Quick, you know?"

She nodded. "Totally."

"Well, I think we've taken up enough of your time. If you'll just give me the phone number," CC said, holding her own phone.

Glancing away from her manicure the twelve-year-old rattled the number off so quickly I didn't know if CC got it.

CC frantically tapped it into her phone and then stepped back from the doorway.

"Got it! Nice meeting you," CC said and turned to leave.

"If you ever make it to Oak Creek, we have a killer manicure salon with lots of Kiss me Quick," I offered, as if CC hadn't spoken.

"That's good to know," she said. "I had to change manicure salons twice last year because they stopped carrying Kiss me Quick."

CC stalked back and grabbed my arm. "Sorry. We're in a bit of a hurry," she said to Jamie's delightful ex-roommate and dragged me away.

"I'm serious. If you're ever in town call me. Claire Miller. Ask anyone and they will know how to find me." I raised my voice so she could hear me since CC had continued to pull me down the hall and around the corner, away from my new friend.

"I liked her," I said to no one in particular.

CC snorted, "You liked her manicure."

"Yeah, it's the same thing," I said.

CC ignored me and continued down the stairs. Going down was easier than going up so we made it in no time. CC charged through the foyer and out the doors. Nell and I trailed behind, following her toward a quieter area of campus.

CC dialed the phone and waited while it rang. And rang. And rang. CC listened, fidgeting, and then shoved the phone at me. "She's not answering, leave a message."

Flustered, I almost dropped the phone but managed to get it to my ear in time to hear the beep.

"Hi, my name is Claire Miller and I'm looking for Jamie Wilson. I work for Brown and Son Insurance Company and have some documents I need to go over with her pertaining to a policy we have. Please call me back at your earliest convenience." I disconnected the call and handed the phone back to CC.

"That sounded very professional," Nell said, smiling.

I smiled back, but the expression faded when I realized she was surprised I sounded professional. "Hey! I am a professional. I can be professional all day long." I placed my hands on my hips and stuck out my tongue. "See, totally professional."

CC rolled her eyes.

"Ah-ha!" I pointed my finger about a millimeter from CC's nose. "That's where she gets it from."

"Gets what from?" CC asked, slapping my hand out of her face.

"The eye rolling. Duh." Oops, more than implied, again.

CC literally snorted. "Please, you are the queen of eye rolling. It's obviously from you."

"Well, I never."

Before I could get good and mad CC continued. "Besides, she looks up to you and wants to be just like you."

I stopped and considered this before nodding. "Excellent point."

Turning to Nell, I caught the very end of her eye roll. "Not bad sweetie, but if you want a quality eye roll you have to—"

CC's phone rand we all froze.

Nell looked at the number and said, "It's her! It's Jamie! Answer it."

A game of hot potato, with CC's phone as the potato, ensued. Finally, CC gave up. She kept the phone and pushed the answer button.

My victory dance was short lived. CC held the phone to my ear instead of her own. Habit kicked in and I said, "Hello?"

"Uh. This is Jamie. I got a message from Claire Miller at this number?"

I wasn't sure why she'd phrased it as a question. "This is Claire Miller. Jamie, the insurance company I work for has been trying to contact you about a life insurance policy you are the beneficiary of. Could we meet to speak in person?"

The silence on the other end of the phone made me wonder if she'd hung up on me. I was about to hang up on my end when I heard her say, "I don't know anything about a life insurance policy. I think you have the wrong Jamie Wilson."

"Jamie, our records had your dorm room listed. Unless you lived with another Jamie Wilson, it's you." I said with a touch more force than I should have.

Afraid the girl was about to hang up, CC grabbed the phone out of my hand. "Jamie, my name is CC, and I can guarantee you are who we're looking for. We drove all the way to your college to find you. We are from the small town of Oak Creek and one of the townspeople died recently. His name was Harrison Johnson. I don't know if that means anything to you, but if we could just talk to you, I think we could get it all straightened out. If we are wrong, you will have to meet with us to convince us of that." CC sensed Jamie was weakening and pressed her advantage. "Besides, the police are interested in talking to the Jamie Wilson listed on the policy. If you don't meet with us, we'll have to give them your phone number. It won't take long for them to track your phone and show up to talk to you."

"Okay, okay. I can meet you," Jamie said, sounding panicked. "I guess I can meet you at the coffee shop on the corner of Fifth and Ryker at three o'clock," she offered.

CC smiled even though Jamie couldn't see it. "That's great Jamie. We will see you there."

She hung up "Well, that's taken care of," CC said. "What should we do until three?" She looked very proud of herself and was practically bouncing on the balls of her feet, just like Eve when she got excited. CC was obviously more excited about meeting Jamie than I was. She looked ready to head to the coffee shop now and wait over an hour for Jamie to show up. Unable to think of something to distract her until we could meet Jamie, I turned to ask Nell what she wanted to do, only to realize she was no longer standing next to me. I spotted her nearly surrounded by three boys several feet away.

It must be her perfect hair, I thought, smoothing my ponytail. Or maybe her sweet smile.

I smiled at a passing student who scurried away as if I had the plague. Maybe it was the fact that Nell is nicer than she is beautiful. And since she's really beautiful, that makes her very nice. I felt a little left out and debated joining her, but decided I'd be a third wheel. Fifth wheel?

CC was still looking at me expectantly and I realized she was still waiting for an answer. "Shouldn't we ask Nell?" I gestured to where she was standing with the boys.

There was a lot of laughing and arm touching going on over there. I found myself frowning toward the boy who was a little too close to Nell. His back was to me so mostly I saw broad shoulders and wind-tossed brown hair. He probably wasn't good enough to talk to Nell. I debated going over and dragging her away from this miscreant when he shifted, giving me a better view. Sizing him up quickly, I saw he was gorgeous, but that didn't impress me much. However, after finishing my full inspection, I started planning their wedding. This boy was perfect for Nell! They would be happy together and have gorgeous babies, which would make CC happy.

"Why are you humming the wedding march?" CC asked, suspicion in her voice.

"What? I am not." I said.

CC frowned at me and then transferred her gaze to Nell. "She hasn't even started going here. She's only been talking to those guys for half a minute. It's too early to plan a wedding."

"But did you see him? He's perfect."

"You just like his shirt," she said.

"You say that like it isn't a good enough reason to marry someone. I mean, did you see it? *I mustache you a question, but I'll shave it for later.* That's hilarious."

"What happens on laundry day when he only has a plain shirt?"

I drew an audible breath. "He would never." I was shocked that she would even say such a thing about Nell's husband. Determined to prove her wrong, I marched toward the group. Nell saw me coming and started doing some sort of semaphore with her eyebrows, but I was on a mission, and I didn't have time to decode her eyebrows.

"Excuse me," I said, coming up to the group, "but I just had to tell you what a great shirt that is."

Nell's husband looked down at his shirt and said, "Thanks, my brother gave it to me. Laundry day. You know, everything else is dirty."

I felt my smile slip. Recovering a little, I said, "Well, we have to go." I linked arms with Nell and walked away with purposeful strides.

Once out of ear shot, I consoled her. "Don't worry sweetie, he wasn't good enough for you. You'll find someone else."

Nell rolled her eyes and allowed me to lead her away.

"So, where are we going?" CC asked from my other side.

"Wherever Nell wants. She just escaped a bad marriage." I patted her reassuringly.

Nell rolled her eyes again but didn't comment. It was getting to be a habit. "Sweetie, if you overuse the eye roll it will lose its potency."

Our aimless wandering led us to the front of a massive brick building. I knew it was just a building, but it was really pretty. "Can you live here?" I whispered with no small amount of reverence.

"No," Nell said.

Nothing else, just no. "Why not?" I asked, my eyes still glued to the building.

"Because it's the library," Nell said, distracted by another group of college kids. These were evenly mixed between boys and girls and were playing a game that looked like a frisbee and a football had a baby.

"Let's go in!" I said, already dragging Nell up the steps.

We entered the well-lit library where rows of shelves, two stories tall and filled with books, towered over us like sacred Egyptian monuments. I'd never seen so many books in all my life, and we hadn't even made it past the circulation desk. I set off toward the bookshelves as if in a trance but was blocked by a turnstile contraption.

"What?" I said in surprise when I bounced off it. "Why won't it turn?" I pushed at it repeatedly as if that would somehow make it open.

A voice from my left said, "You have to scan a student ID card to get in."

I turned to face the mystery speaker. She must be a librarian. Her brown hair was pulled back into a bun at her nape. She wore retro cat's eye glasses. They perched on the bridge of her nose in that way all librarians seemed to have, and were attached to one of those decorative chains that draped around her neck. A string of pearls peeked out from her light blue sweater set.

I mean who wore a sweater in this weather? I couldn't tell if she was twenty-five or forty-five. I squinted at her, as if that would help me determine her age.

Nell distracted me from thinking—or more likely saying—something I would regret, and probably get smacked for. "May we go in and look around, please? I'm starting here next week and hoped to just take a quick peek."

Nell was impossible to resist. She was sweet, kind, charming, and earnest. I faced the turnstile expecting to be allowed through, my eyes once more drawn toward the imposing bookshelves.

"I'm afraid that's not possible," The librarian said, no trace of flexibility evident in her voice.

What? Someone could tell my sweet baby no? I didn't even understand what was happening.

"I understand," Nell said, but she looked disappointed.

At least someone understood. "We'll have to wait until next weekend when all the other families are here." Nell tried to console me. "I know it will be busy then, and it will be harder for the librarian to give us any attention, but it will be ok."

Nell patted my hand and then turned to the librarian. She leaned closer while still gesturing toward me, "I'm sure it will be fine. I mean, she's not really good with patience, being quiet, or focus, but with all the other families here maybe it won't be so bad. I'm sure it won't be like what happened at the grocery store when she knocked over a whole display of—"

"I don't think she wants to hear this story," I said. The librarian, however, looked interested in Nell's story.

"A whole display of what?" she asked, ignoring me.

"Canned peas. They rolled all over the store and a bunch of them popped open spilling peas everywhere. Poor Mr. McIntyre was sweeping up peas for months." Nell finished and shook her head sadly.

The librarian let out a gasp, while somehow looking both horrified and mesmerized at the same time. Her gaze darted to the very tall and very full bookcases. "I suppose," she glanced to the left and right, "since classes haven't begun and you start next week, I could make an exception and give you a guided tour." She placed meaningful emphasis on guided, while looking directly at me. CC and Nell smiled as she reached into her desk drawer and pulled out an ID card.

She stood and walked toward the turnstile. She scanned her card and allowed me to push through. CC and Nell were scanned in behind me, but I was too busy admiring all the books to pay them much attention.

Some people thought that since I struggled to keep my inner thoughts to myself that I was not very bright. Obviously, those people were ridiculous, but I loved books. Books of every kind. Picture books, young adult novels, westerns, mystery, Sci-fi, biographies, really everything is my favorite kind of book, and I was pretty sure I was standing in book heaven. I skipped down the rows between bookshelves, lovingly stroking the spines as I passed. I paused to read some of them or pulled a book out to examine it closer. The librarian, who had been trailing me, winced every time I did so, but I ignored her, so engrossed was I in the books.

The bookshelves suddenly gave way and revealed a set of stairs. Craning my neck, I saw a whole other floor of books. I couldn't suppress a giggle when I heard my own squeal of joy echo back at me.

The librarian shushed me but seemed to realize she had found a kindred spirit.

Unable to contain my joy and enthusiasm, I practically sprinted up the stairs to discover more books. After what seemed like only a few brief minutes during which I had admired the library and all the books, CC assured me it had been at least an hour and dragged me out.

My last view was of the librarian as she resumed her post at the circulation desk. She smiled at me, and I thought she looked like every high school and college boy's librarian fantasy come to life. The door closed, cutting off my view of heaven on earth.

"We have to meet Jamie, remember?" CC said excitedly, still leading me away from all the books.

I kept craning my neck around, if only to see the outside of the library and allowed CC to steer me clear of whatever obstacles we encountered. When the building itself was finally out of sight, I heaved a sigh full of remorse and loss, faced forward, and continued the trek to the car.

Chapter 16

I t didn't take long to find the coffee shop Jamie chose. Pulling into an open spot in a mostly empty parking lot, I surveilled the shop. Two people stood behind the counter, presumably employees. An old lady waited for her coffee, and a hipster sitting at a table near the front windows appeared to be the only patrons. The huge windows meant we could see out, but someone else could easily see in. I thought a table in the back would work to our advantage.

"Claire, it's not a spy movie. We are just meeting Jamie, a recent college grad, not an assassin." CC said.

I realized my inner thoughts may have become my outer words again. Oops. It was slightly embarrassing as I might have been thinking in a stereotypical cartoon spy voice. To cover my discomfort, I swung open the car door headed for the entrance, pretending that embarrassing scenario hadn't just happened. Also, I really wanted some coffee.

Approaching the counter, I ordered a coffee and, spying the pastries in the glass-fronted display counter, a giant slice of pound cake. Nell ordered tea. Ridiculous, we were in a coffee shop, not a tearoom! CC ordered coffee. I knew I liked her for a reason. We took our cups and my cake to a table in the back and settled in to wait. It wasn't a bad wait. I had coffee and cake, so I was a pretty happy camper.

It was a little after three when a slip of a girl entered. She stood about five-foot-two, but her hunched posture made her look even smaller. She was wearing a nondescript outfit of slightly baggy jeans, an uninspired t-shirt, and her long brown hair partially obscured her face, which made it hard to see her facial features. She hesitated on the threshold and seemed ready to turn and bolt.

I nudged CC. "Do you think it's Jamie?" I whispered out of the side of my mouth. CC glanced at the door, but I decided to play it cool and not scare her.

I waved wildly and yelled, "Jamie?"

Her head snapped up and she flinched as if expecting a blow. Not giving her a chance to run, I leaped to my feet and rushed over. Linking my arm with hers, I steered her toward our table. "Hi, Jamie. I'm Claire, this is CC, and CC's daughter Nell."

CC gave me a disapproving frown before she smiled at Jamie. "Hi, Jamie. I'm so glad you could make it. Would you like something to drink?"

Jamie still looked like she wanted to bolt, so I hadn't released her arm. Nell stood and extracted Jamie from my grasp. I mean, one minute I have a firm hold on her and the next she's sitting next to Nell in the booth.

"I'm impressed," I said to Nell, who smiled at me without comment.

"With what?" Jamie asked in the small voice we'd heard on the phone.

"Never mind," I said and took my seat next to CC. "Tell us about yourself, Jamie."

Jamie, who I still hadn't gotten a good look at because her hair continued to obscure her face, shrunk in on herself even more, which I hadn't thought possible.

"Auntie Claire," Nell admonished me like she was the grown up here. "Can't you see you're overwhelming her?"

Turning to Jamie, Nell said, "We're all just really curious why you are the beneficiary of Mr. Johnson's life insurance policy. You see, we live in a small town where everybody knows everybody and their dog. So, it's kind of a mystery, but we don't mean to come on too strong."

While Nell talked, Jamie's shoulders relaxed a little. "I don't know Mr. Johnson," Jamie said. "I think you have the wrong Jamie Wilson." She finally looked up enough for me to see her face. Her hair still obscured most of it, but I could make out one hazel eye looking at me in fear and confusion, but also earnestness. She really believed we'd made a mistake.

I reached across the table and covered her hand where it was fidgeting with the silverware on the table. "Jamie, it's you. It has to be. Your name was on the form and the address of record was your college dorm room last year. Do you know any other Jamie Wilsons at your school? Because we asked at the college information desk, and you were the only one."

Jamie slumped and the tension left her body. "But I don't know him!" she said with more volume than I thought her capable of.

"Well, he knew you," I said. "That's why we want to hear about you. Maybe something you tell us can help us figure out the connection."

Jamie nodded and flopped back in her seat. "Okay. Uhm, I was born and raised here, in McKinley. I never knew my dad. Apparently, as soon as he found out mom was pregnant, he took off. My mom's name is Louise Wilson. Her parents are still alive, but they live across the country and always have. Mom moved here for college and then stayed after she got pregnant her junior year. She would have come here with me, but she's been working double shifts to help pay for my college loans." Jamie looked ashamed to admit her mom was helping her pay for college but continued anyway. "Now that I've graduated, I want to get a job so she can cut back on her shifts. She's already done so much for me."

"What is your degree in?" CC asked.

"I double majored in teaching and psychology."

"Wow!" I said, "That couldn't have been easy."

Jamie seemed to relax as we talked, and for the first time, she smiled a fleeting smile.

"No, it wasn't," she agreed, "but it will be worth it. I love kids and want to help people. I know how difficult childhood can be even when kids come from loving homes, and I want to be able to help them." Jamie looked a little embarrassed after her passionate response.

"I think that's amazing," CC said. "I love kids, too." After a laugh, she explained, "I guess I'd have to, since I have seven of them."

Jamie smiled at CC. "I'd like a big family too. Maybe because I'm an only child."

"CC and I are only children, too," I said, kind of surprised at the coincidence.

"How many kids do you have?" Jamie asked.

Nell either snorted or laughed, it was hard to tell which. But she quickly schooled her features when I glared at her.

Jamie looked back and forth between us, a frown between her brows.

"Auntie Claire doesn't want children. She is the child." Nell continued.

The death glare came back in full force, but Nell somehow escaped unscathed.

"Claire is a wonderful Aunt to my children and would be a wonderful mother." CC tried to smooth over the situation, but I continued to glare at Nell, pointing two fingers at my eyes and then flipping them toward her.

She sipped her tea, apparently unconcerned.

"If you are only children, how can you be sisters?" Jamie said, looking between CC and myself.

I stopped death glaring at Nell and dissolved into a fit of giggles. After several minutes I managed to say, "Sisters! We aren't sisters. I mean look at her. She's five-foot-nothing, blond hair, blue eyes, and looks like a pinup model, and I'm five-foot seven, brown hair and—"

CC interrupted to tell Jamie, "We aren't sisters. We've been best friends and neighbors since we were five years old, though."

Jamie nodded but eyed me like I was crazy. I got that a lot, but I wasn't sure why.

"Perhaps it's been long enough," CC whispered under her breath.

I rewarded her treachery with a swift kick to her ankle. Sadly, she has known me since we were five and moved her foot so that I only struck a glancing blow. Disappointed, I considered kicking her again.

"Claire are you going to get more coffee?" she asked.

Instantly diverted from whatever I had been thinking, I nodded with enthusiasm. "Yep, I sure am," I said, and headed for the counter.

When I returned, Jamie and Nell were carrying on a riveting conversation about the best study carrels in the library. While I loved a good library, this had descended into extreme nerd-dom.

Nell shot me a censorious gaze which told me I might be having inner thoughts that were outer words again.

"I've given it a lot of thought and nothing you've told us connects you to Mr. Johnson," I said, settling into my seat with a fresh cup of coffee.

"You've given it a lot of thought, hmmm?" CC asked, disbelief in her voice. "You heard her story less than twenty minutes ago."

She thought she sounded reasonable, but I wasn't fooled. I glared at her, but otherwise ignored her ridiculous interjection. "What else? Have you lived anywhere else? Any weird uncle figures? Anything else along those lines? There must be something!"

Jamie was already shaking her head. "No, it was just my mom and me. I've only ever lived here. My mom really kept to herself. I don't know if she was always like that or just after I was born. Most of the kids she went to college with moved on, or even if they didn't, they lived different lives. By the time she graduated, my mom had a toddler, and her friends weren't even considering marriage or motherhood. They just drifted apart." Jamie shrugged her shoulders.

I slumped back in my chair. "It's right there," I said, "the answer is right in front of us, and we just aren't seeing it." I allowed the conversation to swirl around me, which was mostly Nell and Jamie discussing college tips and tricks. I might have sat there all day, but Jamie's cell phone rang and jarred me back to the present.

Jamie colored slightly and pulled the phone out of her bag. "Sorry, it's my mom," she said to us.

"Hi Mom," she said before it could ring again. Jamie turned even redder as she listened to whatever her mom was saying. "I'm fine Mom. I'm just at the coffee shop with the people who called earlier." Another pause and even more red colored her cheeks, "No Mom, I'm fine. I was just giving some tips to Nell about college."

Jamie shrunk down in her seat and tried to become invisible and inaudible at the same time.

The devil in me enjoyed her discomfort, so unlike Nell and CC who pretended they couldn't hear Jamie's side of the conversation and were respectfully avoiding looking at her. I stared at her intently.

Seeming to feel my gaze, Jamie looked up and met my eyes. I didn't think it was possible, but she colored an even deeper shade of red. She was starting to resemble a tomato. I mean if tomatoes could look mortified and wished the ground would swallow them whole.

"Ok, Mom. I'll be home soon. Promise," Jamie said and quickly hung up.

"Sorry," she said. "Mom worries."

"All mothers do," CC said in a soothing tone, "besides, we have to be going also. It's a long drive back home."

CC and Nell started to gather their things in preparation for leaving. I wasn't sure what they had to gather, since I didn't remember them getting anything out, but they seemed to be gathering things and putting them in their purses. I grabbed my purse and slung it across my body, ready to go before the others had finished gathering whatever it was, they were gathering. In the flurry of goodbyes, and nice to meet yous, Nell and Jamie exchanged phone numbers so they could text each other. About an hour after they began getting ready to leave, we were finally standing on the sidewalk. CC insisted it had only been a few minutes, but I stood by my original estimate.

"For Pete's sake, Claire, stop being a drama queen." CC said.

Ready to defend myself, I took a deep breath and prepared to tell her off, but she handed me a thermos and said, "Why don't you say goodbye and go put your coffee in the car?"

"Oooh, coffee."

"Bye, Jamie, nice to meet you," I called over my shoulder, already turning toward the car. Nell and CC joined me a few minutes later and we all climbed in and headed home. Although we still had our car trip tunes blaring, I was too preoccupied to sing along.

Driving mostly on autopilot I managed to get us to my driveway safely, even though I didn't remember any of the trip.

"What are we missing?" I asked CC as we all piled out of the car and stretched. "I know it's staring us in the face. I just can't see it."

Before CC could answer, a deep voice from my front porch said, "Can't see what?"

The voice was sexy but filled with an underlying threat. I felt my shoulders slump as the sheriff sauntered toward us. Nell smiled at the sheriff as she scooted around him and entered the house. CC tried to do the same, but I reached out and snatched her arm before she could get away.

Recovering quickly, she smiled at the sheriff as if she hadn't been trying to flee. "Good evening sheriff. Can I get you some lemonade?"

Although I wasn't looking at the sheriff, I could feel his gaze on me. It burned, like standing too close to a fire, and I fidgeted under his scrutiny. I still didn't meet his gaze and actually felt relieved when he shifted his attention to CC.

"I'd appreciate that."

Before I even knew what was happening, CC somehow escaped my grasp and headed toward her kitchen door. I looked back and forth between where CC had been and where she was now, incredulous that she escaped. Maybe she was Houdini reincarnated. That would explain why she didn't usually get in the water at the pool.

"That's not how he died in real life. He actually died of a ruptured appendix, not drowning during a performance. Hollywood took some license when they made the movie," The sheriff said.

Stupid inner thoughts need to stay in I think to myself. I took a deep breath, squared my shoulders, and finally meet the sheriff's gaze. "Why were you waiting on my porch?" I asked, crossing my arms over my chest. I was afraid that instead of looking tough, I probably looked like I was trying to shield myself, which I was. The sheriff always made me uncomfortable and now with Kyle's sketch and the line dancing fresh in my mind it was even worse.

The sheriff shifted from one foot to the other, cleared his throat, and said, "I ah, I wanted to ask you something."

I felt my breath come faster as I panicked a little. This sounded serious, like maybe he was going to ask me out. What would I say? I started to feel lightheaded, and his words come through as if I was underwater.

"Has Rose said anything to you?"

"Wait, what?" My lightheadedness and hearing cleared up immediately. "Why are you asking me about Rose? What do you think she would say to me?"

The sheriff rubbed the back of his neck, which I realized was a sign of deep embarrassment.

"I don't know. Anything? Maybe about me?" His cheeks began to turn pink.

"Umm, she asked what I thought of you," I answered, still uncertain as to what he was driving at.

"She did?" He sounded surprised. "What did you say?"

Now I felt my cheeks flushing. "That you were tall."

He processed this and then looked at me like he didn't believe me. "I'm tall? Someone asks what you think of me, and you say I'm tall?" He sounded kind of angry—at me.

"Well, you are. You must be over six feet. And she surprised me. There I was trying to eat my lava cake from heaven in peace, and

Rose came over and, out of the blue, asked what I thought of you. I was taken off guard." I was getting defensive. "What would you say if somebody asked what you thought of me?"

Surprisingly, he answered without hesitation. "That you're a menace to society. You are a hard worker and fiercely loyal to those you love. You are as much a part of the Moore family as any of the rest of them. You're responsible enough to keep a job you hate instead of being unemployed. You have a soft spot for the underdog and the misfits. You're more intelligent than most people realize, and you might be the most beautiful woman I've ever met." He finished at a near bellow, glaring at me. "I have to go," he said, and abruptly walked away.

Taken aback by his outburst, I could only stare at his retreating back.

"Your mouth is open," CC said, magically by my side as soon as the sheriff disappeared. "What was that all about?" she asked, handing me a glass of lemonade.

"I wish I knew," I said, still staring after the sheriff. "I wish I knew. He wanted to know if Rose asked me anything about him, and then got mad that I said he was tall."

"I heard the rest," CC said, "you guys weren't exactly quiet." She sipped her own glass of lemonade while we both stared at the spot where the sheriff had disappeared.

"Are you going to stare after the sheriff all night, or are you going to come eat dinner?" Jake called.

I took another minute and then a deep breath before I turned toward Jake. "Well, I guess I could stare at you." I said and waggled my eyebrows at him.

He smiled back at me and then winked.

"Sometimes I regret letting you have Jake," I told CC, linking arms with her.

She snorted like Miss Piggy. "You didn't let me have Jake and you know it. You wanted Sampson."

I sighed at the memory. "I wanted Sampson so I could be Prom Queen, but you're right. Jake and I were never going to happen. Still, that doesn't mean I can't enjoy the view." I flashed her a devilish grin.

"Trust me, you aren't the only one," CC said as we joined the rest of her family at the picnic table set up on the patio. As I squeezed in between Kyle and Frank, I recalled what the sheriff said about me being as much a part of CC's family as the rest of them. It was somehow comforting that others recognized the value of our relationship. Sometimes I worried about what people thought of our little family unit.

Jake placed a platter of burger patties on the table, dropped a kiss on whatever heads were in range and then settled across from me. I smiled what I hoped was a regular *I love you guys* kind of smile. He smiled back and then the normal cacophony of so many people eating together filled the air. Watermelon, chips, buns, cheese, lettuce, tomatoes, and condiments were passed. Three or four conversations swirled around the table. I caught snippets of conversation about a pickup baseball game, the newest princess movie, and Ms. Schwartz.

"Wait. What about Ms. Schwartz?" I asked around a huge bite of cheeseburger.

"She had a major hissy fit at the market today," Frank said. "She showed up to shop in a shabby housecoat and with her hair in major disarray. When Mr. McIntyre asked if she was ok, she started yelling at him. Then she cleared off a shelf. I mean, just swiped it all onto the floor. She almost ran over one of the Jenkin's twins with her shopping cart. When she made it to the produce department, she started throwing apples at anyone who came near her. The sheriff had to be called in. I think he arrested her."

I was speechless. Until I wasn't. "Why am I just now hearing about this!" I asked. "The sheriff was just here and didn't say anything!"

"That's not true," CC noted. "He said a lot, just nothing about Ms. Schwartz."

I waved away this unimportant information. "I'm really tired of not getting the benefits from small-town gossip," I said. "I put up with everyone knowing everything about me, but this not knowing about them isn't fair. First, it's Old Tom retiring and now this!" I felt myself working up to a rant of epic proportions when a bowl of chocolate mousse appeared in front of me.

"Yum! My favorite!" I said, grabbing the spoon. About a minute later, I scraped the last delicious bite from the bowl and asked, "What were we talking about?"

"You were saying—" Eve began, before a hand clamped over her mouth.

I felt my eyes widen in fear. Who had the audacity to treat Eve that way? An old school rhyming song played in my head. The hand bone is connected to an arm bone. The arm bone is connected to a shoulder bone. The shoulder bone led me to the face of the person who risked angering Eve. I was shocked to see Ann was the culprit.

"Eve," she said as if she hadn't risked her youngest sibling's terrible wrath, "why don't we have a tea party?"

Now I was even more confused. Why would Ann risk a tantrum? And why would she willingly volunteer for a tea party? Miraculously, Eve's belligerent expression turned joyous in a heartbeat. She nodded and the girls excused themselves and headed inside.

"That was weird," I said.

No one said anything, but the rest of the kids excused themselves, clearing the table as they left. This was also weird. I squinted at CC and Jake who were acting way too nonchalant.

Before I could investigate further, Jake asked, "Did you find Jamie Wilson?"

I nodded. "Yup, but we still don't know how Mr. Johnson knew her," I said. "She's lived her whole life in McKinley and her mom was an only child. Her grandparents live across the country and always have."

Jake frowned. "What about her dad? Any connection through work, or groups?"

I shook my head. "Her dad took off before she was born and never made contact." It was my turn to frown as I thought through the group and work angles. "Any jobs she's worked would be in McKinley and I don't think Mr. Johnson went to McKinley. She didn't mention any groups, but we didn't ask either. Mr. Johnson never struck me as the type to take an interest in others." I said, looking at Jake, but wracking my brain to remember what I knew about Mr. Johnson, which wasn't much. He was a crotchety old man; self-centered and extremely tight fisted.

"Have you considered that Mr. Johnson could have left Jamie the money without knowing her? Maybe as a scholarship type thing?" Jake asked.

"He was a crotchety old man; self-centered and extremely tight fisted," I reminded Jake.

CC frowned at my assessment but didn't contradict me. Giving up on this apparently pointless speculation I asked, "Do you think the sheriff had to tackle Ms. Schwartz to subdue her and, more importantly, do you think they have it on surveillance video?" I smiled widely at Jake, who returned it immediately. CC tried to look serious, but the quiver of her mouth told me she was fighting a grin.

"Gosh, I hope so." Jake said, earning a smack on the arm from CC and a high five from me.

Deciding to call it a night before CC started to lecture me, I slid off the picnic bench and headed home. Benji met me at the door and proudly presented me with a candle and then bowed. I accepted his gift and show of respect, and gave him a scratch behind his ears in return. I set the candle on the counter on the way through the kitchen and headed upstairs for bed. After changing, I settled in amongst the usual menagerie as best I could, which translated into cirque du soleil contortions. The benefit was that I couldn't toss and turn.

Chapter 17

Shuffling, zombie-like, into CC's kitchen the next morning, I collapsed onto a bar stool and accepted the mug of coffee CC handed me. She was in a robe with a towel wrapped around her head. She seemed quite happy for this early in the morning, but I wasn't willing to ask why and kept sipping my coffee.

Jake walked in just as I finished my first cup. He also wore a robe along with a very satisfied smile. You'd think after all these years and children the honeymoon period would have faded.

Before I could say anything snarky or sarcastic, Jake refilled my mug and I forgot whatever I was going to say. CC put an omelet down in front of me, but I was curious how she made it without me noticing. I considered myself a crack observer and nothing escaped my notice. Still pondering how CC could've cooked an omelet without me being aware, Eve appeared out of thin air and stuck a fork piled with a chunk of my omelet into her mouth. Did she have some sort of portal?

Regardless of where she came from, I had to protect my food. Scooting the plate away from the munchkin-sized spawn of Satan, I shoved a huge bite into my mouth. Maybe if I could consume it fast enough, she wouldn't be able to get another bite. Secure in my plan I chewed frantically and moved to scoop up another bite, only there wasn't another bite. My omelet had disappeared! I looked down in case it had somehow slid off the plate. Eve sat nearby her cherubic face sported tell-tale bulging cheeks.

I death-glared at Eve. "You stole my omelet!"

Eve finished chewing and swallowed. "I was hungry," she said, shrugging her shoulders as if that excused her behavior.

"So was I," I said, "only I still am because someone ate my breakfast."

"You snooze, you lose," Eve said and then skipped over to a nearby cat lounging on the floor by the banquet.

I turned to CC in hopes that she would step in and discipline her youngest. She refilled my coffee cup but said nothing.

Jake whispered what sounded like, "The attention span of a gnat."

Hmm, that seemed like it came out of nowhere. Nell appeared in the kitchen wearing grubby clothes, which still looked fabulous on her. Her hair was perfect in a no-nonsense French braid.

"I'm out of boxes and I still need several more."

Boxes for what? I wondered.

"Packing for college," Nell said, looking at her parents.

Already? *It's still weeks away*, I thought.

"Less than a week. You are dropping me off in six days." Nell said, still looking at her parents.

It was weird how she kept randomly answering my thoughts. Wait, maybe she inherited her mother's ability to read minds? *What am I thinking?*

"That I can read your mind," Nell said, finally glancing my way.

"I knew it!" I crowed in victory.

"For crying out loud, Claire, she doesn't have to read your mind. Everything you think, you say. You've been talking this whole time."

I deflated on my stool. "Every time I think I am finally keeping my inner thoughts in . . ." I trailed off with a sigh.

Jake refilled my coffee cup, but before I could even pick it up, let alone drink my fourth cup of the morning, CC snatched my cup and dumped it down the drain.

"No!" an anguished voice screamed. Since everyone was looking at me, I guessed it was my anguished voice.

CC continued without pity, "Go get dressed in work clothes. You promised you would help Nell pack."

"But the coffee!" I gestured to the sink. "You just dumped it!"

"Go get dressed."

When I didn't immediately comply, she got the look in her eye.

Nell and Jake took a slow step back, obviously trying not to draw attention to themselves. It wasn't necessary though; CC was looking at no one but me. Self-preservation set in and I jumped off the bar stool and rushed out the back door before CC could do anything I'd regret.

Chapter 18

Rushing into my kitchen, I surprised Benji, who was standing on the counter.

"What are you doing?" I asked, not believing my eyes.

Benji looked at me like a deer in headlights and then slid down the cupboards like Jell-O, as if that would somehow fool me into thinking he hadn't been on the counter.

"Is that what you do when I leave? Just hop up on the counter and hang out?"

Benji covered his face with his paw as if ashamed. It almost convinced me he was sorry, but his wagging tail told me he's just sorry he is in trouble. Giving him one more disapproving scowl, I ran upstairs to find some work clothes before CC decided to track me down for taking too long.

Grabbing an old pair of jeans that probably had more holes than denim, and a shirt covered with smears of the same China blue as my walls, I threw them on. I ran a brush through my mass of unruly hair and quickly French braided it. Wisps of hair were already escaping when I made it back to CC's house.

Jake came out the kitchen door, also dressed in work clothes. "I'm on a mission for more boxes," he said with a wave.

I glanced over my shoulder and checked out the fit of his old jeans. I put two fingers in my mouth and wolf whistled, which Jake acknowledged with a jaunty wave without changing course. Smiling, I turned and found CC standing in the doorway with her arms crossed and an inscrutable expression on her face. I felt my smile slip, realizing my best friend had caught me checking out her husband. Again.

"I was always jealous that you could wolf whistle," She finally said with a smile.

I smiled too, following her inside and up to Nell's room where it looked like everything she owned was packed into large cardboard boxes and plastic totes. I sniffled as I took in the scene. Something wet slipped down my cheeks and I collapsed onto the bed clutching a stuffed bear to my chest.

"Auntie Claire, you knew this day was coming. We've talked about it. A lot." Nell said.

She was trying to sound reasonable, which she obviously wasn't. I sniffed again, and more tears slipped down my cheeks.

"Remember the college boys? You are going to come visit and help me check out the college boys, right?"

"What's this about checking out college boys?" Jake asked, coming into the room with several moving boxes.

"Dad, be cool. Frank actually has a girlfriend, so I can check out college boys," Nell said.

"Hey, I wasn't worried about you. I was worried about Auntie Claire," Jake said.

"That's it!" I shouted, jumping to my feet.

"I was just kidding Claire," Jake said, already taping the first couple of boxes together.

"No, you don't understand. I figured out the connection between Mr. Johnson and Jamie." Now I have their attention. "Jamie's mom got pregnant her junior year of college."

"That's not going to happen to me," Nell said.

I waved her away, "I know, but it happens right? It's not the first time it has happened. What if it happened with Mr. Johnson? What if, when he went to college and was out from under his parents' collective thumbs, he met someone? What if he had a kid out there somewhere? Stunned silence meets my questions.

"Why haven't we heard about him having a kid?" Nell asked.

"You're too young to remember his parents, but they were even meaner and more judgmental than Mr. Johnson. A baby born six months after a hasty wedding would have been bad enough, but if the girl in question didn't come from a good family it would have been unacceptable," Jake told Nell.

"And what if they made it go away? Maybe Mr. Johnson didn't even know he had a child," CC said. "I mean, I can't imagine not having any contact with my kid. If he knew his girlfriend was pregnant, I don't think it would still be a secret. He would have found a way to at least visit, and somebody would have seen or heard something over the years. Especially after his parents died"

"What if he found out later, like years later, maybe even decades later?" I kept brainstorming.

"Then why wouldn't he leave the money to his kid?" Nell asked. "Jamie is too young to be his daughter."

"She could be his granddaughter," Jake said.

"According to Jamie her mom isn't from here and her mom's parents have only been here to visit them occasionally. So, it's probably Jamie's unknown father," CC said.

I was determined to get to the bottom of this mystery. "We'll have to find out who her dad is."

"Yeah, because it's been this big secret all her life but when a couple of strangers show up asking, it won't be any big deal to tell them."

"I felt like that was a little insincere," I said to Nell.

"It was," She sounded unconcerned about my reprimand.

Lucky for her I was a peaceful person. Also, I was distracted. Contemplating how to find out who Jamie's father was, I started chucking things into the nearest box.

I wasn't sure how long I'd been packing when Nell exclaimed, "Auntie Claire, please stop."

I looked up, surprised. "What? I'm helping you pack. Like you wanted." I reminded her.

Nell took the packing tape out of the box. "You are just throwing whatever you touch in the box. I'm pretty sure I won't need this—" She held up Eve's half-dressed barbie doll, "or this—" she fished out a hamster ball with a hamster still inside.

"I didn't pack those," I said. "It was probably your mother. She's getting emotional with you leaving and not thinking clearly." I lowered my voice.

Obviously, I hadn't lowered it enough because CC looked up from where she was sitting on the floor near the bookcase. "Honestly, Claire. I can't even reach that box."

"Well, if you are going to use logic," I said, using one of my regular stall tactics. "I'm just trying to figure out how we can find Jamie's dad." I flopped down on Nell's bed again. I might've have laid there all day, contemplating both the problem at hand and the ceiling above my head, but the baying of a thousand hellhounds instantly roused me.

"Not again," I yelled, racing down the stairs, out the kitchen door, and toward my house with my hands over my ears. I hurried in my own back door, grabbed the picnic basket cookie jar, and rushed to the front door and Agatha. Waving a dog biscuit in front of her nose caused her to pause long enough to snatch the treat. Before she could start again, I tossed a handful of cookies into the kitchen behind me and she bounded after them. As expected, I opened the front door and found the sheriff, who's face wore a chagrined expression.

"I know. I know. I forgot. It's habit." He rubbed his neck.

I shifted uncomfortably, not sure what to do or say. Last time I saw him he was yelling nice things at me.

"I came to apologize about last night," he said, staring in the direction of my feet. When I didn't answer, he raised his gaze to my eyes. I'm not sure what he saw, but he rubbed his neck again and continued. "It's just . . . Rose got into my head and made me a little crazy. I guess I took it out on you."

"Why?"

"Probably because you were there."

"No, I mean, why did what Rose said make you crazy?"

He sighed. "I guess grandmas are like that, at least mine is."

"Grandmas?" I repeated and felt my eyes widen. "You mean Rose is your grandma?" It was weird, but it looked like the world was tilting.

"Whoa," the sheriff said. He reached out and grabbed my arms.

Startled, I stiffened and then stared into the sheriff's eyes, which were surprisingly close to my own. After a minute, the world righted itself.

"Steady. Do you need to sit?"

He was so close I could see flecks of copper in his eyes. He stared at me carefully, as if trying to determine something. I stared back, unsure what was happening.

He said, "Yes, Rose is my grandma. She raised me from the time I was seven years old after my parents died."

I was having trouble focusing. His hands were warm on my arms and his face was so close it blocked out everything else. He wasn't looking at me with the intensity from Kyle's sketch. If he had been, I don't know what would have happened. Probably nothing appropriate for my front porch in the middle of the morning.

"Do you need something? Water?"

He was still staring at me and I realized I hadn't said anything for quite a while. "No, I'm fine," I said, but I wasn't so sure about that. Neither of us had moved, so he was still standing close and holding my arms. A thudding noise behind me startled us both. He dropped his hands from my arms and took a protective stance. He seemed jumpy.

I took the opportunity to turn away and collect my thoughts. Okay, I didn't have enough time for that because my thoughts were scattered all over, but I tried.

As soon as I opened the door, Benji shot out and proudly presented the sheriff with a kitchen dish towel. The same dish towel that had been on the counter. The sheriff accepted the towel and Benji flopped onto his back, begging for a belly rub. The shameless wretch. An obvious sucker, the sheriff scratched Benji, which caused him to writhe around in ecstasy.

Geez, you'd think I never petted him or anything. I started to feel slightly uncomfortable watching the pet-fest happening, not sure if I was still needed or how to leave if I wasn't.

I prepared to flee, but before I could, the sheriff straightened and looked at me again. His eyes sparkled with happiness and lips that previously had never smiled are smiling. I knew this could become a habit if he wasn't careful. I smiled back at him. How could I not? I was a sucker for a man who loved animals. As I watched his eyes darkened and took on a different intensity. I felt the shift in mood as his expression started to resemble the look from Kyle's sketch.

"Why sheriff, how nice to see you again," CC said from behind me.

"Ms. Miller, nice to see you as well," he said. "Sorry to have interrupted your," he paused and eyeballed my work clothes, "morning."

CC waved this away. "We were just helping Nell get packed for college. We're dropping her off next weekend." CC linked her arm through mine and smiled. "We were about to take a break for some lemonade. Would you like to join us?"

"No thanks, ma'am. I should get going." The sheriff gave me one more inscrutable look and then left.

"Did I mention I was jealous you could wolf whistle?" CC asked with a sigh.

I wrenched my eyes away from the retreating sheriff's backside and realized we were both checking him out. "Jake is going to be jealous," I told her.

"I won't tell him if you don't," she quipped.

I was sorely tempted to tattle on her, but knowing Jake, he would just take it as a challenge to regain her attention in some kissy-face manner, and I just wasn't up for that right now. I still felt too confused by the sheriff.

Heading back to CC's house, we met Jake coming back with more boxes. *Jeez, how many boxes did Nell need?* I wondered to myself.

"A lot," Jake said, which made me think my thoughts weren't just to myself. "Was that the sheriff?" he asked, adjusting the boxes in his arms.

Neither CC nor I offered to carry any. "Yeah," I said, still off kilter from the sheriff's visit.

"Did you ask if there was security footage of him tackling Ms. Schwartz?" He finally set the boxes down instead of continuing to juggle them.

"Oh Man! I completely forgot to ask!" I said, slapping my forehead.

"Huh, he must have had a pretty important reason to visit if it made you forget him tackling Ms. Schwartz."

I felt his judgment attacking me. "Rose is his grandma!" I blurted, surprising myself as well as Jake and CC if their faces were anything to go by.

"Huh, that explains the free food at Bake my Day," CC said, casting Jake an inscrutable look that promised more on the subject later. She headed back into the house and Jake and I fell into line behind her like good little ducklings.

I wondered why I wouldn't get to hear more on it later, confident I was more confused and out of the loop than Jake.

Chapter 19

After Nell's room was mostly packed, with just a few items of clothing and other necessities left out, we headed downstairs for lunch. A huge batch of nachos awaited us, even though CC had been only minutes ahead. I grabbed a plate from the stack and started scooping up tortilla chips covered with melty cheese and ground beef. Not even bothering to find a seat, I shoved a huge bite into my mouth and chewed with real contentment. CC and Jake started passing out plates and serving various children as they filtered into the room. CC handed the last plate to Kyle just as the oven timer dinged, indicating the second batch was ready. I headed toward the oven for a second helping.

"Don't even think about it," CC said standing between me and the oven. "Remember last time?"

I gasped, sucking in air for a strident protest.

Before I could launch into my tirade, CC grabbed the second batch out of the oven and said, "Besides if you dropped them, you couldn't have seconds."

I harrumphed but held out my plate for seconds without further comment. I had only taken one scrumptious bite when the hairs on the back of my neck stood up. Panicking, I searched everywhere for signs of any threat, but nothing jumped out at me, figuratively or literally.

And then, the click of doom reaches my ears. Wasting no time, I jumped onto the counter, being careful not to spill my nachos. I had barely settled onto the countertop when the danger floof appeared in the doorway. His happy, panting face seemed sweet and innocent, but I wasn't fooled. From the safety of my perch, I smirked at him. When he spotted me, I could have sworn his eyes took on a demonic cast. Others said he was happy to see me, but I didn't believe them. He wanted my soul.

My victorious smile slipped as he rushed toward me. Despite my higher vantage point, I leaned back in instinctive fear—fear that seemed justified when danger floof put his front paws on either side of me. His doggy breath hit my face moments before his tongue began swiping my cheek.

"Help me!" I cried, hoping at least one of the heartless curs in the room would come to my rescue. In desperation, I tossed a precious nacho chip behind danger floof. His head snapped around to track the morsel and then he dropped to the floor and scrambled after it.

"Auntie Claire, you know you aren't supposed to feed Bear at the table," Jane said, her gaze censorious.

"Where were you when he was trying to eat me?" I asked. "If he ate me off the counter would that also be seen as feeding him at the table? Hmm?" I ate what was left of my nachos. Jane had no further comment, proving my superior argumentative skills.

"A couple of my friends are getting together to hang out before we all leave for college," Nell said, clearing her plate. "Can I go?"

"Sure, Honey. I mean, why would you want to spend what little time we have left together." I said.

"Claire, you're being ridiculous. Nell can spend time with her friends," CC said with a scolding tone.

"Her other, not as cool friends," I mumbled, wondering why everybody was picking on me today?

Nell heard but chose to ignore me. Instead, she smiled at her mom.

"Thanks, Mom. I might not be home for dinner, but I'll text you."

"Can I get a ride?" Frank asked, also clearing his plate. "I'm meeting Amelia." They headed out together with good natured jostling.

I miss her already, I thought.

"Me too," CC said, giving me a side hug.

Jake wrapped us both in his arms and rested his chin on my head.

We might have stayed like that forever, offering comfort to each other, but Dean pulled Jake away to work on a Rube Goldberg project and Jane asked CC to help her with her newest pet, an owl with an injured wing. I ended up alone in the kitchen, just like I would be in real life when Nell left.

"Auntie Claire, you'll never be alone," Kyle said, touching my arm.

"Thanks sweetie," I said, wrapping him in a hug. His muffled struggles indicate it might be too hard of a hug.

"Auntie Claire, I think you are squishing him," Eve said from my other side. "He's turning kind of blue."

I immediately released Kyle. "Sorry, sweetie," I said, making sure his coloring returned to normal.

"I don't know why you are so sad, Auntie Claire," Eve said. "You'll still have me, and we all know I'm your favorite."

I snatched her up and snuggled her squirming body. Her protests about being crushed to death, along with her pointy elbows, finally prompted me to release her.

After the children fled my love or, as they called it, being crushed to death, I was alone in the kitchen, but this time really alone. Left to my own devices I contemplated how to figure out who Jamie's dad was. I figured asking her mom might be awkward, but I thought it was still an option. I mean, Jamie had a right to know who her dad was.

I supposed we could look at public records to see who was listed on her birth certificate, but her mom might not have listed him, especially if she wanted to keep it a secret. I was still deep in thought when CC returned to the kitchen. She brought me a glass of iced tea before settling on the stool next to me.

"What's got you looking so serious?" she asked, taking a sip from her glass.

I sighed. It may have been over exaggerated, but I didn't think so. "I was trying to figure out how we can find out Jamie's dad's name. So far, I've come up with asking her mom, or pulling public records." CC's expression confirmed my ideas weren't that great. I dropped my head on the counter feeling defeated. I may have wallowed in self-pity for the rest of my life, or at least the rest of the night, until CC's chipper voice interrupted my pity party.

"Sheriff Armstrong."

"I thought of that CC, but it's not like he could make her confess."

"Who am I going to make confess? And confess to what?" a deep, sexy voice said, sounding like it was right here in the kitchen with us.

My head snapped up off the counter and I stared in disbelief at the sheriff, who was standing at the backdoor with Jake. I'm sure my face resembled a fish, with bugged-out eyes and mouth hanging open. This belief was reinforced when CC reached over and gently pushed my chin up. That snapped me out of my stupor.

"What? Nobody and nothing!" I deflected his query with subtle rejoinders.

The sheriff arched an eyebrow, making me think my subtle responses might not have had the desired effect. Also, I was very jealous. I've always wanted to be able to raise one eyebrow like that. I tried again. "I mean, it's not like you could torture the truth out of somebody, right?"

The sheriff continued to stare at me with an unreadable expression.

"Right? You don't torture people, do you? Wait, don't tell me. It would probably be one of those 'If I tell you I'll have to kill you' situations, wouldn't it?"

Was the sheriff ever going to stop staring at me? He was taking it to an almost hypnotic level. I actually felt my peripheral vision disappear while my complete attention focused solely on his face. In fact, his face seemed to loom larger and larger each second. I smelled his aftershave and felt his breath on my face, I realized he actually had been getting closer. As in he probably walked across the kitchen to stand in front of me.

"Who am I going to make confess? And confess to what?" he repeated in a deep voice so smooth it reminded me of velvet.

The need to confess was strong, but since I didn't know what I was confessing to, I managed to remain mute. Our gazes were locked and since he was approximately five inches from my face, I could see those few tiny flecks of copper in his eyes. Our silent battle of wills might have gone on all night. My will was strong, most of the time, anyway. Sometimes I crumbled like a cookie—mmm cookies—but since I had no idea what the sheriff wanted me to confess, I felt confident in my ability to resist.

"I egged Mr. Russell's house," I blurted out.

I might have been a little overconfident in my ability to win this battle of wills. The sheriff arched his eyebrow again and CC's muffled laughter escaped through the hand clasped over her mouth. Jake was much less subtle and laughed out loud. Rude! I death glared at him over the sheriff's shoulder. I had to stand on the rung of the bar stool to see over his shoulder, but I was nothing if not dedicated to a good death glare. Jake, somehow unaffected by the death glare, continued to laugh.

"When did this take place?" The sheriff interrupted my glare.

"Uhm . . . never?" I tried to state it with confidence, but it came out more like a question. The interrogation continued without letup, and I crumbled again.

"Ok. It was Halloween 2001. I was out with my friends."

"Not me," CC clarified for the record.

I continued as if she hadn't interrupted. "And it just sort of happened." I shrugged.

"You just happened to egg somebody's house?" the sheriff asked. "Was there a stray chicken that happened by and laid a bunch of eggs in the middle of the sidewalk, and you weren't sure what to do so you thought hmm, I guess I'll just throw these at somebody's house?"

I narrowed my eyes. "I dislike your tone and that's not quite how it happened," I said. "It was more like Mr. Russell was a jerk who gave me detention for no reason." By now, I was standing nose to nose with him with my hands on my hips. It was a little awkward since he was so much taller than me, but I stood on the barstool rungs again and made it work.

"Why is Auntie Claire yelling at the sheriff?" Eve asked.

The sheriff and I both ignored this pint-sized intruder and continued to glare at each other.

"Maybe we should give Auntie Claire and the sheriff some privacy to discuss things," CC said. She scooped Eve up and beat a hasty retreat with Jake.

I mean, I assumed that's what happened since I didn't hear anything else from them, but I never broke eye contact so they might just be very quiet.

After several minutes the glare changed. It was still intense, but now it was less angry and more … I don't know, but more. My mouth was suddenly so dry, I swallowed what felt like a ball of tissue, and then licked my lips. The sheriff's eyes dropped and followed my tongue's path. That made me the winner of the staring contest. However, I was too distracted to crow about it.

The sheriff leaned closer, which was surprising since he was already so close. *He's going to kiss me* I thought, both panicking and anticipating at the same time.

A sharp yap startled us apart. We both turn to see Benji standing on the counter.

"What are you doing?" I asked in shock, relief, and disappointment.

I was shocked that Benji was at CC's and on her counter. I was relieved the sheriff didn't kiss me and disappointed that the sheriff didn't kiss me. I was a complicated person, but I planned on examining those feelings later. Probably all night.

Benji wagged his tail and panted, his tongue lolling down the side of his mouth.

"Well did you at least close the door, or am I going to have a bunch of bugs in the house?" Benji cocked his head and then jumped off the counter, onto the barstool, and then down to the floor. He ran out the open door without a backward glance, presumably to close my back door.

"No offense, but your dogs are kind of weird," the sheriff said, taking a step back and putting a respectable distance between us.

"You should meet my cat," I said.

"So, I think I can let you off with a warning on the house egging, but I'm going to need to know who I'm going to make confess, and to what."

I debated not telling him and making up a story.

"You better tell me the truth, no making up stories," The sheriff warned.

Boy, for only just having met me he sure seemed to know me well. I sighed and gave in to the inevitable. "Fine," I said. "CC, Nell, and I went to the college and found Jamie Wilson. She says she doesn't know Mr. Johnson. Her mom moved to town to go to college, got pregnant with her and stayed. They have never been to Oak Creek. Jamie doesn't even know her dad's name. Which is what got me thinking. What if the connection to Mr. Johnson is through Jamie's dad?" I finished slightly winded from explaining everything in one breath.

The sheriff looked a little shell-shocked. He opened his mouth as if to speak and then closed it again. Then he opened his mouth again, but still didn't say anything. I nodded, hoping to encourage him to use his big boy words. His frown and glare told me I might have said that part out loud.

"How in the world did you get all that information out of a perfect stranger?" he finally managed to say.

I buffed my fingers on my shirt. "I have many talents," I said with a cat ate the canary grin. His eyes dropped to my lips, which were formed into a satisfied and gloating smile, which slowly wilted under his gaze. *It was getting hot in here* I thought, fanning myself. The sheriff shifted closer to me, still staring at my mouth.

"Is it safe to come in?" CC asked from outside the door.

The sheriff stepped back.

"I was just filling the sheriff in on what we learned from Jamie," I told her, feigning nonchalance.

Her expression told me she didn't buy my act. "Oh," she responded in a believable nonchalant tone, curse her hide. "Does he have a way to figure out who Jamie's dad is and if there is a connection?"

"I don't know, he hasn't said," I told her.

"He is still standing right here," the sheriff said, as if we could miss him. I mean, he's six feet of gorgeous.

I panicked in fear that I said that part out loud, but when nobody mocked me, I assumed I hadn't. We both turned to look at him expectantly.

"Well?" I asked when the sheriff didn't immediately tell us his plan.

"Give me a minute. You just told me all of this, remember?"

"Fine, I'll wait while you process," I said, tapping the Jeopardy theme song on the countertop with my nails. His glare bounced off me and I smiled shamelessly at him. I'm a lot braver when CC was there as a witness, or conscious, whatever the situation called for.

"I'll look into it," he finally said.

The Jeopardy song ceased. "That's it? That's your brilliant plan?" I asked. "That's the brilliant plan we have waited for?"

"Hey, I just found out about all this. You've known about it for over twenty-four hours, and you still don't have a plan."

"Yeah, but it's not my job to investigate stuff. That's your job. Plus, I already found Jamie Wilson and got pretty much her whole life story. Nell and her are texting buddies now, too. So, if we are keeping score, it's me one, Sheriff Armstrong zero." I finished with an air punch of triumph. His scowl told me I might have gone too far.

Before he can respond, Jake reappeared. "Sheriff, can I get you a beer?"

He wasn't a good room reader, I thought. And since he detoured to ruffle my hair, I suspected I might have said it out loud. Curses!

The sheriff's smirk might be even more annoying than the hair ruffling, and I hated having my hair messed up.

The men folk disappeared out the back door with a couple beers. Presumably they were going to talk about men's things. Boring.

"So, what do we know about Mr. Johnson, the young years?" I asked CC as I resettled onto the bar stool.

"Nothing," CC said. "We weren't even born then."

"Come on, CC. It's a small town. Surely, we've heard something." We both contemplated what we might have heard about him over the years. After some deep thought, over a span of about twenty seconds, I admitted defeat. "You're right. I got nothing,"

CC didn't comment, but that determined gleam in her eye was back and I knew we would be visiting every old biddy in town as soon as CC could manage it.

A loud thump reverberated from upstairs, followed by several voices yelling, "We're fine!"

CC rushed upstairs presumably to check on the kids. I refilled my glass and sipped tea while casually glancing out the window into the backyard. Not to catch a glimpse of the sheriff. Nope. That would be pathetic and maybe a little desperate. I was simply enjoying their beautiful backyard.

"I think they are in the garage." A voice at my elbow made me jump and spill my drink.

Turning, I glared at CC, who was smirking. "If you must know, I was just admiring your flowers. You know I struggle to just keep Mom's roses from dying." CC's face instantly softened, and I hid my grin at deflecting her attention behind the rim of my cup as I took a sip.

CC rubbed my shoulder and then wrapped me in a hug. "I know what will cheer you up." CC said, "Let's go for a drive."

As always, the thought of taking a drive in my baby cheered me up. "Let me change out of these grubby clothes and I'll be ready," I said, already turning to the door.

I didn't see the men as I traversed the well-worn path between our houses. Not that I was looking for them. Nope, not even a little bit. Just making an observation.

I changed into my jean cutoffs and another great t-shirt. This one read lettuce turnip the beet. I thought it was especially on point since I had made such a big deal about CC's garden. Outside, CC was already in the car. Smiling, I settled into the driver's seat.

"Let's drive out by Oak Creek Bridge," CC suggested. "It's so pretty out there, especially this time of year."

Not really caring where we went, I shrugged and pointed my baby's nose toward the park.

After driving a few blocks in companionable silence, CC said, "Oh look! There's Ms. Fitzpatrick. We should stop and say hello. I haven't seen her in ages."

"Ms. Fitzpatrick, how are you?" She continued with her plan without waiting for my response.

That forced me to either pull over or be inexcusably rude. The ancient Ms. Fitzpatrick meanwhile has turned toward us and smiled, which caused the many, many wrinkles on her face to shift upward.

"Why CC and Claire, it's been ages since I saw you two. You are both just as lovely as ever."

Ms. Fitzpatrick greeted us in a surprisingly rich voice. Most old women seemed to take on higher pitched and less forceful voices, but not Ms. Fitzpatrick. Her's was still as strong and smooth as bourbon. Although miffed that my drive had been cut short, I'd always liked Ms. Fitzpatrick, so I smiled warmly in return.

She was dressed in a flowing muumuu that dwarfed her trim frame. Her once-black hair was solid white and shaved so short the natural curl had been cut off. "You look just the same as you did the day I met you," I told her honestly. She had been old then, too.

"Oh you!" Ms. Fitzpatrick flapped her hand at me with a coy smile. "You met me when you were five years old. That was so long ago you can't possibly remember what I looked like." She brushed off my compliment. "What brings you two out this way?" she asked, her keen brown eyes penetrating my very being as if to determine the truth.

CC, however, was cooler under fire and answered before I could ruin the moment. "We're just out for a drive. You know how Claire loves her car."

Ms. Fitzpatrick smiled again and said, "Yes, I do. I still remember when you ran over Mr. Johnson."

My smile faltered a bit. "He crossed in the middle of the block. Who does that?" I declared in my defense, but no one was listening.

"I'm sure you heard about Mr. Johnson." CC's face was a perfect blend of respectful sorrow and interest in whatever Ms. Fitzpatrick might have heard.

"I did," Ms. Fitzpatrick replied, "such a shame."

"Claire and I have been reminiscing about Mr. Johnson, but of course we only knew him later in life. You must remember him when he was younger, during his college days. maybe? I bet he wasn't always so—" CC floundered slightly, searching for the right word. "—reserved."

I would have gone with jerk, demonic, or maybe even evil, but CC always had more tact than me.

"Well sure, Honey," Ms. Fitzpatrick said. "What specifically did you want to know?"

"Oh, you know, just some stories about him. Maybe from his visits back home from college." CC said, as if it were the most natural thing in the world.

"Well, his mama kept him pretty well tied to her apron strings, even after he went to college. And he was never exactly a barrel of monkeys, so I probably don't have a lot of fun stories about him. But let me think."

CC and I waited patiently; smiles plastered in place.

"Well, there was the time Mr. Russell filled his car with the mice from the science department. It took poor Mr. Smith weeks to get them all out of the car, and even after all that effort Mr. Johnson never drove the car again."

CC and I smiled, picturing the two old men as mischievous kids.

"Was that what started their feud?" CC asked.

"Oh, heavens no! Those two had been feuding since they were in diapers." Ms. Fitzpatrick laughed.

"Do you remember any stories about Mr. Johnson and a girl-friend maybe?" CC asked, making a subtle turn to the direction of our conversation.

Wow, I was impressed with her smooth skills. I wondered how many times she had used that same smoothness on me to ferret out information. I tried to catch her eye, but she was focused on Ms. Fitzpatrick.

"He didn't get a lot of freedom to meet girls, but I seem to recall there was talk about a girl from McKinley one spring. His mom hushed it up real quick and he ended up staying home after that summer break. The official story was his dad needed him to help at the bank."

"I haven't heard that gossip before," CC said. "Do you remember her name?"

Oh, she's good I thought to myself. So far, so good, on keeping my inner thoughts in today.

"That was a long time ago, Honey. Let me think. She wasn't local of course. It might have been Stone, or Rockwell. Oh, I can't remember, but it was something like that. Maybe."

This didn't seem like a solid lead, but I guess it was more than we had this morning. Maybe.

"Nana!" Delighted squeals sounded from behind us. Turning, we saw a couple of adorable kids spilling out of the car that had pulled into Ms. Fitzpatrick's driveway. The smile that spread across her face was blinding.

We drove away unnoticed as Ms. Fitzpatrick greeted her grandkids, or maybe great grandkids. After all, she was super old.

"Good thing we already drove away before your inner monologue became your outer words again," CC said.

"I know, I was pretty impressed with how long I was able to keep them in." I nodded.

"Ms. Keller, how nice to see you," CC called out the passenger window as we approached another very old woman.

This one was out walking her tiny and very yappy dog in a purple track suit. The woman wore a purple track suit, not the dog. The dog was wearing a sailor suit, of all things.

"CC, Claire, what are you two doing?" Ms. Keller approached the car.

"We are just out for a drive on this beautiful day. You know how Claire likes to drive."

"Yes. I do," Ms. Keller said, eyeing me in a less than friendly manner.

"How are Mitchel and Ralph?" I asked.

Her look became even less friendly. "They're fine. Now."

"We ran into Ms. Fitzpatrick a few moments ago," CC began, but then saw Ms. Keller's horrified expression and quickly clarified, "not with Claire's car or anything. We drove by while she was out watering her garden and stopped to talk about what happened to Mr. Johnson. She was telling us about some of the pranks Mr. Johnson and Mr. Russell used to pull on each other. She also mentioned something about a girlfriend of Mr. Johnson's from college. Maybe a Stone or Rockwell. Do you remember her?"

Wow, CC was smooth. Ms. Keller didn't even look suspicious while she was being pumped for information.

"Now that you mention it, I do recall something about that. If I remember correctly, he brought a girl home to visit. I never met her, but I think her name was Stone. Jenny Stone. I think she was only here for the weekend and the next thing anyone knew, she was gone. Mr. Johnson's mother hushed it all up like she was never here. Very strange indeed. I think that was just before he had to stay home and help his dad at the bank."

The incessant yapping from Ms. Keller's dog is like an ice pick through my brain, and the cacophony finally prompted Ms. Keller to action.

"Well, I'd love to stay and chat, but I have to get Prince home for his din-din. Yes, I do. Yes, I do. Mummy has to get her little Prince home for din-din." Ms. Keller finished with some baby talk to her dog.

If I was honest, it made me a little uncomfortable. Don't get me wrong. I love dogs, but this was a little weird. We pulled away from the curb as Ms. Keller turned away to finish her walk. I said, "This was your plan the whole time, wasn't it? You knew all the old biddies would be out, so you lured me into driving around to find them."

"Honestly Claire, it's not like I lured you into robbing a bank. I asked if you wanted to take a drive because it was nice day and we did. What is wrong with being friendly while we're out and about?"

She sounded so reasonable, but I wasn't fooled. She had an evil plan from the start. Not seeing any more old biddies, we completed the loop of Oak Creek Bridge and headed back to CC's house. Jake was manning the grill. The kids were going back and forth to the kitchen bringing out salad, dressings, plates, napkins, cups, and other various needs for dinner. We all settled at the picnic table just as Jake brought the platter of grilled chicken to the table. Jane kept feeding small pieces to something under the table. Worried she was spoiling Benji, I peeked and discovered it wasn't. It was a fox. Huh.

"I asked the sheriff about the security footage at the market," Jake said, which grabbed my attention. "He said if there was a video it would be evidence and not available for public view."

"Well, that's a non-answer if I ever heard one," I said. "I really need to see that video."

The kids finished eating and cleared the table, leaving the adults alone in the backyard. We enjoyed the calm for about thirty seconds before Eve declared she would only take a bath if Daddy helped.

Unable to ignore his summons, Jake headed inside and presumably upstairs to the bathroom.

"And then there were two," I said stretching out my legs. A sharp bark from the back door told me Benji thought I was breaking curfew and should be home in bed.

"I have to go CC, or else I'll get grounded," I said and slunk home before I got in trouble. After getting ready for bed, I tossed and turned, just like I predicted, reliving the incident with the sheriff in the kitchen. I didn't know what to think of him, how he made me feel, or what I wanted to happen. Luckily, my attention span was about as long as the lifespan of a fruit fly and my mind wandered until I fell asleep after about five minutes.

Chapter 20

I woke up with my head hanging off one side of the bed and my feet off the other. Perplexed by this turn of events and disgusted with the dust bunnies I saw under my dresser, I levered myself up like Greenpeace saving a beached whale, and eventually made it off the bed. Pulling back the shower curtain, I let out an involuntary squeal when I discovered Blackbeard was already in the tub. Benji, hearing my squeal, dashed to my rescue, but when he arrived and discovered only Blackbeard, he sat down on the tile and stared at me. Heaving a sigh at my pets, and life in general, I turned on the shower and stepped in around Blackbeard.

Although the hot water pouring over me felt amazing, I knew I had to get ready for work. Turning off the water, I wrapped a towel around myself and pulled back the shower curtain. Another involuntary squeal burst from my lips when I came eyeball to eyeball with CC. Benji again rushed courageously to my side. I didn't even need to look at his face to know he was judging me.

"Honestly, Claire, you haven't even had coffee and you are already twitchy."

"Maybe because I didn't expect you in my bathroom. Standing outside my shower. While I was showering." I was upset, but still grabbed the cup out of her hand and took a big swig.

"When you didn't come for breakfast, I got worried," she said. "Eve asked if you were dead."

That's sweet, I thought, and took another deep drink of coffee while moving to get dressed.

CC followed me, picked up my sheets and blankets from the floor and then sat on my bed. "She wanted to know if she could keep Benji."

I handed her the empty mug on one of my passes around the room and pulled on wide leg pinstripe trousers, a red silk camisole, and fitted pinstripe short sleeved jacket. I dug out a pair of platform espadrille sandals with long red ribbons from the bottom of my closet. I left the room after deciding it would be safer to lace them after I went downstairs.

CC trailed behind and watched me lace up while sitting at the bottom of the stairs. "Well, are you going to tell me why you didn't come for coffee?"

CC sounded angry. "Jeez, CC, I just took a shower first. It's no big deal." I was being evasive, although I wasn't sure why. I hadn't planned to skip coffee and breakfast. I just got up and took a shower.

"Are you ok?" CC asked with her concerned mom voice.

I mentally deflated. "I don't know CC. I don't know what is happening with the sheriff. I don't know what I want to happen with the sheriff. I don't know how Jamie and Mr. Johnson are connected. I don't know anything." I stared at my knees.

"Come on, Claire, another cup of coffee will help," CC said, rubbing my back and then urging me to my feet.

I didn't believe her, but more coffee was always good.

"See. I told you she wasn't dead," I heard a sweet voice say as I entered CC's kitchen.

"Aw, now I can't have Benji," Eve, the ungrateful spawn of Satan, said. She seemed genuinely dejected that I hadn't kicked the bucket.

The other kids ignored the whole exchange and continued eating. Realizing it is cinnamon rolls I didn't blame them. Snagging a cinnamon roll for myself, I settled on a bar stool and started the serious business of eating. It wasn't long before I was licking the last of the frosting from my fingers. I grabbed the commuter mug and the lunch bag CC held out to me and headed to work.

Chapter 21

Unsurprisingly I was the first one in the office. It felt like it had been weeks since I left last Friday, but everything looked the same. I dropped my lunch in the breakroom fridge and powered up my computer. I managed to go through the motions of a good office manager until lunch.

Realizing Brandon hadn't messed anything up and Steve was still scared of me, I finished a whole day's worth of work before lunch. With nothing to occupy me after lunch, I indulged in a stimulating afternoon of computer solitaire.

Brandon left mid-afternoon for a so-called meeting, and I didn't anticipate seeing him back today. When Steve's three-thirty appointment showed up, I paged him. Instead of coming out to meet ninety-year-old Ms. Blanche and her older sister Ms. Bianca like he would have in the past, he asked me to send them in. After escorting the sweet biddies to his door, I smirked all the way back to my desk. I was really enjoying the peace and quiet afforded me when Steve hid in his office, but also the fact that he quaked in his penny loafers at the sight of me.

The second the clock struck five I grabbed my purse and dashed out the door. I did pause to make sure an unsuspecting sheriff wasn't lurking in the way of the door but saw no one.

Just before I slid into the driver's seat, a hand grabbed my shoulder. Startled, I grasped the wrist, swiveled, and flipped my assailant over my hip, flawlessly applying the self-defense move I had learned at CC's insistence. Shocked that it worked, I stared down at my attacker and met the sheriff's gaze.

His expression was a mixture of shock and annoyance. He might have been slightly impressed, too. "I guess I deserved that," he said and got to his feet.

He took his time to presumably check for injuries. Not sure what to say since I agreed with him, but it seemed inappropriate to say so. I just waited for him to explain why he had snuck up on me, again.

His eyes narrowed, which told me I had probably said that out loud. "I've been looking into Jamie Wilson's father."

"What? You found him? Who is it? Did he admit to knowing Mr. Johnson?" I was practically jumping with excitement.

"As I was saying before being interrupted—" the sheriff said.

He sounded a lot like my second-grade teacher, and my third-grade teacher, in fact, all my teachers. Huh, that was weird. Must be a teacher thing.

"—I have been looking into who her father may be. So far, I'm coming up empty. Is there anything else you can tell me? Did Jamie mention anybody her mom might have been dating? Any mysterious cards or gifts? Any male not quite family, or close friends hanging around?"

I was shocked. *These are great questions,* I thought.

"It's my job," the sheriff said through clenched teeth. "And I'm good at it."

Oops. Not to myself again. I smiled endearingly at him. His jaw was still clenched, so I assumed my smile wasn't as endearing as I had hoped.

"She didn't mention any of that, but I didn't ask either. I could talk to her and see," I said, hoping to smooth things over. "She and Nell text all the time now, so it really wouldn't be a big deal. And she might feel more comfortable with Nell than with the police."

"That's not necessary," the sheriff said. "As I mentioned, it's my job."

Not sure how to respond to that, I said nothing. We stood there, just looking at each other.

"Well, I must be going," I said, perhaps a bit too loud. I turned and practically jumped into my car.

The sheriff stepped closer and leaned down as if he was going to say something through my window. However, when the engine roared to life he jumped back as if he thought I might hit him or run over his foot.

Rude! I only hit him and ran over his foot once, so he was totally overreacting. I chose a hasty getaway over confrontation and pulled out of the parking lot without injuring anyone.

Only after shutting off the engine in my driveway did I realize I hadn't shared the possible name of Mr. Johnson's possible girlfriend with the sheriff. Mentally shrugging, I headed inside to change. Today's t-shirt read, 'surely not everybody was Kung Fu fighting.' It seemed appropriate given the awesome moves I had demonstrated on the sheriff.

Heading downstairs, I realized Benji hadn't greeted me on arrival. Hopefully, he was visiting CC's. I walked into her kitchen and spotted Benji doing backflips, much to Eve's delight.

I dropped onto a bar stool and said, "So, your self-defense moves work."

"That's nice," CC said, distracted as she put the finishing touches on dinner. "Wait. What? Who did you use the moves on? Not Steve?"

I shook my head. "No. No, it was the sheriff."

"What!" CC shrieked. "You attacked the sheriff?"

"No. The sheriff attacked me. That's why it was self-defense." My explanation emphasized the words self and defense.

CC's frown told me she was unimpressed with my tone of voice, but she wanted to hear the story too badly to call me on it at the moment.

"What happened, exactly," she asked, setting the biggest casserole dish in the world on the stove top.

"Well, I was leaving work, and because of the unfortunate door incident, I always look around before rushing out of the office. I didn't see anyone, so I went to my car. Just before I sat down a hand grabbed my shoulder. I was understandably startled, but my instincts took over, and I grabbed my attacker's wrist, swiveled, and applied the self-defense move from that self-defense class I suggested we take."

CC's face showed she thought I had embellished the story, and also that she still thought it was her idea to take the self-defense class. Silly girl, didn't she know all the great ideas were mine?

"It worked just like it was supposed to and when I turned to deliver the follow-up kick and immobilize my assailant, I realized it was the sheriff. He congratulated me on my skills and, since it was all his fault for sneaking up on a ninja, he apologized profusely."

CC's expression communicated her disbelief. "Somehow I don't think it happened quite like that," she said, preparing to carry the world's biggest casserole dish to the table. As if by magic, or maybe her children, the table was already set. In my mind, the house magic theory was gaining credence.

Jake walked in before CC could get a proper grip on the huge dish. "Let me carry that," he insisted, coming over to kissy-face CC.

After about an hour, they finally arrived at the table with dinner. "Honestly, Claire."

My inner thoughts were still running amuck out loud. However, since I was starving and dinner smelled great, I ignored her and held up my plate. I was sitting between Kyle and Jane, who had a small monkey on her shoulder.

"Where did you find a monkey?" I asked. I bobbed and weaved as the monkey started sifting through my hair, apparently looking for bugs to eat.

"The biology department had her," Jane answered, which raised a few more questions.

Before I could ask them, Ann launched into a story about how she beat the neighborhood boys in some sort of obstacle course. Dean followed with an update on his Rube Goldberg project behind the garage. Although he explains it in excruciating detail, I still didn't know what it was supposed to do.

Frank helped Eve get a second helping of casserole before clearing his plate and heading out to meet Amelia for ice cream. *Mmm, ice cream*, I thought. Frank turned at the door and flashed me a quick smile, which made me think he could read my mind, or I was still voicing my thoughts aloud. Probably the mind reading thing; it seemed to run in the family.

CC's eye roll told me she disagreed and that she was still reading my mind.

The other kids started drifting away one by one as they finished.

Stuffed from the delicious dinner, I watched Jake and CC put leftovers away and otherwise clean the kitchen. On one of his passes around the room, Jake dropped off a glass of lemonade for me. I had been feeling a little thirsty—maybe he can read minds, too.

I concentrated on chocolate with all my considerable focus. I visualized Jake bringing it to me. My eyes were closed to block out distractions, but I heard footsteps approaching and peeked between my eyelashes. Sure enough, Jake had brought me chocolate. I smiled at him and grabbed a piece, which quickly found its way into my mouth.

Jake returned my smile. Did the kitchen temperature rise slightly?

CC brought the pitcher of lemonade and refilled my glass.

I took a sip and thought, *I could get used to this reading my mind thing. Of course, I would have to keep my thoughts pure and never think of the gifts I get them. After suitable consideration, I determined the benefits would outweigh any downside.*

"Claire, for the last time, we aren't reading your mind. You say everything you think."

Huh. Well, I suppose that could be true. I mean the sheriff wasn't related and it seemed unlikely that all of CC's family and the sheriff were mind readers. I resolved to give it some thought.

CC and Jake settled across from me with their own glasses of lemonade. "You never told me why the sheriff went to see you after work," CC said, taking a sip of her lemonade.

"The sheriff came to see you again?" Jake asked.

"Yup. And I flipped him to the ground like the ninja I am," I declared with a measure of pride.

"That's a story I'd like to hear," Jake said, so naturally I obliged him.

CC interrupted frequently, stating that I was clearly exaggerating.

"I think the sheriff sees you more than he sees his deputy," Jake said when I had finished.

"I wonder why that is?" CC asked, before answering herself. "Because he likes her. You should have seen the way he was looking at her at Bake my Day. Not to mention Kyle's sketch. Even drawn in pencil it's intense enough to scorch."

Jake and CC exchanged some sort of silent communication for several seconds before CC nodded decisively followed by an agreeable nod from Jake.

I wasn't sure what they had said in their secret language, but it made me suspicious. Before I could go on the attack, Jake passed me the chocolate and I pop one into my mouth.

"What were you saying?" I asked. CC smirked at me, but Jake's smile was genuine.

"Why did the sheriff stop by to see you?" he asked.

"He wanted to know if Jamie said anything that might help him find her dad," I said before taking a sip of my lemonade.

"What did he say about the possible last names we heard?" CC asked.

"I forgot to tell him." I hoped the rim of my glass would muffle my response.

CC's look made me squirm uncomfortably. "What? I had just thrown him to the ground. I was a little distracted."

"Yet, the sheriff, the one who had been accidentally flipped to the ground, still remembered to ask about any clues Jamie might have mentioned about her dad."

Before we could work up to an epic staring contest, a voice called out from upstairs, "Mom!"

CC gave me one more long look before heading to investigate.

Jake smiled and said, "Did you really flip the sheriff to the ground?"

I nodded with a big smile. "I sure did! I knew those self-defense classes would come in handy."

"I thought CC insisted you take them, and you complained every week that you had to go?" Jake said.

"That's not the way I remember it," I stated, perhaps a little too forcefully.

He held up his hands in the universal I surrender gesture. "Hey, I'm not attacking you. Don't use your epic self-defense moves on me."

We smiled at each other, enjoying a happy moment of détente, and then another voice from upstairs called out, "Dad!"

"Well, that's my cue. See you tomorrow."

I drained the last of my lemonade and popped another chocolate in my mouth before heading home with Benji at my heels.

For once, I fell asleep quickly and got a good night's rest without any confusing dreams to plague me.

Chapter 22

Despite the good night's sleep, I still arrived zombie-like in CC's kitchen for coffee and breakfast. I chugged my first mug while CC served breakfast. She had made a little breakfast sandwich with eggs, sausage, bacon, and cheese on a biscuit. *Yum*, I thought, taking a huge bite. None of CC's children are in the kitchen, which I only realized after I started on my second mug of coffee.

"Where is everybody?" I asked, looking around as if they were simply playing hide and seek.

"They are still asleep. Jane found a stray dog yesterday and she had puppies last night. Everyone wanted to stay up with her."

"You have puppies and I'm just now hearing about it?" I asked.

"There is no point in telling you anything before your second cup of coffee," CC reminded me.

I knew she was right, but still, puppies. "Well. Where are they?" I asked.

"In the guest bathroom," CC said and led the way out of the room. I crowd behind her, practically pushing her down the hall toward the bathroom. Wisely, she stood aside at the door, so I didn't accidentally bodycheck her in my haste to see the puppies.

Spying the momma dog curled up in the shower stall, I baby talked my way closer to her. Her short tail wagged as I approached. I dropped to my knees in front of her and crooned sweet talk to her while I stroked her head. She appeared to be an Australian Shepherd mix of some kind. She had five different-colored puppies snuggled against her belly, all sleeping soundly. I carefully picked up the closest, a chocolate merle colored one, and cradled it to my chest. I murmured softly while momma kept a wary eye on me. I might have stayed all day if CC hadn't reminded me about work. Sighing, I returned the pup to its warm spot near momma and headed home to get ready.

At work, I went through the motions of being an office manager. Of course, I was an amazing office manager, so even with minimal effort, I still nailed it. It helped that Brandon spent the day napping in his chair and Steve was still afraid of me.

When five o'clock finally rolled around, I grabbed my purse and headed out. I looked around for the sheriff, not only during my exit, but also while crossing the parking lot. Fool me once shame on you, fool me twice shame on me and all. Especially since we were on fool me four times. Seeing no one lurking—meaning the sheriff—I made my getaway without incident.

Once home, I changed quickly. Today's t-shirt featured a golden retriever's head holding a couple tennis balls and read *don't stop retrieving*. I thought it was hilarious, not to mention that it honored the baby puppies. I rushed next door to visit them. Breezing through the kitchen with a distracted wave to whoever happened to be there, I headed straight to the guest bathroom and the sweet puppies. Momma dog wagged at me in greeting, and I give her a few pats while crooning to the puppies. I scooped up the chocolate merle puppy and cradled it to my chest. All the puppies were adorable, but this one was my favorite.

Two seconds after snuggling the puppy, CC came and dragged me to dinner. She assured me it had been over twenty minutes. I resisted leaving, but CC reminded me that Jake and the kids had their bowling tonight, so sundaes were on the dinner menu. I debated taking the puppy with me or asking CC to bring my sundae to the bathroom, but the puppies started squirming around to eat so I grudgingly put the puppy back with its littermates and followed CC to the kitchen.

I settled onto the barstool in front of my huge sundae. It had a scoop each of chocolate fudge, chocolate mint, and chocolate peanut butter ice cream, topped with fudge sauce, caramel sauce, whipped cream, chocolate chips, and a cherry. If that wasn't enough, it was garnished with a brownie and a chocolate chip cookie. Thinking this would be a restful evening hanging out with my best friend, I began eating, but as soon as I placed the last spoonful in my mouth, I realized how wrong I was. CC whisked away the dishes and replaced them with two laptops.

"What's this?" I asked, perplexed.

"This is the online yearbook for the years Mr. Johnson was at college. I thought we would look through for any possible girl friends with rock sounding names."

"That's a good idea," I said, apparently sounding surprised because CC frowned at me but didn't comment. We both started skimming through photos and names. I cracked up at the ridiculous hairstyles everyone sported back then. After skimming through a couple pages, CC reminded me that I wasn't looking for funny hairstyles I needed to look for Mr. Johnson's girlfriend. Buckling down, I started at the beginning again.

After two eons, CC called out, "I found her! I found Jenny Stone!"

"What! Where?" I asked, peering over her shoulder. Sure enough, there was the smiling face of an attractive girl—with a ridiculous hairstyle and horn-rimmed glasses.

"How do we know if she was really dating Mr. Johnson? I mean just because Jenny Stone went to college with him doesn't mean they were a couple." I ask, causing CC to frown.

"That's a good point," She conceded. "I wonder if we can find a picture of them together," CC said, looking a little daunted by the prospect. We both sighed and went back to looking through the yearbooks. Page by page. For all eternity.

"Honestly, Claire. It's been two minutes," CC said.

I sighed a deep sigh worthy of Eve and returned to looking at the yearbook pages. "This is hopeless," I moaned, dropping my head onto the counter.

"What's hopeless?" Jake asked, coming into the kitchen with the kids.

"We found Jenny Stone in the online yearbooks you found for me, but we still don't know if she was dating Mr. Johnson, so now we are trying to find a picture of them together," CC explained as the kids filed upstairs to bed, except for Jane. She made a detour to check on the puppies. I was about to follow her, but Jake had cut off my escape route by coming over to kissy-face CC. Ugh! *I could be here awhile*, I think.

Jake and CC pulled apart, and CC's frown and Jake's mischievous smile told me I probably thought out loud again.

"Let me work on it and I can probably get a program to search for the names Johnson and Stone and it will flag the pages they are on."

"That was an option?" I practically shrieked. "Why didn't we just do that in the first place?" I asked.

Jane re-entered the room with momma dog trailing behind. They passed through and headed to the backyard. Apparently, it was potty break time for momma. *I better go check on the puppies*, I thought as I hopped off my barstool and headed that way. I picked up the same chocolate merle puppy. I couldn't help that I had a favorite. He was so cute. Wait, maybe I should say she's so cute. Shrugging, I kept snuggling until Jane came back and chased me from the room. Huffing out a breath, I went back to the kitchen.

"Oh, my eyes! I need the bleach!" I said, finding CC and Jake smoochy face kissing. This time, they ignored me, so my options included: continue to be annoying until they stopped, stare at them awkwardly until they stopped, or go home. Although I'm sorely tempted by the first two choices, I picked the last one and went home to bed. I just hoped CC and Jake made it to theirs. I eat in that kitchen.

Chapter 23

M y alarm clock seemed muffled when it went off the next morning. Worried I might have developed some horrible medical condition that affected my hearing, I snapped my eyes open. Oh my gosh, I couldn't see anything! I was blind! And losing my hearing! I was too young to die! I reached toward my face and felt fur. Oh no! I was growing a beard! I wouldn't be able to have an open casket. I continued prodding my fur-covered face and caused a disgruntled meow. Wait, I didn't meow. All at once, my vision and hearing returned but a heavy weight began to crush my chest. Looking toward my sternum, Blackbeard's one eye glared at me. Whew! What a relief, I wasn't dying after all. My cat was just trying to smother me in my sleep. Wonderful.

I tried to get out of bed but since about seven hundred pounds was on my chest, I couldn't. In desperation, I strained my lungs as hard as I could and said, "I can't turn on the shower with you on top of me."

Blackbeard stopped grooming his paw and blinked, or is it a wink, since he only had one eye? In any case, he jumped off and sauntered into the bathroom. Thrilled with the ability to breathe again, I took a few deep ones and then got out of bed to turn the shower on drip. I thought of showering since I was already here but didn't want a repeat of stalker CC. She knew I hated the Psycho movie and her standing outside my shower hit a little too close to home on that one I thought with an involuntary shiver.

I left Blackbeard to his shower fun and headed next door with Benji at my heels. CC was manning the waffle makers. Yes, she had two waffle makers going at one time. Otherwise, it would take forever to make enough waffles for the family. Spying a plate with a waffle, I grabbed it on my way to the counter where my coffee awaited.

I took a huge swallow before deciding what toppings to put on my waffle. CC had laid out syrup, butter, chocolate chips, strawberries, whipped cream, peanut butter, mixed berries, bananas, powdered sugar, and caramel sauce. Weighing my options, I chose peanut butter, chocolate chips, and powdered sugar for my breakfast masterpiece. Licking the last bit of peanut butter from my fingers, I seemed to be wearing as much powdered sugar as I'd put on my waffle. Shrugging, I silently congratulated myself on not getting dressed first.

"What happened to Auntie Claire? Did a powdered-sugar bomb go off?" Eve asked when she joined us in the kitchen.

I narrowed my eyes, but before I could respond to her rudeness, CC poured me more coffee.

"More coffee," I whispered while raising the mug to my face for a big swallow.

CC handed Kyle two plates with waffles on them and he helped Eve add enough whipped cream on hers to rival Mount Kilimanjaro.

I finished my coffee and hopped off the stool and headed home to shower and get ready for work.

Pulling back the shower curtain I saw Blackbeard sprawled in the tub. Since he was approximately the size of Shamu, I wasn't sure how I could shower and not step on him. Gingerly stepping around him, I eased my way into the shower and turned it on full blast. Even though he had been in the shower for hours (that might be an exaggeration) Blackbeard was still disgruntled when I turned it off. I towel dried my hair, put it in a French braid, and then pulled on some work-appropriate clothing before heading to the office.

Since CC was manning the waffle makers, she wasn't standing by my car to hand me lunch. However, Jake was there, and he handed me the sack with a smile before he wrapped me in a hug and kissed the top of my head. "Go get 'em, slugger," he said and then sauntered toward his own car.

I thought about giving him a teammate-style slap on the rear but decided the rumor mill had already enjoyed enough fun at our expense lately. Better to give them a break. So, I simply waved and drove to work.

The office was empty when I got there, which came as no surprise. I was surprised to get a message that Steve was home sick today. Usually, he was sick on Fridays and Mondays. I spent the morning rescheduling his appointments and doing other office managery stuff. When lunch rolls around I realized Brandon wasn't coming in today either. *Why didn't I get the skip work memo*, I thought, heading to the break room for lunch. The rest of the day drug on with no excitement. Without either of the guys here to mess things up, I finished the day's tasks early and played an epic computer solitaire tournament until five.

Once home, I quickly changed, selecting an awesome t-shirt that featured a lemon sitting on a pear's shoulders and the words 'Whoa, we're halfway there.' I went straight to the puppies, looking forward to a snuggle with my favorite. Momma dog wagged her tail in greeting, and I gave her some pats since the puppies were nursing. Rats, I couldn't hold my puppy!

CC called me for dinner, and I dragged myself away from the puppies. The kitchen was empty, so I looked out back and saw everyone seated at the picnic table. I chose an empty seat and sat down. Before Jake could bring the grilled bratwurst and corn to the table, the sheriff came through the back gate.

He really was following me; maybe he did like me after all, I thought. A quick look around assured me I hadn't said that out loud.

CC greeted the sheriff and took the bowl he offered. A bowl? What was going on here? The sheriff stepped aside, and I saw Rose behind him. Rose here too? *Now I was really confused.*

"You always are," Eve said.

Before I could figure out what was happening, CC was gushing about how glad she was that they could make it to dinner and orchestrating everyone's assigned seats. I ended up between Kyle and the sheriff. Coincidence? I think not!

Ann was regaling Rose, a new audience member, with a gripping tale about how she beat the neighborhood boys at, well, everything. Eve was singing one of her princess movie songs to herself, but at the volume of a rave. CC tried to shush her, but Eve wasn't one to be thwarted. Frank and Nell talked quietly with Amelia, who I just now realized was here. Dean was asking Jake about something technical above my level of understanding, which wasn't very high. Kyle was quiet, of course, which left Jane as my only hope of avoiding conversation with the sheriff.

"Jane, what are the names of the puppies and the momma dog?" I asked, taking a huge bite of bratwurst.

Jane smiled. She was always happy to talk about her animals. "The momma is named Marmee, and the puppies are Josephine, Meg, Beth, Amy, and Laurie."

"From Little Women?" the sheriff asked.

Jane lit up. Her smile resembled her mother's and caused the sheriff to get the shell-shocked look everyone gets when CC gave them her full-wattage smile. Even though she was only eleven, the effect was still the same.

"Yes! Are you familiar with the book?" Jane asked.

The sheriff shifted in his seat, appearing uncomfortable, which caused his knee to bump mine. That caused me to shift uncomfortably, which prompted Kyle to give me a knowing smirk.

"I read it in school, but that was a long time ago. What kind of dogs?" The sheriff changed the subject.

"They are an Australian Shepherd mix of some kind," Jane said, warming to her favorite subject: animals. "After dinner you can meet them."

Before he could respond, a huge plate of brownies started circulating around the table. "Brownies! Best day ever!" a voice called out. Since everyone turned to look at me, I assumed it was my voice. I ignored their rude staring and grabbed a brownie. I reached for a second, but Kyle passed the plate before I could grab it. *Rude!* Twin smirks on Kyle's and the sheriff's face told me I probably said that out loud. I consoled myself with my lone brownie. Popping the last bite into my mouth, I stared at my empty plate. But wait, instead of empty there was a brownie sitting on it! I was shocked. *Are brownies just appearing now?* I wondered. That would be fabulous.

"I was full but didn't want to hurt grandma's feelings, so I took one. You can have mine," the sheriff said.

I beamed at him, evoking the shell-shocked look people got when CC smiled at them. Before I could fully process this interesting occurrence, his face took on the strangely intense look that always seemed to raise the temperature and suck oxygen from the room. Since we were outside, this seemed even more unlikely. Still, I was short of breath, so it must be true.

The sheriff's face was getting closer, and I wasn't sure who was leaning in, him or me. Before I could embarrass myself, Kyle nudged my knee and broke whatever spell the sheriff had cast on me.

"Uh, thanks," I mumbled to my brownie before taking a bite.

The delicious flavor took all my concentration, so I was able to ignore the sheriff and my unsettled feelings about him. Not really, but I pretended anyway. Licking the last bit of brownie from my lips, I realized most of the family had drifted away, but the sheriff was still sitting by me, and his gaze was locked on my lips. My breath shortened as I returned the sheriff's gaze. This time, I was pretty sure we were both leaning closer to each other.

This was it, I thought. He was going to kiss me. Did I want him to kiss me? I mean, of course I wanted him to kiss me, but was it a good idea?

"Do you ever think anything you don't say?" the sheriff asked, so close his lips were almost brushing mine.

"I don't think so," I said honestly, "but I'm working on it."

Before either of us could say or do anything else. Jane reappeared with Marmee, the momma dog. Marmee jumped between the sheriff and I, and because we were so close, I found that impressive. It broke the moment, and I wasn't sure if I was relieved or disappointed. Using the sheriff's distraction to my advantage, I slipped away to snuggle my favorite puppy.

Sitting with my back against the wall and the puppy snuggled on my chest, I tried to sort through all that had happened in the last week and a half. It was a lot. Normally, small-town life didn't have so much going on in a year, let alone a couple of weeks. Marmee appeared and snuffled the puppy I was holding before she checked on the others. Setting the puppy down near Marmee so she could have her dinner, I sighed.

"Those are some nice-looking puppies," the sheriff said from right next to me. "I like them a lot better than Fluffy."

I smiled, remembering the ill-fated incident with Jane's snake.

"Me too," I said as the sheriff settled beside me to watch the puppies.

"I like the chocolate merle one the best," he said.

"Me too." I watched the puppies wriggle around.

We sat there and enjoyed the companionable silence, contemplating deep thoughts. *Was the sky really blue, or did we just perceive it that way? What would happen if Batman and Catwoman had a child? Why couldn't the coyote order food instead of chasing the road runner?*

A chuckle sounded from beside me and brought to mind a brook tumbling over a rocky riverbed. "You are a deep and complex woman," he said, smiling at me.

I wasn't sure how long we both sat and smiled stupid smiles at each other, but at some point, Rose interrupted. "There you two are! I wondered where you had snuck off to. And together no less."

I couldn't read her expression to determine whether she was happy or horrified at finding us together. Not waiting to find out, I yelled, "Coming!" I scrambled up and said, "Sorry, I heard someone calling me." A quick glance at Rose's smirk told me she knew I was lying.

However, when I reached the kitchen, CC said, "It's about time you get here. Jake finished the algorithm thingy, and it has marked all the pages that have Stone and Johnson on them. Come look."

I rushed toward the bar and we started scanning pages that popped up. "Wait, look! There they are! We have proof," I said with growing excitement.

"Proof of what?" asked the sheriff.

How I had forgotten he was here I didn't know.

"Jake set up a program to search for all the pages in these online yearbooks with the names Johnson and Stone on them, and we found a picture of the two of them," CC explained, still looking at a picture of the two of them embracing.

"Who is Stone?"

"Mr. Johnson's girlfriend in college," CC explained to the sheriff, while frowning at me. "Didn't Claire tell you on Monday what we learned from Ms. Keller?" CC the traitor asked.

She knew I hadn't. We had even talked about it.

The sheriff said, "She did not."

"You saw each other on Monday?" Rose asked in the background, her expression unreadable.

Not enjoying that I was the center of everybody's attention, I shifted around, feeling uncomfortable. "Well," I said, "it might have slipped my mind when he attacked me."

Rose's eyebrows shot up, which was the opposite direction taken by the sheriff's.

"And then he started asking me questions and it slipped my mind," I finished with a mumble.

The incredulous stares from everybody implied they expected more from my mind. Foolish mortals. After several stunned seconds, everyone chimed in at once. Snippets of conversations filtered through to me, "Attacked . . ." "Slipped her mind . . ." "Sorry . . ." "Ridiculous . . ."

Deciding discretion was the better part of cowardice, I snuck away and headed home. I knew I would pay for it later, but my sense of self-preservation was strong.

Chapter 24

Trying to pretend nothing happened the day before, I was super cool and smooth entering CC's kitchen for coffee. I absolutely did not spy through the kitchen window, slink inside, or use Kyle as a human shield to reach my mug of coffee. Picking it up to take a huge swallow, I realized it was empty.

"What! CC where is my coffee?" In my pre-caffeinated state, I couldn't help but be outraged.

"People who act like children and sneak out don't get coffee," CC said.

I whimpered. It was a cheap ploy, but caused her to relent and pour me a cup. Well, half a cup, which was better than nothing. I gulped it down and held out my cup, going for the Tiny Tim look, the pitiful little kid in A Christmas Carol.

CC's stern gaze told me it wouldn't be happening, so I used my firm, commanding voice. "Please, CC. I'm desperate." That wasn't firm or commanding, but it might work if I kept playing up my pitiful state. "Fine, I forgot to tell the sheriff about Jenny Stone. I told you that. You threw me under the bus when you asked the sheriff if I had told him. And then Rose accused me with her eyes. You know I hate conflict," I said, giving her my best sad-eyed, puppy dog look.

"You hate conflict when it's directed at you. You have no trouble making it or watching others squirm."

I sucked air between my teeth, but then admitted the truth. "You're right," I got up to give her a remorseful hug. While she was distracted, I refilled my coffee mug.

CC finally caught on and scowled at me, but I had coffee so I didn't really care.

"You're impossible!" she said.

"Well, well, well. If it isn't the disappearing woman," Jake said, walking in and dropping a kiss on my head.

"I'm here all week." I sotto voce, taking another swig of coffee. Jake smiled at me, which caused my breath to hitch and my temperature to rise. Luckily, he didn't seem to notice, busy as he was kissy facing with CC. I took the opportunity to pour another cup of coffee and help myself to fruit, yogurt, and granola parfait CC had put out for breakfast. I ate while staring at them making out.

Five years later—okay, maybe five minutes—they realized I was watching them like I might watch a movie. CC's scowl and Jake's satisfied smile are all the thanks I needed. It was time to head home for a shower before work. Remembering Jake's smiles, I made it a slightly cold shower.

Sadly, both Brandon and Steve were in the office when I arrived. Brandon paged me about twenty times for random things like getting him coffee—not my job—to ask stupid questions, or to explain things I already knew. Finally, he got a call from his daddy and left me alone after that.

Steve still avoided me but was getting braver. Occasionally, he would leave the safety of his office, but would always maintain a ten-foot distance from me. I found it oddly satisfying to move a step or two closer to him just so I could watch him scramble backward. When five o'clock rolled around I was so ready to leave, I actually had my purse in my hands as I watched the secondhand sweep toward the twelve. I set the answering machine at five o'clock on the button and dashed for my car. Knowing the sheriff's affinity for hanging around my office and scaring the living daylights out of me, I was ready for him to leap out of nowhere.

"Aah! Don't do that!" I said, clutching my heart after the sheriff did exactly that.

"I didn't leap out at you. I simply walked around the corner of the building," the sheriff said in what I'm sure he thinks is a non-patronizing tone but isn't. "And I would think after your disappearing act last night you would be expecting me." He crossed his arms over his chest.

"So, I forgot to tell you Mr. Johnson's college girlfriend was named Jenny Stone! You attacked me and repeatedly told me that investigating was your job, and you didn't need my help." I crossed my arms over my chest, too. "Besides, CC didn't tell you either."

Our stare off lasted long into the night, but eventually I was victorious and left the sheriff weeping in shame on the sidewalk. Actually, I crumbled after about three seconds. "Fine. Sunday, CC and I went for a drive and ran into Ms. Fitzpatrick." Seeing him about to jump me with his menace to society rap again, I said, "Not literally. I did not hit her with my car."

Seeing the sheriff back down a tad, I continued, "she thought there had been a rumor that Mr. Johnson was dating a Stone or Rockwell. Then we saw Ms. Keller," I emphasized saw so the sheriff couldn't accuse me of hitting anyone else with my car, "and she came up with the name Jenny Stone. Jake found some online yearbooks from Mr. Johnson's years at college. CC and I searched through them, and we found a picture of Jenny Stone, but that alone didn't prove they were dating, just that she went to school there. Jake said he could work some computer magic and it would tell us the pages where both names were listed. Last night we found a picture of them embracing, supporting the hypothesis that Mr. Johnson was dating somebody and that somebody may have gotten pregnant and had a baby, who then got Jamie's mom pregnant making Jamie Mr. Johnson's granddaughter." I was slightly out of breath from the long explanation.

"Why do you insist on trying to do my job for me?" the sheriff asked, pinching the bridge of his nose.

I squinty eye glared at him. "First off, I didn't insist on doing your job for you. CC insisted I do your job for you. Second, you constantly tell me not to do your job and that you don't need my help. Third, if you were good at your job, I wouldn't be doing it for you. You would be doing it. I'm getting all this information after working all day. What do you do all day? Eat brownies?"

I realized my tone had turned shrill and further, I was standing toe to toe with the sheriff, on my tip toes. and almost eye level with him. This put our mouths very close together. I felt the emotional shift from annoyance to something else, but I was frozen like a deer in the headlights and couldn't move. Whether I should move closer or farther away, I wasn't sure.

A car nearby backfired and the moment was broken. The sheriff pushed me behind him and reached for his gun. After he realized it wasn't gunfire, he relaxed his stance a little. Jumpy much?

I seized the opportunity and fled before the sheriff could turn around. By the time he did, I was in my car and backing out. I could see him watching me until I turned the corner.

I would never complain about small-town life being boring again, I thought to myself.

After changing, I made the dinner pilgrimage to CC's with Benji jumping all around me.

"I will never complain about small-town life being boring again," I said as I entered the kitchen.

Since everyone was already at the table, I slid into an empty seat and grabbed the nearest Chinese food carton and dumped some fried rice onto my plate. Sweet angels passed other containers my way, so I also got beef and broccoli, cashew chicken, chow Mein, and egg rolls. Using chopsticks, I dug in.

"Why?" asked Eve, using a fork.

Loser, I thought, shuttling another bite of rice into my mouth with chopsticks.

Eve's scowl told me I might have said that out loud.

"Because boring is great. I don't have to drive all over town talking to people who hate or judge me,"

"That's the whole town," A smart aleck murmured.

Not sure which one said that I glared at them all before continuing. "And the sheriff doesn't jump out at me every day after work."

"Why does the sheriff jump out at you?" asked Amelia.

"Good question, Amelia. That's what I'd like to know."

"What did you do to him this time?" CC asked, confiscating Ann's chopsticks, which she was using like a sword to battle Dean.

"Nothing!" I said, upset that she would take the sheriff's side.

"Honestly Claire. You've hit him with your car, slapped him, run over his foot, hit him with a door, given him a black eye, punched him in the . . . well punched him, and flipped him to the ground. You met him less than two weeks ago."

Well, when she put it like that. Staring at my plate, I picked at my rice, contemplating this turn in events. Was I the problem? *I didn't believe so*, I thought as I scooped up the last of my rice, while everyone else started clearing the table.

"Mom, we're going to meet some kids in town for a kind of going away get-together," Nell said as her, Frank and Amelia, headed toward the door.

"Isn't it kind of early for a going away get-together?" I asked. "You don't leave for like a month," I reminded Nell.

"Two days, Auntie Claire. You are taking me to college in two days." She seemed annoyed for some reason.

"I feel like she's trying to tell me something, but I'm not sure what," I said as CC cleared my plate.

"I know sweetie," she said, sounding kind of condescending.

Before I could call her on it, she brought me a brownie. "A brownie!" I smiled at my best friend.

"There were some left from the batch Rose brought last night and I saved you one."

I beamed at her, and she returned my smile while she and Jake put away the food. The three of us sipped lemonade and visited until the kids called for their parents and Benji told me it was time to go home. He didn't talk, he just barked at me, but I knew what he meant. Agatha and Blackbeard were already asleep, but I was happy to see they had left me almost half the bed.

Chapter 25

I wasn't my usual crabby self when the alarm went off, because today was Friday! I managed a relatively normal walk to CC's for coffee. Strolling in, I found the kitchen is empty, which was unusual. With some concern, I rushed to check on my best friend. Thankfully he was fine. Relieved that Mr. Coffee was working and full, I filled my mug and looked around for breakfast. Not seeing the usual breakfast buffet, I debated whether I should yell for CC or just eat a pop tart. I had poured my second cup of coffee and was still pondering my breakfast strategy when CC breezed in.

"Where have you been, young lady?" I asked with my best matronly tone.

CC rolled her eyes at me, but when Jake walked in behind her, his satisfied expression told me exactly where she'd been, and what she'd been doing. Before I could come up with some good mocking, CC handed me a breakfast burrito. I took a bite while holding my cup out for Jake to refill, and then headed for the door, which Jake helpfully opened since my hands were full. However, Gentleman Jake wasn't on my back porch, so I was left stymied by my own kitchen door. *Where was Benji when you needed him*, I thought. With a shrug, I shoved the last of the burrito in my mouth and let myself in.

Benji was not only in the kitchen he was standing on my counter again. Pointing my now free hand at him I said, "We've talked about this."

He slid off the counter, apparently ashamed, but I didn't believe him. He was shameless.

Anticipating an easy day at the office—Brandon rarely came in on Fridays, and Steve either doesn't come in, or takes a half day—I whistled as I pulled on clothes and twisted my still-wet hair into a bun. I found my lunch sitting in the passenger seat of my car, so I jumped in and drove to work.

It turned out I was right about my coworkers. Brandon didn't show at all, and Steve arrived late and left early. That made for a quiet day, and I accomplished so much. I beat KoolKat23 at online Scrabble. Take that, English teachers who said I'd never amount to anything. I browsed online shopping and loaded my shopping cart with things I wouldn't ever buy, but thought were pretty. I planned a fantastic vacation to Hawaii, which I forwarded to CC—a nudge in the right direction before we had a repeat of the last vacation. Camping is not a vacation. It was one step above homelessness. Sleeping on the ground, cooking over a fire, public bathrooms (if you were lucky), and bugs. Yuck! She obviously needed my planning assistance.

As five o'clock approached, I set the answering machine, double-checked everything was ship-shape for Monday and grabbed my purse. Pausing at the door, I scanned the surrounding area and listened for approaching footsteps before locking up and hustling to my car. Surprised I hadn't been surprised by the sheriff, I made my getaway. Another surprise was that it didn't bring the relief I had anticipated. In fact, I was disappointed the sheriff hadn't shown up. Deciding I would mull it over tonight instead of sleeping, I let it go and cranked up the radio.

I remembered to pull on my cowboy boots when I changed. Tonight's clever t-shirt read 'when you dip, I dip, we dip' and had a picture of a chip loaded with dip. I cracked myself up. If only those around me could appreciate my shirts as much as I did.

Benji rushed ahead and opened the back door for me before he dashed out and jumped the fence between our yards. I wondered why we even had a fence between our yards. Then I wondered why I had never wondered why we had a fence between our yards. Deep thoughts.

Before I could ask CC why we had a fence, I was distracted by homemade macaroni and cheese. Fixing my plate, with a slice of ham and a pile of noodles covered in rich cheese sauce and breadcrumb toppings, I grabbed a seat and took a huge bite. Everyone was talking at once and I did my best to keep up with the snippets of conversation while I ate.

"Right, Auntie Claire?"

"Right. Wait, right about what?" I asked, looking around to see who was talking to me.

"If you die, I get Benji," Eve said.

"I'm a little worried you spend so much time planning my death," I said.

Eve rolled her eyes. "I don't have to plan for your death. You're a walking menace."

Those words were not only hurtful, but they sounded familiar. Where had I heard them before?

"Eve, that's not nice to say," CC tried to instruct her evil offspring in proper manners.

"But it's true," the evil offspring insisted.

Not for the first time I think, *Eve might be short for Evil.* CC glared at both Eve and I, so I assumed I said that last part out loud.

I decided I had better check on the puppies and headed that way. Marmee wagged her stubby tail at me, and I give her a pat before grabbing the chocolate merle puppy. I should really ask Jane what her name is.

"Claire, let's go!" CC called from the kitchen, so I reluctantly put the puppy back.

On the way, CC reminded me that Dana will be on the war path since I ditched her idea of my perfect date last week. Scowling, I realized that was probably true. We didn't see her when we arrived, so I put off the inevitable confrontation. CC and I were greeted warmly by the regulars as we fell in line and danced. I had always enjoyed line dancing and the stress release it provided, not to mention the workout. When the band finally took a break, I was both disappointed and relieved. We headed to the bar to get a drink and I scanned the room looking for Dana but didn't see her.

"She couldn't come tonight." CC could still read my mind. "Gwen said she had to work late."

I sighed in relief, even though I knew it was temporary, like a stay of execution. We both chugged our water and sipped our Sex on the Beach. I wasn't sure I liked the drink, but I loved ordering it. I also enjoyed everyone flitting to and from our table to visit.

Gwen didn't flit so much as sit right next to me the entire time. CC gave me a meaningful look but didn't comment. I ignored her and listened as Gwen told me about the new cat she adopted. She had named him Schrödinger. I got it, like Schrödinger's cat, right? *Funny* I thought or said. Who knew anymore? She seemed to be doing a lot of smiling and arm touching, which prompted CC to give me that look again. I ignored her, again.

When the band started tuning up, we all fell into our lines. CC was on one side with Gwen on the other. I forgot everything except the dance and for the first time in what felt like forever, I relaxed and let go of all the confusion that surrounded the sheriff. Which reminded me, last week the sheriff had been here. I wondered if he was here this week. I scanned the room as the dance turned me every which way. I didn't see him and once more relaxed into the dance.

When the band took another break, I decided I needed another drink. I bellied up to the bar and spotting the bartender, the extremely attractive Erick, I said, "I'd like Sex on the Beach, please. Do you think you could help me?" I threw in a flirty smile for good measure.

He leaned over the bar and said in a low, sexy voice that sent a shiver down my spine, "Darling, that's my specialty." He winked one gorgeous hazel-green eye, made all the more striking by his dark complexion, before he turned away to make my drink.

I turned and leaned against the bar to scan the room again, but all I saw was black. Worried I was losing my vision, I blindly reached out and was surprised to touch a hard surface. I felt around, trying to determine what had happened. Something grabbed my hand and held it pressed flat against the hard surface. Raising my eyes, I realized the sheriff was standing very close and that his black shirt was why everything looked black. I also realized his chest was the hard surface I had been exploring with my fingers. I felt my face heat up, both with embarrassment and something more. We stared at each other, communicating something. I wasn't sure what, but I felt like he was trying to tell me something with his eyes. Before I could decipher what it was, Erick came back with my drink.

"I believe you ordered Sex on the Beach, and I can deliver the best you've ever had," he said with what I'd call a smoldering look. Someone down the bar called for a drink and Erick left to take their order, which was good because I wasn't sure I could handle two hot guys giving me hot looks. I took a hasty swallow with my free hand to cool off. The other one was still held against the sheriff's chest.

"He's hitting on you," the sheriff said, his voice gruff, almost angry.

I laughed, but it sounded like a snort. "He is not," I said to reassure him. Taking another sip of my drink, I wondered if I'd ever get my hand back.

"I don't think you are the best judge of when someone is hitting on you," he said.

"Well, since he's already in a relationship with someone—"

It was the sheriff's turn to snort.

I narrowed my eyes but continued. "Besides, I'm not his type."

The sheriff gave me a skeptical look, using that eyebrow thing.

"I'm serious," I said, tugging on the hand that was still trapped against his chest. He didn't take the hint. "Look," I said, gesturing down the bar to where Erick is kissing a beautiful blond. "That's his type."

The sheriff turned to look and then sighed, relaxed his shoulders, and turned back to me. "I see," he said.

I giggled because Erick's hot blond sported a scruffy beard. "He's gay," I said, although further clarification was probably unnecessary.

Before the sheriff could respond, Gwen appeared beside us. She didn't look happy about my hand, still pressed against the sheriff's chest, and I was reminded that CC thought she had the hots for me.

I was feeling very popular tonight. The sheriff didn't even look at her, so I decided to introduce them. "Gwen, this is the new sheriff. Sheriff this is Gwen." Neither one of them looked away from my face, which made me a little uncomfortable. "Well, I must be going," I said. This time, the sheriff released my hand, after a slight tug-of-war, and I took my drink and sauntered back to CC. In truth, I practically ran like a scared rabbit.

"Well, I think we should call it a night," I said abruptly as I rejoined the group at the table with CC.

"Before the band quits?" A chorus of voices reminded me that I always said anybody who left before the band was a loser.

Trapped by my own words, I drained the last of my Sex on the Beach in one huge swallow. CC handed me a glass of water, which I also chugged.

The band started back up and we fell into our lines. I was able to follow the steps and not mess up, but I didn't exactly do justice to the dance moves, either. I refused to look around for the sheriff but felt eyes on me no matter which way I turned. It made me itchy, and not just because I had worked up a sweat.

When the band finally called it a night, I was relieved. Everyone drifted toward the parking lot. Saying goodbye, Gwen gave me a longer than usual hug. Not sure if she was trying to stake a claim, cop a feel, or simply comfort me, I returned the hug and then became aware the sheriff was watching. Was Gwen hugging me because she liked me, or to rub it in the sheriff's face?

CC extracted me from the hug in a way that felt natural without ruffling any feathers and then steered me toward my car.

"Wait, this is the wrong side," I said. "There's no steering wheel." She buckled me in anyway.

"I'm not letting you drive. You chugged several drinks and are obviously distracted by the sheriff, again."

I huff out a breath and settled into the passenger seat. It felt weird, but CC drove us home, which allowed me to contemplate some deep thoughts. *Did the sheriff like line dancing? Why did he show up every week, but never dance? Did Gwen grab my butt by accident or on purpose? Why would Schrödinger put a cat in a box? Is Blackbeard even a cat, or some mutation? Why are the mutant turtles ninjas? Turtles aren't known for their speed.*

"You have a lot going on in your head, don't you?" CC asked, pulling into my driveway.

"Yep," I answered, even though I think her question was rhetorical. Jake opened the kitchen door and waved at us, well, probably at CC.

He was shirtless and I might have leered at him.

We both leaned against the car and once he realized neither of us were moving, he walked barefoot toward us. My leer was joined by an eyebrow wiggle and Jake adjusted his course and came to me instead of CC. I knew if given enough time he would make the right life choice.

He crowded into me, which forced me to tilt my face up to maintain eye contact. "You're hot," he whispered, his breath fanning my face.

I swallowed convulsively, unable to manage any form of response.

He reached up to brush strands of hair away from my face.

I froze like a deer trapped in headlights. All I could do was wait for whatever he was going to do next.

He leaned even closer, his lips brushed mine and he said, "I mean you are sweaty."

I felt my knees wobble before his meaning filters through my brain. "Rude!" I said pushing him away.

CC and Jake chuckled and then wrapped their arms around each other and waved over their shoulders as they headed home.

Disgusted with them, and my sweaty smell, I went inside to shower.

Chapter 26

I felt a sense of doom permeate my very soul. As if all joy had been stripped from my life, and possibly the world. Even Benji seemed to sense it as he whined at my side. I gathered the last of my strength and rolled out of bed. Staggering toward CC's, I wanted my last moments on Earth to be with those I love.

Bursting into CC's kitchen I made a beeline toward my favorite person in the whole world: Mr. Coffee.

CC watched me cuddle her coffee machine. Even in my weakened state, I felt her judgmental eyes on me. She must've grown bored watching me coo at the coffee machine because she handed me a mug of coffee and a plate with a slice of quiche. Releasing Mr. Coffee, I accepted the plate and mug and found a barstool. I ate my quiche, drank my coffee, and stared with longing at Mr. Coffee.

"Don't you feel a sense of doom?" I asked, holding out my cup for a refill. I was despondent, not dead.

"It's Saturday," CC said, as if that explained everything. Which it didn't.

"I know. It should be a good day. No work. We can go to the pool—"

"It's Saturday," CC repeated. "As in the day we take Nell to college." Her tone implied she thought my mental faculties were lacking.

"CC," I said, my tone also implying a lack of mental faculties, this time on her part, "that's weeks away."

"It's today, Claire."

We engaged in a silent staring contest, each striving to bend the other to our will. My will was powerful, so I anticipated CC would crack under my gaze at any moment. "Gah!" I broke eye contact after about five seconds. I saw CC's smirk out of the corner of my eye but chose to ignore it.

Nell popped into the kitchen, almost dancing.

I reached out and clutched her to me. "I can't believe you're leaving! Why didn't you warn me this day was coming?" I began to sob.

"Auntie Claire, I have been reminding you of this day all summer."

Nell lied right to my face. Well, to my shoulder, since I had her in a death hug.

"Did she forget it was today?" Jake asked from over Nell's shoulder.

"I think it's some sort of coping mechanism," CC said, handing him coffee and a slice of quiche. She stared at me while holding a plate of quiche.

"CC, I can't eat now. Nell is leaving me forever."

"It's for Nell," CC said.

"How could she possibly eat it while hugging me?" I asked with an implied duh. "Duh." Oops, not implied. One second, I was holding my precious baby in what some might call a desperate embrace and the next I was empty handed while she walked away with her plate.

"Are you a witch?" I asked CC, my eyebrows raised in suspicion. "If you are, no judgment and I promise I won't burn you at the stake."

"How comforting," CC said. Before I could latch onto Nell again, CC asked, "Have you seen the puppies yet today?"

I changed direction immediately and went to the guest bathroom. "Who's a good girl?" I crooned, stroking Marmee's head. I picked up the chocolate merle pup and snuggled her to my chest. After several minutes of snuggling, a thought forced its way through the veil of puppy love. CC had used these sweet babies to distract me from my precious child leaving. I placed the pup back with her siblings and went to confront CC. With my scathing rebuke of her behavior on my tongue I strode into the kitchen, where she handed me a full coffee cup.

"Thanks," I said, and took a deep drink. Jake, who had the paper open, shakes his head. I wondered what headline he disagreed with but didn't care enough to ask. The moment I finished my coffee CC swooped by and took my cup.

"Time to get dressed," she said.

I nodded agreeably at her, but she didn't move. We both look at each other.

"For you," she said. "It's time for you to get dressed."

"Oh, right. I knew that," I said and headed home to do so.

Having showered the previous night, I pulled on, you guessed it, jean cutoffs and a great t-shirt. In no time, I was back at CC's.

She frowned at my t-shirt choice but refrained from commenting.

Jake, however, snorted out a laugh. "What are you trying to say, Claire?" he asked, gesturing to my t-shirt.

I pulled out the hem so I could see the image of a seal saying 'Booooo!' and the words 'seal of disapproval.'

"What? Oh, I just grabbed whatever shirt was on top," I lied.

Jake smiled at me even though his eyes were calling me a liar.

We started loading boxes and plastic bins in our cars and before I was quite sure what had happened, CC's mom mobile was loaded with boxes as was my baby. Jake and CC were in the mom mobile and Nell was sitting next to me. We backed out and Frank and the other kids waved from the yard as we passed by. *It was like a funeral procession*, I thought.

"Auntie Claire don't be a downer," Nell said, adjusting her sunglasses and turning up the volume on the radio.

Lucky for her I had the attention span of a gnat and loved good road tunes. Nell and I sang our way to McKinley. Following CC's mom mobile to Nell's dorm, we passed dozens of other families dropping off their children. *I could actually feel their pain like a knife to my gut.*

"Auntie Claire, try to be cool. I have to go to school with these kids."

I sniffled but didn't comment.

"Besides, you don't want the college boys to remember you as the crying lady. Puffy eyes, blotchy face, not exactly attractive." Nell shook her head, her face downcast.

She had a point. I should be brave for Nell. This was an important moment in her life. Even though she was overwhelmed with sadness at leaving me, she had to go to college to become a doctor. I didn't want to make this harder on her than it already was. I turned to rest a comforting hand on her arm and show my support, only to find the seat next to me empty. Looking around, afraid Nell had been kidnapped, I spotted her talking to a group of other college kids. Some of them were boys. Boys that weren't good enough for my precious baby.

Before I could untangle myself from the seat belt that was holding me prisoner, CC laid a restraining hand on my shoulder. "Let her be," CC said. "She's ready, and we need to be too."

Sighing, I watched the group of kids and suddenly realized Jamie was one of them. Finally breaking free of my seat belt, I got out of the car. Nell and Jamie broke free of the group and headed back our way. Jamie smiled her shy smile and then ducked her head so low I couldn't see any part of her face.

We all grabbed a box and headed up to Nell's dorm room, which was, thankfully, on the second floor. On my third trip, and Jake's tenth, I noticed Jamie pull out her cell phone, look at it, and then shove it back in her pocket. She hunched her shoulders more than usual. I was almost surprised her head didn't completely disappear into her shoulders. She grabbed another box and rushed away with it. I was about ready to grab another box myself, but Jake appeared and grabbed it. *Well, I tried*, I thought, looking around at the other families unloading their children into the dorms. CC appeared as if by magic (I knew she was a witch) and handed me a box. Heaving a sigh, I hauled it to Nell's room. I passed Jake as he was coming down for another box, and then he passed me with that box on the way back up.

"Show off!" I called, not even bothering to try and keep that thought in. He smiled at me as he turned the corner for the next flight of stairs. That put his rear end at my eye level. Now I was the one to smile, although mine was more lascivious. I dropped my box on the first flat surface I could find, which happened to be a counter Nell had just cleared off. She gave me an inscrutable look, but I chose to believe it was thankful. Out of the corner of my eye, I saw

Jamie slide her cell phone back into her pocket and look even more scared than usual.

"Is everything ok?" I asked Jamie, which caused her to cast a panicked look around the room. CC and Nell were now looking at Jamie with concern also.

"Yeah, why?" Jamie mumbled in response.

"What's going on? Why don't you think Jamie is ok?" CC asked like the mother hen that she was.

"Well, it's the second time I've seen Jamie check her phone and quickly shove it back in her pocket and then hunch her shoulders so hard she looks like the headless horseman." My apt description was apparently not up to CC's standards of care and concern because she glared at me.

Jamie continued to fidget, and Nell wrapped her in a supportive side hug. "It's just some guy who keeps calling and texting me. I don't know who he is or how he got my phone number, but he won't stop. I've tried blocking his number, but he just gets a different one."

"What does he say?" I asked.

"He wants me to meet him. He says it's important and that it's about my family. But he won't tell me his name and wants me to come alone. It just seems so creepy," Jamie said, what could be seen of her face looked miserable.

"That's fantastic!" I said, practically bouncing with excitement.

"I don't think that word means what you think it means," CC said. "Having a stalker is not fantastic." CC sounded as if she was explaining something to a very small, slow minded child.

"Yes, it is CC. If that stalker's mother was Jenny Stone."

Dawning understanding appeared in CC's eyes. "Oh! You think while we've been looking for him, he's been looking for her?" CC asked, pointing at Jamie.

"He's looking for me? Who is he?" Jamie asked, starting to hyperventilate.

CC rubbed Jamie's shoulder while Nell kept her arm wrapped around her.

"Jamie, Mr. Johnson was dating a girl named Jenny Stone while he was here at college. When he took her home to meet his family it didn't go well. His mom was not nice, and we think she ran Jenny off. We also think Jenny was pregnant, with your father. It would explain why Mr. Johnson left his money to you."

When she still looked confused, I clarified, "Because you are his granddaughter."

If I thought Jamie was pale before, this new revelation completely leached the color from her face. She swayed slightly, but Nell and CC were on both sides of her and managed to keep her upright.

"I think you should meet with him," I said.

Jamie's head snapped up, which caused her face to emerge from the hair that usually obscured it. Her mouth opened and closed, but no sound came out. Her hazel eyes were a little wild and cast about the room as if looking for an escape.

"We would be there with you," I said, reaching out to take her hands and try to offer some measure of comfort. "So far, we haven't been able to locate Mr. Johnson's son, but he has located you. If he is already calling and texting, you can bet it won't be long before he just shows up. It would be better to control the meeting." My explanation caused Jamie to hunch in on herself so much I was a little surprised she didn't just disappear.

"Claire's right, Jamie. He will keep contacting you," CC said.

Turning to me she said, "You should call the sheriff, Claire."

"Me! Why me?" I said. The look she shoots my way implied that perhaps Jamie had more reason to whine since she was being stalked, and I just didn't want to talk to someone. I huffed out a breath. Pulling out my cell phone, I dialed the sheriff's office since the sheriff hadn't given me his phone number.

"Sheriff's office." Barbara answered on the second ring.

"Hey Barbara, it's Claire. How are your kids?" Asking about one's family is a prerequisite to any conversation in Oak Creek.

"Hey, Claire. They're great. Nancy just competed in her regional dance contest and got second place overall. And Zack has been away at camp but comes home next week. How are CC's kids?"

"They're great, Barbara. We are dropping Nell off at college."

"Already? Wow time flies. It seems like just yesterday she was off to high school," Barbara said.

"I know! That's what I keep saying. Is the sheriff available?" I asked.

"As far as I know. I haven't heard any rumors that he is dating or married. I haven't answered any calls from a girl," Barbara answered, lowering her voice. "But I wouldn't wait to make a move. A good-looking guy like that won't be available for long."

"Uh, that's not what I meant," I said, feeling color rise into my cheeks. "I mean, can I talk to him? It's about a case he's working on."

"Oh, well let me check," Barbara said in a tone I couldn't decipher.

I waited, fighting the urge to hang up. Barbara might just tell the sheriff it was me on the line and then it would be even more embarrassing.

"This is Sheriff Armstrong."

I felt my knees weaken, but I locked them in place.

"Hello?" The sheriff's voice asked, obviously thinking no one was on the line after what I realized must have been a prolonged pause.

"Hi, Sheriff. This is Claire. Claire Miller. Um, we are dropping Nell off at college and Jamie is here helping. Anyway, Jamie has been getting calls and texts from some guy wanting to meet her and we think it might be Jenny Stone and Mr. Johnson's son. I know we don't know for a fact they had a son, but it makes sense. I mean, why else would some strange guy keep bugging Jamie? She's blocked his phone number, but he just keeps getting new ones. Probably disposable phones, so they can't be tracked."

"Claire," the sheriff interrupted my rambling, but then didn't say anything else.

I pulled the phone away from my ear to see if I'd lost the signal. Holding it back to my ear I heard the sheriff sigh. I imagined he was rubbing his forehead in exasperation, which caused me to frown.

"Ok. I'm on my way there. Don't do anything until I get there. Give me your phone number."

I'm flummoxed. Maybe he does like me. Kind of an abrupt way to ask for it. Maybe he doesn't have a lot of experience with women. His interpersonal skills were lacking.

"Claire. Your phone number. In case I need to get hold of you before I make it to the college. Oh, and what dorm is Nell in?"

Well, that makes sense. I gave him my number and the dorm information and then hung up. Meanwhile, my face remained red from embarrassment.

"He's on his way," I said to update everyone.

"Who is on his way?" Jake asked, carrying another box into the room. I realized he must have been unloading the cars all by himself the whole time we'd been talking.

"The sheriff," CC told him.

"Oh," Jake said with a lot of secret meaning and a wiggle of his eyebrows.

"Jamie's being harassed by a strange man. We think it might be Mr. Johnson's son, the one we've been looking for. Claire called the sheriff to let him know what's happening and he is on the way here." CC caught Jake up on what he had missed while he was single handedly unloading the cars.

"Well, I've got a few more loads to go," he said walking out of the room.

CC shot me a look that said I should help. She was apparently too busy patting Jamie's arm to unload boxes for her daughter. With a sigh, I headed down to the car, passing Jake on his way up. At the car, I grabbed the smallest box I could find. Jake had already grabbed another big box and beat me to the stairs. Before I reached Nell's room, he passed me going back down. I wasn't sure why CC thought he needed my help. He seemed to be doing fine on his own.

When we finally coordinated our trips to be at the cars at the same time, I asked Jake, "It's kind of hot and you've been doing a lot of lifting. Do you want to take your shirt off? You know, to cool down."

Jake paused as if thinking about it. "You know it is kind of hot. Maybe I will take off my shirt." He stalked toward me while grabbing the collar of his shirt in preparation for pulling it over his head. A hint of washboard stomach peeked out at the bottom of his shirt as he raised his arms.

My gaze was riveted on this tantalizing bit of skin, and I felt short of breath.

"You know. It's not that hot after all," he said, dropping his shirt back into place.

My gaze flew to his face and saw his evil grin. "You were teasing me the whole time? You never intended to take your shirt off!" I said with a hint of outrage.

"Why did you want Jake to take his shirt off?" the deep voice I've come to know well in the last two weeks said from behind me.

Closing my eyes in resignation, I turned toward the sheriff. "You made good time," I said, avoiding his question.

"Sheriff, good to see you again," Jake said, extending his hand for a handshake, which the sheriff returned.

He seemed genuinely happy to see Jake. *Maybe it was only me he found exasperating*, I thought. Jake's hastily covered laugh turned into a cough, and the sheriff's inscrutable look told me I probably said that last bit out loud.

"Well, these boxes aren't going to unload themselves," I said, grabbing one and starting toward the stairs. Jake and the sheriff both passed me carrying boxes larger than the one I had. I should be mad, but took the opportunity to check out both their rear ends. The stairs did a great job of putting them at eye level. Since neither of them laughed at me, I must have kept my thoughts from becoming words. Silently congratulating myself, I continued up the stairs.

I set my box on the counter Nell had just cleared off again and earned another glare. The sheriff emerged from another room. I stood on my tiptoes to try and see behind him, just now realizing there weren't any beds in this dorm room.

He shifted to one side, which allowed me to glimpse a very small bedroom with two beds, which was now half full of Nell's boxes. Looking around, I spied another room with two beds in it. I realized Nell had scored a prime four-person room, although I was surprised none of the other girls were here.

"Hi Jamie, I'm Sheriff Dominic Armstrong. I've left you several messages."

"You're the stalker?" I said with an audible gasp. "And I led you straight to her! I can't believe it."

The sheriff glared at me, but otherwise ignored my outburst and continued talking to Jamie.

"I understand that a strange man keeps contacting you, trying to get you to meet him?" He demonstrated his slight-of-hand skills by making a pad and pencil appear in his hands. "Why didn't you report this?"

"Hey, don't make her feel bad. She's the victim," I said, walking over to wrap a supportive arm around Jamie.

The sheriff shifted his gaze to me and managed to respond between clenched teeth, "I have handcuffs and I'm not afraid to use them."

"That is so inappropriate! There are children present and you're talking about your sexual proclivities." I covered Jamie's ears.

"CC, cover Nell's ears."

"Everybody is an adult here, Auntie Claire. Remember, I turned eighteen months ago. You came to the party. I'm going to college—"

"That's not for a while, Nell. Don't worry, college will come before you know it."

"—but I don't think that's what the sheriff meant."

The sheriff pinched the bridge of his nose and seemed to be counting to ten. I read his lips to know how close he was to ten. Dirty tree? That's not a number.

"Claire, why don't you help Nell pick her bed," CC said.

Nell cast her mom an inscrutable look and led the way to her room. I heard the murmur of voices from the main room, but was focused on ensuring Nell got the best bed. I surveyed the two options, but I wasn't convinced either were up to snuff. I decided to check the beds in the other room and swiveled on my heel.

I passed through the main room just in time to hear the sheriff assure Jamie he would be close by. Jamie looked terrified and unconvinced. CC was holding her hand and trying to calm her fears. It wasn't working. Jamie looked like she was about to throw up.

"He's really great at hiding nearby and jumping out at people," I said, hoping to soothe Jamie. Her green tinge as well as the sheriff's scowl told me it hadn't soothed and might have actually ruffled the sheriff's feathers.

Trying to fix it I continued, "I'm serious. He hid behind my car, so I hit him with my car. Then he suddenly appeared at my office, so I hit him with the door. He appeared at my work parking lot twice, which made me flip him in a self-defense move."

I stopped, realizing this might not be portraying me in the best light. Even though I mastered that self-defense move. *I mean, he was way bigger than me and I flipped him like a rag doll.*

Jamie's expression was incredulous, and the sheriff was working up to a full-on death glare. This made me think I might not have stopped talking while thinking about flipping him.

Jamie's phone chirped, interrupting the staring contest I'd been having with the sheriff. He looked at Jamie while she pulled out her phone. I smiled in victory having won the staring contest. Jamie read the text and shrunk in on herself even more than normal, which I hadn't thought possible.

"It's him," she whispered, handing her phone to the sheriff.

He read it and then said, "Jamie, this is the best way to make him stop. If you don't set a meeting we can control, he will just show up. I promise I won't let him hurt you."

Jamie nodded, resigned to following the plan, and the sheriff immediately started typing on her phone. He showed it to her and asked, "Does this sound like something you might say?" Jamie read and nodded. The sheriff pushes the send button, and then pulled out his own phone while moving to the other side of the room for a relatively private call.

I tried to eavesdrop, but Jake threw an arm around my shoulder and steered me out of the room and back to the car to get more boxes. The never-ending torture is never-ending. The sentiment was a little redundant, but accurate. After three trips from me and about a dozen from Jake we were finally done unloading the cars, and the sheriff was no longer on his phone.

Through the open door, I saw Nell in her room. Not waiting for me to help her select a bed, Nell had claimed the one closest to the window. She was starting to unload another box; this one of clothes.

A commotion at the door signaled one of Nell's roommates had arrived.

"Hi, I'm Violet and these are my parents, Samantha and Kevin. You must be my roommate," the new girl said.

"Oh, no I don't go here," I said, causing Violet to look away from Nell and toward me, "but Nell does," I gestured toward Nell.

"Uhm," Violet looked back and forth around the room.

"I'm Nell and this is my Aunt Claire," Nell said, saving Violet from further embarrassment. She was obviously a little slow-witted. "And these are my parents, CC and Jake, my friend Jamie, and Sheriff Armstrong."

Now, Violet's parents looked worried.

"Nice to meet you. I'm a friend of the family and came to help them."

The sheriff lied smoothly. I felt my eyebrows rise and I filed away the fact that the sheriff was a very convincing liar.

"Technically, he and Jake are friends, and he did help carry some boxes, and he is going to help Jamie with her problem." CC whispered.

She had a point, I conceded, while watching Nell and Violet get to know each other. Soon, they had disappeared into Nell's room with Jamie and giggles trickled out.

CC, Jake, and Violet's parents had drifted together in the kitchen area, which left the sheriff and I alone. We remained silent, contemplating deep thoughts. Like, did Violet have sisters named Rose, Iris, or Daisy and maybe a brother named Sage.

My deep thoughts were interrupted by the sheriff's quiet voice, "Do you keep any thoughts in, or do you say everything you think."

Realizing I had once again been talking instead of thinking, I shrugged. "Mostly if I think it, I say it. But sometimes I can keep my inner thoughts in."

For some reason this caused the sheriff to smile.

"It really is becoming a habit," I said.

"What is?" he asked.

"You, smiling. When I first met you, I thought your lips looked like they had never smiled, ever, like seriously ever. But then you did smile, and it was really nice." I felt my cheeks blushing again and looked away from the sheriff, whose smile had turned a little wicked and self-satisfied. I realized Jake and Violet's dad had been bringing up her boxes for a while now. Afraid I would be drafted into more box hauling, I moved to join CC and Violet's mom in the kitchen, plus I was hoping for coffee.

Violet's mom smiled when I walked into the kitchen. Her smile lit up her face and made her warm brown eyes dance. She had light brown hair with gray streaks. Instead of detracting from her looks, the gray accents made her even more beautiful.

"Claire, CC was just telling me some stories about you."

"She lies. She's a big liar. Don't trust anything she says," I blurt in a panic.

CC rolled her eyes and Violet's mom smiled even wider, which I hadn't thought possible. Her laughter was rich and warm like melted chocolate and made me like her immediately. I thought we would be good friends, Violet's mom and me. It might become awkward if

I forever called her Violet's mom, since I had already forgotten her name, but I thought it would be alright.

"Samantha was telling me about how excited Violet is to be going away to college," CC said, catching me up on the conversation I had missed and subtly dropping Violet's mom's name into the conversation as well.

She knew me so well. I winked at CC to let her know I appreciated her sneakiness.

"Do you have something in your eye?" Samantha asked.

"Uh, no. I think it's okay now." I said to deflect Samantha's suspicions. I almost winked at CC again but stopped myself in time.

Violet's dad stopped by the kitchen to drop off a box.

"Thanks, Hon. Is the car almost unloaded?"

"Just a couple more boxes," Violet's dad said, dropping a kiss on Samantha's cheek before leaving to finish uploading.

Wow! No shame in that game. Deflected any possible request for help and redirected the laborer back to work. Nice!

Jake dropped a box off, and before he could say anything I asked, "Is the car almost unloaded?"

"We have a couple more boxes," Jake said, throwing his arm around my shoulder. "Thanks for offering to help." He steered me out of the kitchen and down the stairs.

I was confused. How did this happen? It worked when Samantha did it. I mulled over what could've gone wrong. Maybe the lack of kissing? When we arrived at Violet's family car, I saw Violet's dad and the sheriff were already there, grabbing more boxes. Jake grabbed one too and they all trooped off with their loads. I sifted through the possible box options, looking for something small and light, but was distracted by a movement out of the corner of my eye.

Looking in that direction, I saw nothing. I mean, I saw stuff. I hadn't suddenly gone blind, but I didn't see what had caught my attention. I thought it was something at the edge of the lawn, among the trees and bushes. There was no wind, so it wasn't the branches moving. I was staring so intently I didn't realize the sheriff was back until he spoke from right over my shoulder, and I mean so close his cheek was almost touching mine.

"What?" He seemed to accept that I saw something concerning.

"I don't know," I said, still trying to calm my pounding heart. "I thought I saw something move over there, but when I looked, I couldn't see anything. I just had this weird feeling," I said, shrugging my shoulders. But I didn't look away from the bushes.

The sheriff moved toward them cautiously, his posture alert. I watched as he looked through the vegetation and then returned.

"There is no one there. I did find some footprints, but I don't know how long they've been there." He frowned. "What do you think you saw?" he asked.

"I did see something," I insisted, placing my fists on my hips, ready to fight.

"I believe you. I want to know what you saw," The sheriff said.

I relaxed a little. "I'm not sure. I got this weird feeling and . . . I turned and looked. I think something moved. Maybe. No, I know it did, because I remember thinking there was no wind, so it couldn't have been the branches moving. But then when I looked, I didn't see anything," I rubbed my arms to combat a sudden case of goosebumps. "It makes me feel really weird and uncomfortable," I said, feeling miserable. "I mean, Nell will be here all alone. Well, not alone, she has roommates, but I don't know how much help they would be."

"I'll alert campus security to a possible threat," I bristled a little at his word choice, but he continued, "you said yourself you weren't sure what you saw. What could I tell the security people?" he asked, putting his hand on my shoulder.

Of course, he was right, I realized. I also noted we had moved quite far from Violet's family car and toward the bushes. Also, Jake and Violet's dad were grabbing the last of the boxes and locking up before heading upstairs again. Which left us alone. I mean, not really alone. There were a bunch of students coming and going doing studenty things, but they ignored us, so they didn't count.

The sheriff's hand was still on my shoulder and his former comforting and professional expression had started to smolder. My vision narrowed to his face, everything else disappeared and his face loomed larger and larger. His breath feathered across my face and I realized he was drawing nearer to me, or I was getting closer to him. He lowered his head; his lips were almost touching mine. I licked my lips, feeling nervous, and his gaze lowered to focus on my lips, which broke the eye contact we had enjoyed for what must surely have been hours. I waited for him to kiss me, holding my breath. I felt like I'd been waiting forever, or at least two weeks, and now it was going to happen. He leaned even closer, and I closed my eyes, ready for his lips to touch mine. I was not ready for them to slam into me so hard!

"Oww!" we both said at the same time, holding our hands to our mouths.

"Sorry!" a voice yelled. "We did give you a heads up, but you must not have heard." A lot of snickering accompanied this statement, and I realized a couple of guys were waiting for us to throw a soccer ball back. The ball must've hit the sheriff in the back of the head. *Jokes on them. They were never getting that ball back*, I thought, and glared at them. The sheriff, however, was nicer than me and tossed them the ball. I was still holding my mouth.

"Let me see," the sheriff said as the boys wandered off, still laughing.

I glared at their retreating figures, but my ire was interrupted by the sheriff gently prying my hand off my face. His wince told me it's not good.

"You have one heck of a fat lip, but I don't see any blood. Do any of your teeth feel loose?"

I ran my tongue around my teeth checking but they all seem fine, so I shook my head.

"What happened to Claire?" CC said, materializing at my side.

I didn't know she could do that. I knew she could read my mind, so obviously she had powers, but now this? We had been friends forever and she never told me she could teleport. Rude! I told her everything.

"I was hit by a soccer ball," I blurted before the sheriff could say anything. Technically it was true, Newton's theory of relativity and all. Wait, not Newton. He invented fig cookies.

"Oh my gosh! Let me see. Are your teeth, ok? I don't see any blood," CC said as she jerked my head from side to side to investigate my injury.

I swatted her hands away. "I'm okay, it's just a fat lip. The sheriff already checked," I said avoiding her eyes. She's also a human lie detector and I didn't want to tell her what really happened, especially in front of the sheriff.

"How did it hit you in the face? You've got great reflexes and a strong sense of self-preservation," CC asked, looking suspicious.

I preened under her praise. "I know. Remember when I snatched the ball out of the air last week?"

"Yes. I do," she said, crossing her arms over her chest and scrutinizing me.

I felt my smile droop and my eyes got a little wild as I started to panic.

"Claire thought she saw somebody suspicious in the bushes." The sheriff gestured to the general area. "I think she was concentrating on that and didn't see the soccer ball until it was too late."

Ooh, that sounded great. And it wasn't even a lie, so it should pass CC's lie detector abilities. I nodded my head vigorously and agreed with the sheriff. "Yeah, it could have been Jamie's stalker," I added.

That diverted CC. "Poor Jamie. Her world's been turned upside-down recently." CC couldn't help her mother hen tendencies.

"Yeah," I agreed, "it must be horrible to have somebody leave you five million dollars. Thank goodness that's never happened to me."

CC ignored me. "We're heading to town to get some lunch. Would you care to join us, Sheriff?" CC asked. "The café has the best sandwiches."

"Sandwiches? What are we waiting for?" I said, heading to the cars and realizing Jamie, Nell, and Jake were already in the mom mobile. Losers.

"You can ride with Claire," CC said, steering the sheriff to my passenger seat. I didn't even hear him agree to lunch, but there he was, buckled into my baby. I wasn't sure why we didn't all go in the mom mobile, but any excuse to drive my baby worked for me. I jumped in and fired her up.

"Wow!" the sheriff said, feeling my baby's power rumble through her chassis.

"I know, it still gets me every time," I said, running my hands around the steering wheel.

"There must be a story behind this car," the sheriff said, which seemed like he was fishing for information, but not in a pushy way.

I contemplated not telling him, but it wasn't like it was a secret. I took a breath and said, "My dad and I restored it together while I was in high school. He was really into cars and mom wasn't, so I was the one he talked to about it. He brought this girl home when I was a freshman." I stroked the steering wheel to show who the girl was. "She didn't look like much then. She had dents, missing and broken lights and engine parts, and was mostly primer gray, but dad had a vision. He told me she'd be ready to take me to prom. She wasn't, but she was ready to take me to college." I finished my story and realized the world had gone a little fuzzy.

The sheriff reached over and put his hand on my leg, in kind of a regular, comforting way.

The world wasn't fuzzy, I had tears in my eyes, and I blinked to try and keep them from falling.

"I still miss my parents too," he said, not trying to fix it, but just letting me know he understood.

It helped and we rode the rest of the way in silence. By the time we reached the café, my tears were under control.

The commotion of all of us ordering sandwiches amid Nell and Jamie's excited chatter cleared the last of my melancholy mood. CC, however, scented blood in the water like a shark, and kept eyeing me thoughtfully with a hint of concern. Fearing she might be able to read my mind, I started singing The Star-Spangled Banner in my head.

"Are you humming The Star-Spangled Banner?" the sheriff, who somehow ended up sitting by me, asked in a low tone.

"What? No, of course not! Why would I be humming? You must be imagining things!" I was smooth under pressure. His quick smile was disarming and made me suck in a sharp breath. Luckily, I wasn't chewing, or it might have been a choking situation. And while I might not mind the sheriff's arms wrapped around me holding me close, I'd prefer it not involve the Heimlich maneuver and an audience.

His soft chuckle made me think I might have said that part out loud, but since he was the only one laughing, I wasn't sure. Plus, his chuckle was doing funny things to me. My stomach fluttered, like actually fluttered, my pulse raced, and my temperature rose. Taking a sip of my drink to try and calm myself, I accidentally caught CC's eye. She smirked at me before turning back to Jake.

Desperate for a distraction, I blurted out the first question that came to my mind, "When and where will Jamie meet her stalker?" I couldn't bring myself to call him her dad. The sheriff's look implied he didn't think it was any of my business, but undaunted I pressed on.

"What about the investigation into Mr. Johnson's death? Any leads besides Jamie's father? CC and I hit a dead end. I mean, obviously Jamie didn't do it. But she was your top suspect, wasn't she? We thought it might be Ms. Schwartz, Mr. Russell, or even his housekeeper Tessa, but none of them seemed like the one. Ms. Schwartz is mean enough to do it, but she seemed genuinely distraught by his death. It's unlikely Mr. Johnson would have invited Mr. Russell in so it would have had to be premeditated and Mr. Russell doesn't have the mental focus to plan a crime. Tessa is a sweet girl and I can't imagine her pushing him at all, let alone down a flight of stairs. Besides, she quit before he was killed, so she wouldn't have even been at his house. Have you been able to confirm their alibis?"

The sheriff continued to give me a look that implied it wasn't any of my business. He also said, "That's none of your business. I'm the sheriff. You are a citizen. I investigate. You do not."

I wondered if he was using short sentences because he thought I was simple-minded, or maybe he was. We were once again engaged in a stare off. I felt like it was a battle of wills that would determine our whole relationship going forward. Displaying even a hint of weakness was not an option. I focused completely on this battle of wills. And my will was strong. Wait, did someone say coffee?

"Wait, did someone say coffee?" I asked, looking at the other people around the table.

"Yes, Claire. I said I was going to order a coffee before we head back to Nell's dorm. Would you like one?"

Her question was unnecessary as I'd already grabbed my purse and leaped to my feet before she could even finish talking. "Yup. Absolutely!" After beating her to the counter, I placed my order and turned to look at our table. The sheriff quickly looked away, but I caught him staring at me. He can't escape me forever. I'm his ride.

Soon enough, we had all piled back into the cars and drove back to Nell's dorm. The sheriff spent his time looking out the window and I spent my time looking at him. I mean, I'm driving, so mostly I'm looking at the road, but I kept glancing his way. That is until we drove past a shirts and skins game of basketball, then I looked at the cute college boys.

"They're too young for you," the sheriff said, glaring at me.

I glared back. "I'm not planning to date them. I'm just enjoying the scenery. Besides, when did who I date become your business?"

He continued to glare at me but didn't comment. When we parked, we both climbed out frowning at each other. CC linked her arm with mine and steered me toward Nell's dorm. Jake intercepted the sheriff for some man talk. Arriving in Nell's dorm room, we discovered two new girls, four new parents, and about seven hundred new boxes.

Violet rushed over and grabbed Nell. "Nell, Jamie, this is Sarah and Olivia, our other roommates. Sarah, Olivia, this is Nell, her friend Jamie, and her mom and Aunt."

We all murmured greetings before the girls drifted away together. The new parents drifted our way, and we all introduced ourselves. Not that I would remember their names, but I smiled politely while they all chatted.

Way too soon, the time to leave Nell came and we hugged her goodbye. There is a lot of crying, but when CC promised to get me chocolate if I would release Nell from my death grip, I relented.

The last thing I heard as we left my sweet, precious baby behind was, "Your Aunt is a little intense."

Before I could decide which one of Nell's roommates I hated, CC pulled me from the room. I'm sure Nell would set her straight and then ostracize her for life. I allowed CC to steer me down the stairs. The sheriff and Jamie had left earlier to prepare for the meeting with her stalker, so it was just Jake and CC in the mom mobile and me in my baby for the ride home.

Chapter 27

CC and Jake stopped to pick up dinner on the way home, so I beat them to their kitchen. Everything seemed quiet, so I guess Frank had everything under control, either that or all the other children had been kidnapped.

I decided to check on the puppies. They probably missed me. Unfortunately, they were having dinner so I couldn't snuggle my favorite, but I did give Marmee some pats to let her know she was doing a great job. I smiled at the piggy noises the puppies made while feeding and how their little legs kicked and flailed. Leaving them to eat in peace, I drifted back to the kitchen and grabbed a glass of iced tea before relaxing on a barstool.

Something was bothering me, other than the fact that Nell was gone, but I wasn't sure what it was. Something dangled just out of reach, tickling my brain. The more I tried to focus on it the more it eluded me. Sighing heavily, I took a sip of tea about the same time CC and Jake came in the backdoor carrying a stack of pizza boxes each.

"Dinner time," CC called out, which caused a veritable earthquake. Wait, not an earthquake, just a bunch of kids rushing for dinner. They poured into the room like a tsunami, grabbing boxes and plates before receding into their chairs to eat. I guess they weren't kidnapped, and Frank had it all under control. Thankfully, Jake managed to hold onto a box and set it on the counter next to me. I flipped it open and grabbed a slice, not bothering with a plate.

"Claire, we will see her again soon. She's not that far away." CC said, sitting down next to me at the bar.

"What? Oh, yeah, I know." I took another bite of pizza and stared at the wall.

"Why are you frowning?" she asked, obviously realizing it wasn't because I missed Nell.

"I don't know," I answered. "It's just ... something isn't right. Or maybe I'm missing something. I don't know. Something is niggling at me, but I can't figure out what it is." I ate pizza and drank tea as the conversation flowed around me. It seemed the kids had lived a whole lifetime since we'd been gone, and they had to fill their parents in on all of it.

I was so lost in thought that only when Benji barked in my face did I realize that it was dark outside, the children had all left, the kitchen was clean, and Benji was standing on CC's counter.

"Benji! Get off the counter, people eat here. It's not like at home."

Benji wagged his tail at me, barked once more, and then jumped to the floor. He ran to CC's back door and looked at me. When I didn't move, he barked again.

"Apparently, it's time to go home." I said to the empty kitchen, realizing CC and Jake must have gone to bed since the kitchen clock showed it was midnight. I followed Benji home and went to bed.

Chapter 28

My eyes snapped open and I came completely awake in an instant. Sun streamed through the windows.

"How did he get Jamie's phone number?" I asked the ceiling. Agatha didn't stir, unless her snoring counted. Blackbeard cracked his eye open and glared at me, while Benji leaped upright, ready to help in any way he could. Sitting up, I continued my thought process, "We couldn't find her, and we had a legitimate reason. The sheriff couldn't find her, and he had law enforcement databases at his disposal. How did her stalker get her phone number? And if he was what moved in the bushes, how did he know Jamie would be at Nell's dorm? If he was there, he saw the sheriff. Maybe even heard us call him the sheriff. He'd know law enforcement was there the same day Jamie suddenly agreed to meet him. He would know it's a trap!" I realized now what had been bugging me the night before. I threw off the sheets and blankets and dashed next door to CC's.

Out of habit, I accepted the cup of coffee and drank deeply before remembering I was on a mission. "How did he get Jamie's number? Remember how hard it was for us to get it, and we had a starting point. If the stalker was who I saw in the bushes at Nell's dorm, how did he know Jamie was there? He now knows the sheriff was there on the day Jamie finally agreed to meet him! He knows the meet-up will be a trap!" I was almost shouting at CC when I finished.

Understanding spread across her face. "You're right! We have to tell the sheriff. Call him."

I pulled out my cell phone and called the sheriff's office. I waited impatiently, fidgeting while it rang. Finally, it connected, but it was the answering machine.

"It's the machine," I told CC. "No one is in the office on Sunday." I left a message for the sheriff to call me, but I wasn't holding out much hope that he would get it today.

"What now?" I asked CC.

She shook her head. "I don't know. He wouldn't be in the phone book. Maybe we can call Barbra and she could give us his number. It's her day off, but I'm sure she would understand."

"Who would understand what?" Jake asked, wandering into the kitchen looking deliciously mussed, but I was too distracted to notice.

Okay, I did notice, but I couldn't fully appreciate it.

"Claire realized Jamie's father shouldn't have been able to get Jamie's phone number or know she was at Nell's dorm. If he was there like Claire thinks, he knows the sheriff was there too, and that he's been set up. We have to let the sheriff know, but nobody is at the office, and we don't have his phone number," CC said, catching Jake up.

"I have his phone number," Jake said, pulling his cell phone out of his pajama pants pocket.

He's lucky I was so worried about Jamie or there would have been some major teasing about his anchor-printed pajama pants. Especially, since they matched CC's pajama shirt-inspired nightgown. Wait, they were sharing a set of pajamas. I should be grateful CC got the shirt instead of the pants. But I filed it away for teasing on another day.

"Hey, Dominic, it's Jake. Claire has something she needs to tell you. Here she is."

"How did the stalker get Jamie's phone number? If he was who I saw in the bushes, then he saw you too. He will know Jamie was talking to law enforcement on the same day she agreed to meet him. He will know it's a trap. You have to call off the meeting and put a security detail on Jamie," I said, all in one breath.

"I can't call off the meeting," the sheriff said, his voice gruff.

"You have to. Jamie's safety is at stake!"

"No, it's not that I won't call it off. I can't. It was set for yesterday, but he didn't show. Now I know why."

"What? Is Jamie okay?" I yelled, holding the phone tightly with both hands as if that could protect her.

"She was when I left her last night," the sheriff said, "but I haven't talked to her yet today. I'm still in bed."

This caused a wildly inappropriate image to appear in my head. The sheriff was in a huge bed with rumpled sheets, mussed hair, drowsy eyes, and naked chest. I swallowed convulsively and remembered his abs from the pool but forced the image away so I could focus on Jamie.

"I got in late last night after waiting with Jamie and then making sure she was home safe."

I breathed a sigh of relief. "At least she's home with her mom," I said. "I'm glad she's not alone."

"Her mom was still at work when I left," The sheriff confessed, and I pictured him rubbing the back of his neck.

"We have to check on her," I said and disconnected so I could call Nell.

"Hello?" a sleepy voice answered after the second ring.

"Nell, it's Auntie Claire, I need Jamie's phone number. Text her and tell her I'm going to call her. She needs to answer. It's important."

My panic must have filtered through Nell's sleep-fogged brain because her voice became more distinct and tinged with fear. "I'll text you her number now. Is she ok?"

"I don't know Honey, but I'm going to do everything in my power to make sure she is."

"Okay. I'm texting you now."

I heard the phone disconnect in my ear and I handed Jake's phone back to him as I grabbed mine. As soon as Jamie's number appeared, I pressed call. It rang and rang, before going to voicemail.

I took a calming breath before saying, "Jamie, it's Nell's Aunt Claire. It's very important for you to call me as soon as you get this. He knows it was a trap. Don't leave your house and keep the doors locked."

Hanging up the call, I turned miserable eyes to CC. "What if it's too late? Why did it take me so long to figure it out?" I asked, near tears.

"This isn't your fault. No one else figured it out. Not even the sheriff." She wrapped me in a hug and then Jake wrapped his arms around both of us.

I accepted their comfort for a moment before squirming free. "I have to go. I have to check on her," I said, already on my way out the door.

Back home, I grabbed my keys, but then realized I was still in my pajamas. I bolted up the stairs and pulled on cutoffs, sneakers, and the first shirt I touched. I didn't even take time to appreciate the pun. On the way downstairs, I pulled my hair up into a ponytail. It probably looked like a blind, handless chimpanzee fixed it, but I didn't care. Hopping in my car, I started to back out of the driveway but had to slam on the brakes when CC and Jake appeared in my back window.

They jumped in the car as soon as it came to a stop. CC looked less pulled together than usual, but still more than me. She sat in the front passenger seat and Jake climbed in the back. I drove the whole way imagining horrible things happening, or having happened, to Jamie because of me. We arrived in McKinley much more quickly than normal and only then did I realize I didn't know where Jamie lived.

Before I could cry, Jake said, "Take a left on Main. Then left on Fifth. It's a white house halfway down the block."

Not sure how Jake knew where to go, but too worried about Jamie to ask, I followed the directions to a cute white house. It was a small two-story with lace curtains in the windows, and a white picket fence almost obscured by flowers. A big maple tree in the front yard had a tire swing that I pictured a young Jamie playing on.

Skidding to a stop in front of the house, I leaped out and rushed to the door. I pushed the doorbell and waited patiently for Jamie to answer. Just kidding. After maybe half a second I pushed it again and then continued jabbing it until CC pulled my hand off and held it so I wouldn't keep ringing the doorbell. The door finally opened, but it wasn't Jamie. The family resemblance was strong though, so I assumed it was Jamie's mom.

"Where's Jamie?" I asked with a complete lack of finesse.

"Hi, I'm CC, this is my husband Jake, and this is our friend Claire. We're Nell's family and we were hoping to talk to Jamie. It's very important." CC said.

"It's kind of early for a visit, isn't it?" Jamie's mom asked, sizing us up.

"I apologize for the early hour, but as I said, it's very important that we speak to Jamie. We think she might be in danger."

This caused Jamie's mom to open her eyes wide. She opened the door and let us in.

"Jamie," she called up the stairs, "some people are here to see you." When no response came, she called again, "Jamie? Honey?" She was starting to look concerned.

As one, we all headed toward the stairs. Jamie's mom was first, followed by me, then CC, and finally Jake. Jamie's mom knocked on the second door from the landing.

"Jamie?" When there was still no answer, she opened the door. "Jamie?"

I knew it was empty even before I followed her in. Jamie's room was stereotypical of all little girl's rooms and apparently hadn't been updated as she grew. It was comfortable and comforting all at the same time. Her walls were painted a soft peachy pink. Her dresser, desk, bookcase, bedside table, and bed are obviously not a set, but they are all painted a uniform white. Her bedspread looked like a family heirloom quilt but might have been bought at a second-hand store. It was made of soft, wash-worn, pinks, purples, and blues. The lace bed skirt and several accent pillows, in the same shades as the quilt, completed the look. Her room was neat except for the desk in front of the open window. The surface of the desk had papers scattered, a pencil cup knocked over, and the lamp dangling off the desk by the cord. I moved to the window while Jamie's mom stood confused in the middle of the room.

"I don't understand," she said, "Where is Jamie?"

CC wrapped an arm around her and guided her to sit on the bed.

I heard them murmuring about when she last saw Jamie, what time she got home, and so on. Good questions, for sure, but I was distracted by the window. The screen was missing. Looking out, I saw it lying in the backyard. A sturdy trellis was attached to the house and seemed strong enough to hold a person. I felt someone right behind me and when the sheriff's face appeared in my peripheral vision, I realized he too had rushed to Jamie's house.

"I think he came in the window. That trellis looks sturdy enough to hold a man. The screen is down there," I pointed to the yard, "and her desk was messed up."

I wilted, realizing I was too late to save Jamie. The sheriff's strong chest kept me from melting to the floor. He gave me a few moments to collect myself and then rubbed my arms, to reassure me, I thought.

"Ms. Wilson said she last saw Jamie when she left to visit Nell. Jamie wasn't home before she left for work. She got home at three this morning and thought Jamie was in bed." CC filled us in as I remained wilted in the sheriff's arms, utterly defeated.

Sensing I wasn't going to pull myself together any time soon, the sheriff handed my mostly prone body to CC and turned to confer with Jamie's mom.

"I'm too late CC. I failed. How could I be so dumb? I knew something was wrong, but I ignored it."

"Stop right there!" CC interrupted, giving me a gentle shake. "You did not ignore it, you mulled it over all night and were the first one to figure out something was wrong. Now we can get help for Jamie, hours earlier than otherwise. The sheriff will find her. I know it." CC gave me a quick hug and then released me, obviously expecting me to stand on my own.

I swayed slightly, no longer supported by CC. Jake reached out a hand to push me back upright. I locked my knees and pulled myself up by my bootstraps, metaphorically speaking. I was wearing sneakers, not boots.

I stared randomly around Jamie's neat and tidy room, feeling listless. Her bookshelf had a variety of books that she had obviously read and some mementos of her life: a stuffed penguin, a bottle of seashells, a small basket full of hair accessories, a candle, and a paper crane. I drifted over to her bulletin board, where photos, ticket stubs, and other papers were pinned. Most of the photos were of Jamie and her mom, and a cute small dog. I studied them, wondering if Jamie would ever see her room again.

Realizing everyone else had moved downstairs, I started to drift that way, lured by the sound of voices and the smell of coffee. I bumped into Jamie's bedside table, which caused the lamp to wobble. It was the only item on the table besides a single book. I picked up the book and tapped it against my free hand while frowning around the room. When no clue jumped out at me, I sighed and turned to go, forgetting the book was in my hand until I had almost reached the door.

Sighing again, I walked back to set the book down. When I leaned over to place it on the table, a paper fluttered out and drifted under Jamie's bed. I got down on my hands and knees to find it, but when I looked, the paper wasn't the only thing under the bed. A shoebox was there, perfectly situated in the middle of the space under Jamie's bed.

Feeling a little guilty about invading Jamie's privacy, I nonetheless pulled the shoebox out. I sat with my back against Jamie's frilly little girl's bed and opened the box where I imagined she kept her secrets. I hesitated before reaching in to sort through the contents. It was full of magazine clippings and childhood notes scrawled by little kids' hands. The clippings are of families; moms, dads, and kids laughing while picnicking, boating, camping, and having Christmas dinner. Normal families doing normal things. The notes appeared to be from classmates and friends over the years. They were full of sweet sayings, happy memories, and compliments. Not quite the clue I had been looking for, but rather a deep insight into who Jamie was and what she wanted out of life.

Feeling terrible for invading her most secret thoughts, I replaced the lid and carefully slid the box back under her bed. I picked up the paper from the book and placed it on the bedside table. That's when I realized it was a list of phone numbers. Probably the ones her stalker was calling and texting from. Assuming they were worthless, I still took them with me to give to the sheriff.

Wandering downstairs into what had apparently become the command center for finding Jamie, I saw several new police officers had arrived. Ms. Wilson is handing out coffee, probably to keep busy and not panic. I headed her way because I wanted her to feel useful, plus I wanted coffee. Waiting for the sheriff to finish talking to the other officers, I drank my coffee and thought about Jamie. When the sheriff finally turned away from the other officers, I handed him the paper.

"This fell out of a book on Jamie's bedside table. I'm betting the numbers are from the stalker's calls and texts, but . . ." I shrugged.

Before I could say anything else, Nell appeared. "Mom? Dad? Auntie Claire?" she said, looking around. "Where's Jamie?"

Her beautiful face was wreathed in concern and her eyes were swimming with tears. Instead of detracting from her beauty it only enhanced it. The officers seemed to notice too because they all wanted to take her statement. The sheriff's fierce frown dispersed the swarm.

"We aren't sure sweetie," CC comforted her, patting her hair like Nell was a dog. Oh wait, that was my hand patting her.

The sheriff took Nell's statement himself. It didn't take long since we were all together yesterday, and besides Jamie being missing, not much has happened since.

Before I knew what was happening, Jake had escorted us out of the house and to my car. Our first stop was to drop Nell off at her dorm.

"Don't worry sweetie, Jamie will be home safe soon. You'll see," I reassured her as she climbed from the car.

As soon as Nell was out of sight I said, "I hate lying to her."

"Claire! You don't know that anything bad has happened to her. Maybe she snuck out with friends."

My scoffing noise implied to CC that I didn't believe that.

"Even if she was taken, the sheriff is on the case. I'm sure he'll find her safe and sound."

Although her words were full of confidence her tone was not. No one spoke during the drive home and I surmised everyone was contemplating Jamie's disappearance. When we got back to CC's kitchen, we pretended nothing was wrong so as not to upset the children.

"What's wrong, Auntie Claire?" Eve asked as soon as she saw me. Apparently, not all of us were able to pretend nothing was wrong.

"One of my friends isn't home." I tried to keep it simple for her sake.

Eve's adorable face scrunched in thought before she said, "You don't have any friends besides us, and we're all here. Except for Nell, who is at college, which is now her new home, so she is home also."

Well, that was rude, I thought.

"I have friends," I argued. "There's Gwen, and Stacy, and Dana, and —"

"Ha! You only see them at line dancing. Those aren't friends, they are acquaintances. They wouldn't help you move or visit you when you're sick." That little girl could be blunt when she wanted to be,

"Gwen would help me move and visit me when I'm sick." I placed my fists on my hips to emphasize my point.

"That's because she wants to date you, not be your friend."

"How much do you say in front of her?" I asked CC before turning back to Eve.

"A girlfriend is still a friend," I said. "It has friend right in the name." I stuck my tongue out in victory and considered the argument won.

"Whatever!" Eve said and rolled her eyes at me before flouncing off.

The euphoria of the win soon drained from me. Seeking comfort, I went to the freezer and pulled out a pint of ice cream. I grabbed a spoon and headed to the bathroom to hold a puppy. That was where CC found me; on the floor next to an empty carton of ice cream with a sleeping puppy cradled to my chest.

She didn't comment on my sad life choices, but just said, "Lunch is ready."

CC waited for me to get up. It was like she didn't trust me. Probably for the best. I had planned on ignoring her and staying with the puppies anyway. However, since Marmee was starting to nurse them, I bowed to peer pressure, put down the puppy, and followed CC to the kitchen.

I picked at the taco salad CC had made for lunch. I managed to eat all of it, but my normal enthusiasm was lacking. Everyone else ate with more gusto, so they were all finished before me.

The kids took possession of their parents for various family reasons I didn't pay attention to, so I headed home and fell face-first onto my bed and lay there, unmoving. Benji apparently thought I'd died and tried to perform CPR by jumping on my back repeatedly. I found the energy to roll over and caught him in between jumps. Thinking he had saved my life, he wriggled around and licked my face. I didn't have the energy left to fend him off, so I endured the treatment until he had satisfied himself that I was alive and grateful for his help.

After Benji had used my chest as a springboard to vault off the bed, I stared at my ceiling and played the whole thing over in my mind. Mr. Johnson's death, Jamie, her stalker dad. How did they all connect? Or did they? Was it two different events that happened simultaneously? Like Nell going to college and the sheriff coming to town. They happened at the same time but weren't related. I frowned as I mulled that thought over. I felt like I was assembling a puzzle without the picture to guide me, that the puzzle was missing some pieces, and that I might have pieces from more than one puzzle. I wasn't sure how long I stayed there, staring blindly at my ceiling. It might have gone on until my alarm went off the next morning, except Jake appeared in my bedroom doorway.

Thinking I was dreaming, I smiled at Jake. "Did you finally get tired of CC and decide to trade up?" I asked with a leer.

Jake returned my smile, but his lascivious leer was probably a lot better than mine. He seemed to float toward me. He sat on the edge of the bed and reached out a hand to brush strands of hair from my forehead before he leaned toward my face. His eyes searched mine and I realized my breath was coming in short pants. His lips drew closer and closer to mine until they were almost touching. I shivered in anticipation, waiting for the moment his lips brushed mine. When they did, it was feather-light, and they moved as if he was talking. Wait, he was talking— "CC is top shelf. I could never get tired of her. And she sent me to get you for dinner." Then he leaned back, while a mischievous smile played across his face.

"One of these days your teasing is going to cause me to have a heart attack and then you will have to explain to CC why you killed her best friend," I said, leveraging myself up onto my elbows.

Jake reached out and hauled me the rest of the way to my feet. Once I was upright, he wrapped me in his arms and held me close. I could feel his laughter vibrating in his chest, but I returned his hug for longer than normal. I found it very comforting to be wrapped securely in a hug. I hadn't realized how much I needed a reassuring hug until now, but it had been a rough day. Plus, I felt like he deserved some teasing of his own, so I slid my hand down to his jean-clad behind and gave him a sharp pinch. He only laughed harder.

"Honestly, you two. I can't turn my back for a minute. You're worse than the children," CC said from the doorway.

"He started it!" I dropped my arms from around Jake.

He kept one arm around my shoulders tucking me against his side. "Sorry, Honey. I can't help it. She's just so easy to tease," he said with a smile that would melt anyone.

I mean, not me. I have my knees locked, plus Jake was still half-supporting me, so I felt confident I wouldn't actually melt into a puddle at his feet.

CC rolled her eyes and lead the way back to her kitchen.

Sitting among all the chaos a big family brings helped ease my morose mood a little. As everyone started dispersing, which left CC and me alone in the kitchen, I decided going to bed early was a good idea.

As I stood, an idea struck me like lightning. "She's at Mr. Johnson's house!"

"What? Who is? What are you talking about?" CC asked while closing the refrigerator.

"Jamie. She's at Mr. Johnson's house. Think about it. If her stalker is her dad, where would he go? A huge mansion with all the comforts you could want, and no one nearby. Heck, he probably even feels entitled to it. After all, he thinks he should inherit his father's estate. It's the perfect hideout. Let's go!"

CC got caught up in my enthusiasm and followed my mad dash out the back door. It was only as we were driving to Mr. Johnson's that sanity seemed to return. "Shouldn't we call the sheriff? If Jamie is there with her father, what are we going to do?" she asked as I sped along deserted streets.

"I can't, CC, I'm driving. That's against the law. Duh." Oops, the duh was more than implied.

CC frowned at me before digging my phone out and scrolling through the contacts.

Finding the phone number, she held the phone to her ear. "Hello, Sheriff? This is CC. Claire thinks Jamie might be at Mr. Johnson's house, so she wants to go over there and check."

I shot her a look full of retribution. She made it sound like it was all my idea. Just because I had thought of it, told CC to come with me, and am the one driving us there, didn't mean it's all my idea. Okay, maybe it was, but she didn't have to tattle.

CC pulled the phone away from her ear, but I was pretty sure she could still hear the sheriff since he was yelling loud enough for me to hear, too.

"Do not go to Mr. Johnson's house! I am on my way! Do not go there!"

CC hung up the phone without saying goodbye.

"I'm not sure what he meant by that." I said, only slowing down a little before rolling through a stop sign.

"Claire, maybe we should go home and let the sheriff handle it." Apparently, her bravado had left her. I ignored her ridiculous suggestion and kept driving. "Claire—"

"You could just go to bed tonight knowing Jamie might be with a killer, just sitting in that house? Knowing you could have helped her, and you didn't?" My voice rose to epic proportions.

"Okay, Okay," CC said. "Fine, we can go to Mr. Johnson's house."

The rest of the ride was quiet. My silence was tense and determined. CC's seemed tense and apprehensive. I parked down the street and out of sight. We snuck toward the house using my ninja skills. I darted from bush to tree to conceal our approach. CC shadowed me as we worked our way in a zigzag pattern toward the nearest window. I peeked in, but the heavy drapes were closed and blocked my view. I moved to the next window and then the next, but all the drapes were drawn. Working our way around the building, we came to the back door. I tried the knob, expecting it to be locked and was surprised when it turned easily in my hand.

With CC glued to my back, I eased the door ajar enough to peek inside. The door opened into the laundry/mud room. Not hearing or seeing anything, I pushed it open just enough for us to step inside. My super stealthy ninja skills got me as far as the swinging door to the kitchen. As I approached it, my foot tangled in some unseen trap, and I crashed through the swinging door and sprawled on the floor. Swallowing my instinctive scream of terror, I landed somewhat quietly, just a muffled thump as my body bounced off the floor.

CC, of course, came through the door as silent as a ghost behind me. She helped me to my feet, and we listened intently for movement or other signs of alarm. Hearing none, we continued across the kitchen. We investigated the ground floor, stopping at every door to peer into each room, we found no one. I knew watching all those crime shows would come in handy.

CC was following me so close I was surprised she wasn't in my shoes with me. Deciding the back stairs would be a better choice than the main staircase, I headed that way. I remembered the Nancy Drew books my mom read to me when I was little and stepped on the outside of the stair treads, not in the middle where most people would walk. Nancy was right! No stairs squeaked on our way up. As we approached the landing, I heard voices, well, a voice anyway, so I crept along even more carefully.

"Oh my gosh! You were right!" CC breathed in my ear.

I don't know why she sounded so surprised. I'm always right. The voice seemed to come from a room at the far end of the hallway. We continued toward the mostly closed door, listening intently. Stopping on the hinge side of the door, I peered through the small crack but couldn't see anything besides dark, sage green wallpaper. I could, however, hear what was being said.

"Why can't you just do what I say? I'm your father." The voice sounded angry, pleading, and desperate.

The angry and desperate had me concerned. Not hearing a response, I worried about Jamie's condition. The crazy ramblings continued and were now accompanied by footsteps coming closer to where we hid. I held my breath and squeezed my eyes closed in some horribly misguided belief that if I couldn't see him, he couldn't see me. It worked! The footsteps were receding now. Before I could celebrate too much, the footsteps come our way again. Realization dawned on me. He was probably pacing in agitation.

He continued to pepper a nonresponsive Jamie with questions and orders. "Do as I say. Why won't you sign the papers? I deserve the money. Don't you think leaving me his fortune would make up for not being in my life? He was my father. Do you know what it's like growing up poor without a father?"

Apparently, Jamie's father wasn't making a connection between him abandoning her before she was born and him being abandoned. He kept droning on and on about his father abandoning him and being poor. Yada yada yada. I'm not sure how long Jamie has had to listen to him, but it was too long.

Timing it with his pacing, I peeked around the doorframe to see the back of a five-foot-something dirty blond thin-haired man wearing wrinkled jeans and a t-shirt. I ducked back behind the door before he turned to pace my way again. When he turned to pace away from me, I peeked again. This time I spotted Jamie tied to an old leather wing chair by the fireplace. She's too far away from the door to try a quick grab, even if she hadn't been tied to the chair. I tried to mentally project my plan to my mind-reading best friend. Her confused frown told me her powers were on the fritz.

Retreating down the hallway and away from the door, I whispered my plan to her. "We need a distraction so he will leave Jamie alone. I'll go in and untie her and then we will meet at my car."

CC's frown deepened. "What kind of distraction? How are you going to untie her? You are terrible at knots. What happens if he comes back before you get out of there?" She whispered.

I can't believe she would doubt my abilities. "What was the point in coming here if we aren't going to help her? Do you want to tell Nell we left her friend in the clutches of a mad man?"

CC shook her head and with a look of resignation, trepidation, and resolution turned to head back down the stairs, presumably to create a distraction.

I looked around for a good hiding spot, so he didn't see me when he left the room. I debated the various merits of a window seat that looked like it had a storage area underneath, the dumbwaiter, and a nearby statue. Practicality and noiselessness were the most important hiding place qualities, so I finally settled on the floor length curtains that flanked the window seat. Moving behind them, I waited for what I was sure would be a fantastic distraction.

Maybe CC would set off the smoke alarm or bark like a dog. Or maybe she would make siren noises and machine-gun sounds like in that movie we saw last month. That was hilarious. The bad guy was all like 'Oh, no! The Police are here! I better run. It's too late they are firing machine guns at me. I'll throw my gun down and surrender.' Except it wasn't the police, it was one guy who could make cool noises. My silent chuckle was interrupted by a loud crash from downstairs. Concerned, I almost came out of hiding to investigate before I remembered it was part of my plan.

Sure enough, it worked. Jamie's father stopped his pacing and ranting and came to the doorway. He looked around, acted confused, and then headed to the main staircase. As soon as he was out of sight, I rushed into the room where Jamie was being held. Her eyes grew huge when she spotted me, but the tape across her mouth ensured she couldn't say anything.

I struggled to untie the knots holding her to the chair. Darn it, CC had been right on that point. I was terrible at untying knots. Looking around for something to cut them with, I realized Jamie's dad must have been living here. There were clothes scattered near what I assumed was the door to an attached bathroom. The bed was unmade and there were dishes and food wrappers lying about. Good thing Tessa didn't have to clean the house anymore. This place was a pigsty. Not seeing a convenient knife, I turned back to the knots. Jamie seemed to be trying to tell me something with eyebrow semaphore. Deciding I was no good at semaphore, I removed the tape across her mouth.

Once it was removed, she said, "I'm not tied to the chair. The rope is just wrapped around it. Help me get it off."

Surveying the rope instead of just the knots, I realized she was right. We struggled to wiggle the ropes toward the top of the chair and slide Jamie toward the bottom until she was able to slip free.

Just as we turned to go, I heard insane ramblings accompanied by steps on the stairs. Jamie and I exchanged panicked looks before I grabbed her hand and pulled her toward the bed. She ducked underneath while I took a few precious seconds to open the bedroom window before ducking under the bed on the far side.

I had barely managed to duck down before he yelled, "What! Where are you?"

Like Jamie was going to say, 'Here I am, crazy man who is my previously unknown father who kidnapped me.' I managed to swallow my giggle at the absurd notion of her responding to him. I heard him moving around the room in what seemed like a panic. He stopped suddenly and I was afraid he had spotted me since I hadn't had time to get under the bed; I was just crouching next to it. I dared to sneak a peek at where I knew he was standing, near the foot of the bed.

My window ruse was working. He stood still, facing away from me and stared at the open window. He darted toward it and then leaned out, scanning for Jamie, who of course wasn't anywhere to be seen. I managed to swallow my giggle again, but it was getting harder to do so. Apparently, deciding to go after her, he swung a leg over the windowsill. Personally, I would have used the stairs, but to each his own, I guess.

He swung his other leg over the windowsill and floated in mid-air. Jamie's dad could fly! That was so cool! Wait, there was probably a ledge he could stand on. That would make more sense. When he disappeared, presumably moving along the ledge, I counted silently to ten and then eased upright. Moving with ninja-like quietness to the window, I peeked out and saw him about ten feet away carefully edging along toward another window. I slowly and quietly closed and locked the window before moving toward the bedroom door.

Jamie had already climbed out from under the bed and was waiting for me there. We rushed down the main staircase and ran to the front door. Pulling it open, I screamed in terror at the giant figure hulking there with a gun. He took a step toward me and I slammed the door. Unfortunately for him, he had stepped in far enough that the door hit him hard in the shoulder and caused him to lurch sideways and hit his head on the door frame.

"Damn it, Claire!" the monster swore.

Wait, that voice sounded familiar.

"Sheriff, thank goodness you're here!" Jamie said, relief evident in her voice.

"Hey, I was rescuing you just fine before he got here." I glared at the sheriff.

Now that my initial panic had worn off and the sheriff had shifted into the light, I realized I had once more caused him bodily harm. He had a good-sized cut on his temple that was bleeding steadily.

"That looks pretty bad." I said, gesturing to his bleeding temple. "You should be more careful."

His scowl implied he didn't appreciate my concern. "Are you two okay? Where is CC? Where is he?" the sheriff asked us in rapid-fire succession.

"We're fine. CC should be meeting us at my car down the block. He is on a ledge outside the upstairs bedroom."

The incredulous look the sheriff gave me was a little insulting. I folded my arms across my chest to let him know I didn't appreciate his lack of belief in my abilities.

The sound of breaking glass from upstairs made Jamie and I jump to hide behind the sheriff. He was tall and broad, so we were mostly able to get behind him.

The sheriff's gaze laser focused on the staircase. "Stay here." He said quietly, before moving toward the stairs, gun at the ready.

Jamie and I half cowered behind the door and half peered after the sheriff, who was quietly but swiftly moving up the stairs.

When he was about halfway up Jamie's father appeared at the upstairs landing.

The sheriff immediately raised his gun and yelled, "Freeze! Police! Put your hands up!"

His voice was so commanding I fought the impulse to raise my hands.

Jamie's father's face was frozen in shock. Apparently, he didn't expect to encounter a giant of a man with a gun and a badge. He again demonstrated his lack of intelligence by not immediately raising his hands.

"Hands, now!" the sheriff repeated, moving closer to him.

That kick started Jamie's father, but instead of complying, he turned and ran.

The sheriff darted up the stairs after him.

As they both disappeared, I wrung my hands. I knew it would become a habit. Jamie also felt the tension because she latched onto my arm with a death grip. A loud thud from upstairs caused the chandelier to sway and Jamie and I to jump. I was frozen with indecision; not sure if we should stay put, run away, or run to help.

Before I could make up my mind, a voice from right next to me said, "I thought we were meeting at your car?"

I jumped about six feet in the air and clutched my chest. "Don't do that! You almost gave me a heart attack!"

"Do you think the sheriff is okay?" Jamie asked, still peering up the stairs.

Before I could answer, Jamie's father appeared at the top of the stairs again. We all sucked in our breath and clutched each other for support. Before my survival instinct of running could kick in, I realized the sheriff was right behind him, holding his arm and escorting him down the stairs. *Whew, I really hated running. You get all sweaty and plus, I watched the cop shows. That's how you end up murdered.*

"Lots of people run and don't get murdered," CC said, sounding exasperated.

Obviously, I said that part out loud.

The sheriff opened his mouth to congratulate me on a job well done and for saving Jamie. I smiled in anticipation. "I told you not to come here, you little fool. You risked your life and the lives of CC and Jamie. For the last time, you are not a police officer!"

Wait, that wasn't congratulations. I frowned at the sheriff, very much doubting it would be the last time he told me I wasn't a police officer. Since his frown deepened, I bet I said that out loud too. Flashing red and blue lights approached up the driveway and the ensuing commotion allowed me to slip away from the sheriff's anger. I grabbed CC and we retreated to my car.

"Jake is going to be mad at you for this," I said to CC as we drove away from the commotion and gathering crowd. Somehow, we made it through without having to stop and talk to any of the gawkers. CC said it was because people were afraid to approach any car I was driving. Rude, but probably accurate. Pulling into my driveway, the headlights illuminated a grumpy-looking Jake.

He was standing with arms crossed, legs braced, and a ferocious frown. However, as soon as CC climbed from the car, he wrapped her in a tight hug. They hugged for several seconds before Jake reached out and pulled me in, too. We stood like that in the dark driveway for a long time. Finally, we pulled apart and adjourned to CC's kitchen.

Jake pulled out a bottle of whiskey and three glasses. The night did seem to call for something stronger than beer. We sipped silently for a few minutes before Jake said, "Okay, I'm ready to hear what happened."

CC tried to minimize the story. "Well, let's see. After dinner Claire suddenly had the idea that Jamie and her father might be at Mr. Johnson's house. It is big, empty, and doesn't have a lot of close neighbors. She wanted to drive over to see if we could help. I called the sheriff on the way to let him know about the possibility. Claire was right. Jamie was there and the sheriff arrived to arrest her father."

Wow, that sounded not at all dangerous, I thought. Jake's relaxing shoulders told me he agreed. I nodded my head to give credence to CC's story.

"Yeah," I said, "The plan went off without a hitch. CC made a great distraction. I untied Jamie and locked her father out on the window ledge. We would have made it to the car no problem if the sheriff hadn't surprised me at the front door on the way out."

Jake's tensing shoulders and CC's sharp kick to my ankle told me maybe I should have kept my mouth shut.

"Now Jake, it's not as dangerous as it seems when Claire tells it. You know her flair for drama," CC said with a soothing tone. "Besides, the important thing is everybody is safe, and Jamie's father is in jail."

I thought her hugging him with one arm and rubbing his chest with the other did more to distract Jake than her words. I poured him another drink, which he swallowed in one gulp. My throat burned in sympathy, but it seemed to help him calm down.

"I couldn't stand it if anything happened to you. Either of you," he said, wrapping us both tightly in his arms. CC and I returned the hug fiercely as the night's events replayed in our minds.

What if I hadn't been able to untie Jamie and her father caught me? What if Jamie's father had looked around the room instead of out the window? What if I wasn't really a ninja?

Jake's rumbling laugh interrupted my thoughts. He kissed the top of my head. "I'm really glad you're okay. Our family wouldn't be the same without you."

Deciding I should head home for some sleep, I started to pull out of Jake's embrace, but swayed dangerously. Jake's quick reflexes caught me before I fell over. All my energy seemed to drain out and I wasn't sure I could make the long trek back to my house.

Jake looked torn between letting go of his wife and helping me home, or never letting go of his wife and letting me fend for myself. Deciding to save my life, he released CC and half guided, half carried me to the back door. We managed to make it down the steps without incident. Okay, there was an incident when I was unable to walk and mostly fell down the steps, but Jake kept me from getting hurt, so it shouldn't count.

"Dominic," Jake said out of the blue. He must be losing his marbles.

"Jake," the sheriff said, who I realized was standing not five feet away from us. "I'll take it from here. I'm sure CC needs you."

Not even hesitating for a second, Jake passed me off to the sheriff like a sack of potatoes. I'd complain, but it seemed like it would take too much effort. The sheriff deftly managed to catch my mostly limp body. It was like all my bones and muscles had melted. He paused as if unsure what to do next, but then bent and scooped me up in his arms like a princess. I smiled as I snuggled against his chest. I had always wanted to be a princess.

"Off with their heads!" I said, sleep threatening to claim me.

The sheriff managed to navigate both yards and the open gate but got stuck at my back door. His hands were full holding me and if he put me down, I might not be able to support myself. He jumped a little when Benji appeared in the window. He was jumping up to see who was at the back door. Recognizing us, he opened the door.

The sheriff shook his head in disbelief but refrained from commenting.

"Good boy, Benji." I murmured into the sheriff's neck where my face was currently pressed. "Mmm, you smell good," I thought, or possibly said, who knows?

Benji led the way to my bedroom. Not that there were a lot of bedrooms to choose from in my house, but still helpful.

The sheriff seemed perplexed about how to fit me on the bed between Agatha and Blackbeard. Agatha ignored us and snored loudly, but Blackbeard glared out of his one good eye. Benji barked sharply at Agatha who, without breaking her snoring pattern, shifted enough to allow the sheriff to ease my limp body down into the small, recently vacated space. The sheriff disappeared, but since I felt someone pulling my shoes off, I assumed that's where he went. He returned to my field of vision with a blanket, with which he carefully covered me.

He had to bend close to tuck me in and I saw a couple of stitches in his temple. I frowned at him and said, "You should be more careful. You get hurt a lot and you work in a dangerous job." My words were slightly slurred, either from exhaustion or whiskey. Maybe both. It sounded more like, "Oo oud e ore airful. Oo it urt law an oo ork angerouse ob."

His face was about half an inch from mine, and he stared at me intently, searching for something. I'm not sure what, but he must have found it because he moved even closer. He's going to kiss me I thought, but I was too tired for all the conflicting feelings, and my eyes simply drifted closed. When his lips did touch me, it was on my forehead and not my lips. It was the last thing I remembered before sleep claimed me.

Chapter 29

T en seconds after falling asleep my alarm started blaring. I pulled the pillow over my head to block it out. It worked! The blaring stopped. I relaxed, drifting back to sleep. Before I could fall all the way, a troubling thought occurred to me. Every other time I had pulled my pillow over my head, I could still hear the alarm. That was in fact the reason it blared so loudly. If you overslept and showed up late to work fifty times, they threatened to fire you. Completely out of the blue. Geesh, some people. I assumed CC had come to bring me life-giving elixir and I held out my hand while struggling into a sitting position.

"Coffee," I said in my morning frog voice, not bothering to open my eyes. I felt the bed depress where CC sat on it and then a warm mug pressed into my hand. I took a deep drink. After draining the mug, while leaning against the headboard for support, I was finally strong enough to open my eyes. However, it was not my best friend's gorgeous blue eyes I stared into, but the sheriff's chocolate brown ones.

"Gah!" I half-shouted while groping for the blanket to cover my still completely dressed form. His quick smile told me he found me amusing. "What are you doing here?" I asked, my eyes darting wildly around the room as if the explanation was written on the wall or something.

"I was worried about leaving you alone last night. You were pretty groggy and out of it," he explained, all too reasonably for this hour of the morning.

"Huh, I guess that makes sense." I said, while staring into my empty coffee mug.

"I made a whole pot. Come down to the kitchen and I'll get you your own cup," he said and grabbed the mug from my unresisting fingers.

I debated rolling over and going back to sleep, but the lure of coffee was too strong. "Wait. Get me my own cup? Whose cup was it?"

His laughter floated up the stairs, but he didn't explain.

It's his cup! I staggered upright and, listing only slightly sideways, made it to the door. The stairs were a bit of a challenge and when I slipped on the last two, the sheriff materialized to save me from falling. He guided me to the counter where two mugs were filled with coffee, apparently from my coffee maker.

"When did I get a coffee maker?" I asked the room at large.

"How would I know? I found it in the appliance cupboard."

"I have an appliance cupboard?" When did that happen, I wondered.

"Didn't you grow up here?" the sheriff asked, eyeing me as one might an escaped mental patient.

"Yeah, but that was a long time ago." *Ha! Take that!*

He rolled his eyes. Obviously, he had hung around Nell too much, but refrained from further ridiculous comments. He handed me a mug of coffee and I practically snatched it from him and drank deeply. I looked up from my delicious, life-giving brew to find him watching me. He was leaning back against my counter with his long legs crossed at the ankles holding his own cup of coffee. He looked relaxed and right somehow, standing in my kitchen in the morning. I started to feel warm, and it wasn't from drinking hot coffee.

Before I could say anything, probably embarrassing, he said, "I called your office to let them know you won't be in today. I had to leave a message on the machine since nobody was there."

I nodded. "That was nice, but since I'm the first one in in the morning and Brandon doesn't know how to work the answering machine, no one will get the message."

The sheriff frowned. "I hadn't thought of that. I'll have my deputy swing by and leave a note."

I waved this away. "Don't bother, I'll call Missy. She'll make sure everybody knows."

I searched for my phone and finding it in my back pocket, I called Missy. "Hey, Missy, it's Claire," I said when she picked up.

"Oh my gosh, Claire! I heard all about last night from Henry, who heard it from Mary, who heard from Sharon, that you saved that girl at Mr. Johnson's place and caught his killer."

Not quite what happened, but close enough. "Listen, Missy, I got in really late last night and I'm taking a personal day. Could you be sure Brandon knows I won't be in today?"

"Sure, Honey. After last night, I bet you need a day off. Say hi to the sheriff for me. Bye."

The phone disconnected in my ear before I could say anything else. I dropped the phone on the counter.

"Well good news, bad news," I said to the sheriff. "Good news is, Brandon will know I won't be in today. Bad news is everyone will know you were here all night."

The sheriff frowned. "How would they know?" he asked, seemingly more curious than anything else.

"It's a small town. I'm sure someone saw your car out front, assumed you were here, and started the rumor mill. If Missy knew you were here, everyone will know." I held my cup out for a refill.

He automatically refilled it with no judgmental looks for drinking three cups of coffee like CC would have given me.

When he turned to put the coffee pot back on the burner, I noticed the stitches on his temple again. "Sorry about slamming the door on you last night," I mumbled into my cup. When there was no response, I worked up the courage to look at him. He was staring at me as if trying to figure me out. *Good luck*, I thought, *I'm an enigma*.

"How many stitches?" I asked, trying to deflect his attention. Oddly, I seemed to be more comfortable when he was mad at me. It felt less risky then.

"Four," he answered, still staring.

Apparently, deflection didn't work. "Did Jamie get home safely?" I tried deflection again. It was a stupid question. If she wasn't home safe, where would she be? The sheriff chose not to take the bait and nodded, still staring. Now I was fidgeting, unable to bear the scrutiny.

"Why did you go to Mr. Johnson's house?" he finally asked.

I shrugged, "I thought Jamie was there. I wanted to help her."

"Why didn't you call and let me handle it while you stayed home where you would be safe?"

"I couldn't. What if something happened to her and I could have stopped it? I couldn't live with myself if that had happened," I said and wrapped my arms around myself.

The sheriff reached out and pulled me to him, wrapping me in his arms.

I remained stiff against him for a second before giving in to the comfort he offered and wrapped my arms around him, too. My face pressed into his neck and his chin was resting on my head. *He does smell good*, I thought, taking a deep breath.

It ended up hitching a little and then the tears came as I imagined all the ways it could have gone wrong. Jamie might have been hurt, or worse, killed. And I had drug CC into it. What if something had happened to her?

He let me cry and rubbed my back in soothing circles. He didn't try to stop the tears, or fix the problem, he just let me cry. After a few minutes, when it became obvious, I wasn't stopping anytime soon, he scooped me up in his arms and headed for the living room. He sat on the couch and settled me in his lap. I wasn't sure how long we sat like that, but eventually, the tears tapered off into hiccups and finally into silence.

"I was so scared I wouldn't make it in time, and something would happen to you," he confessed.

Not sure what to say to that I remained quiet.

"You were right about Mr. Johnson having a son," he said. "His name was Harry Stone. Apparently, Mr. Johnson didn't know about him until a year ago. Harry's mom died of cancer and on her deathbed, she told Harry who his father was. It seems Harry has been down on his luck his whole adult life and decided to hit his father up for money. Mr. Johnson was shocked to hear he had a son, but Mr. Johnson wasn't a fool and decided to investigate to be sure Harry's story was true. He hired a private investigator who confirmed Harry's story but also reported his criminal record of petty crimes, lack of character, and the daughter he abandoned before she was born. Mr. Johnson gave Harry small amounts of money hoping he would turn his life around. When it became obvious that wasn't going to happen, Mr. Johnson decided Harry deserved nothing more and cut him off. He decided to leave his fortune to his granddaughter, Jamie, who better met his expectations of his family's character traits."

I snorted, since abandoning children, and shunning those deemed not worthy were the family's character traits and it sounded like Harry fit right in.

"When Harry came demanding more money Mr. Johnson refused to give him any and told him he wasn't getting another dime. They argued and Mr. Johnson told him to get out and never come back. Mr. Johnson turned his back, dismissing him, and went upstairs. But Harry wasn't going to give up millions so easily. He followed him up the stairs where they continued arguing. Harry claims Mr. Johnson grabbed him and when he pulled away Mr. Johnson lost his balance and fell down the stairs. Personally, I'm more inclined to believe Harry pushed him, but we will probably never know for sure."

I mulled this over. It made sense, I guess.

"After Mr. Johnson's fall down the stairs, Harry looked through his desk and papers. He found the private investigator's report with Jamie's information on it. Since Mr. Johnson changed his will to leave everything to Jamie, Harry decided he would get Jamie to sign everything over to him. Since he had stolen the report, he was able to get Jamie's location and her contact information. When she was less than willing to meet with him so he could make her sign over five million dollars, he got mad. He decided to confront her, but when he traced her cell phone to college, he saw us and heard I was the sheriff. Realizing it was a trap, he decided to set one of his own. He kidnapped Jamie and took her to Mr. Johnson's house to convince her to give him the money. He's in lock up and has been charged with kidnapping, theft, and murder."

I digested the new data, which was pretty much what I had put together. "I'm just glad Jamie's okay. She didn't deserve any of this. She's a good kid."

We sat in silence, me still snuggled in his lap, exhausted by the adrenaline dump and crying fit, with his cheek resting on the top of my head. It felt good, comforting, and right somehow, but I suspected I would spend sleepless nights trying to figure out how I felt, how the sheriff felt, what I wanted us to feel, and so on.

A loud growling noise disrupted the peace and quiet. I covered my stomach with my hand as if that would erase its rude growling.

The sheriff's chuckle vibrated through me. "I guess it is past breakfast time," he said.

"If you two are hungry, Jake picked up doughnuts," CC called from my back door with near-perfect timing. When she peeked around the corner and spied me curled in the sheriff's lap her smile was mocking, delighted, and full of meaning.

I didn't know a smile could convey so many different things, but hers did. Climbing from the sheriff's lap and probably resembling a drunk flamingo, I ignored her pointed look and eyebrow semaphore.

We all trooped next door to Jake and CC's kitchen. The kids shifted and made room at the banquet for the sheriff to join our family like he had the right to be there. I pondered how I felt about this adoption of a near-stranger as I watched Jake, Dean, and the sheriff engage in a discussion about the tensile strength of various materials, presumably for a Rube Goldberg device. Before they could fully explore the topic and bore the rest of us, Eve bumped my precious coffee mug. As it teetered, precariously close to spilling, the sheriff reached over, caught it, and handed it back to me.

Well, maybe he can stay, I thought to myself as Jane asked the sheriff if he would like one of the puppies when they were weaned. Before he could answer, Ann asked him if he could throw a curveball. Most people were overwhelmed by our family, but the sheriff seemed to take it all in stride. I took a sip of my coffee and allowed the commotion to swirl around me. I sat and thought some deep thoughts about what the sheriff being part of the family meant. Did it make it more awkward or less awkward between us? If we did date and then broke up, who got to keep which friends in the breakup? Maybe go halvsies? Boys versus girls? Every other weekend? What about holidays? *This was going to be hard.*

"What is going to be hard?" asked Jake.

"Nothing! You're hard!" I covered my inner thoughts becoming outer words again and deflected attention away from said outer words. Realizing how inappropriate my response sounded, I felt my face flame with embarrassment.

Jake's warm chuckle washed over me and CC tried to hide her evil cackle behind her hand, but it escaped, which deepened my chagrin.

The sheriff's expression was amused, incredulous, and resigned all at the same time.

I actually got that look from lots of different people. Lucky for me, Eve distracted everybody by loudly demanding a fourth doughnut, which CC denied. Eve sucked in a breath and prepared for another epic tantrum. We all froze in terror, knowing the inevitable was coming and we didn't have time to escape.

Just before the deafening screams emerged from her kewpie doll mouth, the sheriff asked, "Eve, do you think the new princess movie will have a dragon?"

Eve snapped her mouth shut and tilted her head as if in deep thought.

We all waited with bated breath.

Finally, Eve said, "I hope so. It would be really cool if she was friends with the dragon."

The sheriff nodded. "That would be cool. Which movie is your favorite?"

I'm shocked speechless. The sheriff prevented a tantrum. And he's a rookie. How did he know?

"Are you a witch?" I whispered.

The sheriff shot me a huge self-satisfied smile with those lips that previously looked like they had never smiled, ever, but now seemed to welcome the chance. His smile never failed to draw a smile from me, and there we were, smiling at each other while the rest of the family went about whatever it was they did on a Monday morning.

Before you go….

Thanks for joining Claire and CC on their first chaotic case in the Claire's Chaos and Crimes Series. If you'd like to stay in Oak Creek a little longer, there are plenty of ways to keep the adventure going by following Amanda Nelson on social media for behind-the-scenes announcements, publishing updates, and other Oak Creek shenanigans.

Instagram: